The First Collected Tales of
BAUCHELAIN &
KORBAL BROACH

www.rbooks.co.uk

Also by Steven Erikson

GARDENS OF THE MOON
DEADHOUSE GATES
MEMORIES OF ICE
HOUSE OF CHAINS
MIDNIGHT TIDES
THE BONEHUNTERS
REAPER'S GALE
TOLL THE HOUNDS
DUST OF DREAMS

The First Collected Tales of
BAUCHELAIN &
KORBAL BROACH

Steven Erikson

BANTAM PRESS

LONDON · TORONTO · SYDNEY · AUCKLAND · JOHANNESBURG

TRANSWORLD PUBLISHERS
61–63 Uxbridge Road, London W5 5SA
A Random House Group Company
www.rbooks.co.uk

First published in Great Britain
in 2007 by PS Publishing Ltd

This edition first published in Great Britain
in 2010 by Bantam Press
an imprint of Transworld Publishers

A CIP catalogue record for this book
is available from the British Library.

ISBNs 9780593063941 (cased)
9780593063958 (tpb)

Addresses for Random House Group Ltd companies outside the UK
can be found at: www.randomhouse.co.uk
The Random House Group Ltd Reg. No. 954009

The Random House Group Limited supports The Forest Stewardship
Council (FSC), the leading international forest-certification organization.
All our titles that are printed on Greenpeace-approved FSC-certified
paper carry the FSC logo. Our paper procurement policy can be
found at www.rbooks.co.uk/environment

Typeset in 11/13pt Sabon by
Kestrel Data, Exeter, Devon.
Printed and bound in Great Britain by
Clays Ltd, Bungay, Suffolk.

2 4 6 8 10 9 7 5 3 1

Contents

BLOOD FOLLOWS

T HE BELLS PEALED ACROSS THE LAMENTABLE CITY OF MOLL, *clamouring along the crooked, narrow alleys, buffeting the dawn-risers hurriedly laying out their wares in the market rounds. The bells pealed, tumbling over the grimy cobblestones, down to the wharfs and out over the bay's choppy, grey waves. Shrill iron, the bells pealed with the voice of hysteria.*

The terrible, endless sound echoed deep inside the slate-covered barrows that humped the streets, tilted the houses and cramped the alleyways in every quarter of Moll. Barrows older than the Lamentable City itself, each long ago riven through and tunnelled in fruitless search for plunder, each now remaining like a pock, the scarring of some ancient plague. The bells reached through to the scattered, broken bones bedded down in hollowed-out logs, amidst rotted furs and stone tools and weapons, bone and shell beads and jewellery, the huddled forms of hunting dogs, the occasional horse with its head removed and placed at its master's feet, the skull with the spike-hole gaping between the left eye and ear. Echoing among the dead, bestirring the shades in their centuries-long slumber.

A few of these dread shades rose in answer to that call, and in the darkness moments before dawn they'd lifted themselves clear of the slate and earth and potsherds, scenting the presence of . . . someone, something. They'd then returned to their dark abodes

– and for those who saw them, for those who knew something of shades, their departure seemed more like flight.

In Temple Round, as the sun edged higher over the hills inland, the saving wells, fountains and bowl-stones overflowed with coin: silver and gold glinting among the beds of copper. Already crowds gathered outside the high-walled sanctuaries of Burn – relieved and safe under the steamy morning light – there to appease the passing over of sudden death, and to thank the Sleeping Goddess, who slept still. And many a manservant was seen exiting the side-postern of Hood's Temple, for the rich were ever wont to bribe away the Lord of Death, so that they might awaken to yet another day, gentled of spirit in their soft beds.

It was the monks of the Queen of Dreams for whom the night just past was cause for mourning, with clanging dirge of iron, civilization's scarred, midnight face. For that face had a name, and it was Murder. And so the bells rang on, a shroud of fell sound descending upon the port of Moll, a sound cold and harsh that none could escape . . .

. . . while in an alley behind a small estate on Low Merchant Way, a diviner of the Deck of Dragons noisily emptied his breakfast of pomegranites, bread, prunes and watered wine, surrounded by a ring of dogs patiently awaiting theirs.

THE DOOR SLAMMED BEHIND EMANCIPOR REESE, RATTLING THE flimsy drop-latch a moment before sagging back down on its worn leather hinges. He stared at the narrow, musty hallway in front of him. The niche set waist-high on the wall to his right was lit with a lone tallow candle, revealing water-stains and cracked plaster and the tiny stone altar of Sister Soliel, heaped with wilted flower-heads. On the back wall at the far end, six paces from where he stood, where the passage opened on both sides, hung a black-iron broadsword – cross-hilted and bronze-pommeled, most likely rusted into its verdigrised scabbard. Emancipor's lined, sun-scoured face fell, becoming heavy around his eyes as he gazed on the weapon of his youth. He felt every one of his six, maybe seven decades.

His wife had gone silent in the kitchen, halfway through heating the wet sand, the morning's porridge pot and the plates on the wood counter at her side still awaiting cleansing; and he could see her in his mind, motionless and massive and breathing her short, shallow, increasingly nervous breaths.

'Is that you, 'Mancy?'

He hesitated. He could do it, right now – back outside, out into the streets – he knew how to sound depths, he knew knots – all kinds of knots. He could stand a pitching deck. He could leave this damned wart of a city, leave her and the squalling, simpering brats they'd begetted. He could . . . *escape.* Emancipor sighed. 'Yes, dear.'

Her voice pitched higher. 'Why aren't you at work?'

He drew a deep breath. 'I am now . . .' he paused, then finished with loud, distinct articulation: 'unemployed.'

'What did you say?'

'Unemployed.'

'Fired? You've been fired? You incompetent, stupid—'

'The bells!' he screamed. 'The bells! Can't you hear the bells?'

Silence in the kitchen, then: 'The Sisters have mercy! You idiot! Why aren't you finding work? Get a new job – if you think you can laze around here, seeing our children tossed from their schooling—'

Emancipor sighed. *Dear Subly, ever so practical.* 'I'm on my way, dear.'

'Just come back with a job. A good job. The future of our children—'

He slammed the door behind him, and stared out on the street. The bells kept ringing. The air was growing hot, smelling of raw sewage, rotting shellfish and human and animal sweat. Subly had come close to selling her soul for the tired old house behind him. For the neighbourhood, rather. As far as he could tell, it stank no different from all the other neighbourhoods they'd lived in. Saving perhaps that there was a greater variety among the vegetables rotting in the gutters. *'Positioning, 'Mancy. It's all in positioning.'*

Across the way Sturge Weaver waddled about the front of his shop, unlocking and folding back the shutters, casting nosy, knowing glances his way over the humped barrow mound that bulged the street between their houses. *The lingering fart heard it all. Don't matter. Subly'll be finished with the pot and plates in record time, now. Then she'll be out, gums flapping and her eyes wide as she fished shallow waters for sympathy and what-not.*

It was true enough that he'd need a new job before the day's end, or all the respect he'd earned over the last six months would disappear faster than a candle-flame in a hurricane; and that grim label – *'Mancy the Luckless'* – would return, the ghost of old in step with his shadow, and neighbours like Sturge Weaver making warding signs whenever their paths crossed.

A new job. It was all that mattered now. Never mind that some madman stalked the city every night since the season's turning, never mind that horribly mutilated bodies were turning up every morning – citizens of Lamentable Moll, their eyes blank (when there were eyes) and their faces twisted in a rictus of terror – and their bodies – all those missing parts – Emancipor shivered. Never mind that Master Baltro wouldn't need a coachman ever again, except for the grave-digger's bent, white-faced crew and that one last journey to the pit of his ancestors, closing forever the line of his blood.

Emancipor shook himself. If not for the grisly in-between, he almost envied the merchant's final trip. *At least it'd bring silence – not Subly, of course, but the bells. The damned, endless, shrill, nagging bells . . .*

'GO AND FIND THE MONK ON THE END OF THAT ROPE AND WRING his neck.'

The corporal blinked at his sergeant, shifted uneasily under the death-detail's attire of blue-stained bronze ringed hauberk, lobster-tailed bowl helm and the heavy leather-padded shoulder-guards. *Damn, the lad's bloody well swimming in all that armour. Not quite succeeding at impressing the onlookers – the short sword at his belt's still wax-sealed in the scabbard, for Hood's sake.* Guld turned away. 'Now, son.'

He listened to the lad's footsteps recede behind him, and glumly watched his detachment enforcing the cordon around the body and the old barrow pit it laid in, keeping at a distance the gawkers and stray dogs, kicking at pigeons and seagulls and otherwise letting what was left of the dead man lie in peace under the fragment of roof-thatch some merciful passerby had thrown over it.

He saw the diviner stumble ash-faced from the other alley. The king's court magus wasn't a man of the streets, but the cloth at the knees of his white pantaloons now showed intimate familiarity with the grimy, greasy cobblestones.

Guld had little respect for coddled mages. Too remote from human affairs, bookish and naive and slow to grow up. Ophan was nearing sixty, but he had the face of a toddler. *Alchemy at work, of course. In vanity's name, no less.*

'Stul Ophan,' Guld called, catching the man's watery eyes.

'You finished your reading, then?' An insensitive question, but they were the kind Guld most liked to ask.

The rotund magus approached. 'I did,' he said thickly, licking his bluish lips.

A cold art, divining the Deck in the wake of murder. 'And?'

'Not a demon, not a Sekull, not a Jhorligg. A man.'

Sergeant Guld scowled, adjusting his helmet where the woollen inside trim had rubbed raw his forehead. 'We know that. The last street diviner told us that. For this the King grants you a tower in his keep?'

Stul Ophan's face darkened. 'Was the King's command that brought me here,' he snapped. 'I'm a court mage. My divinations are of a more . . .' he faltered momentarily, 'of a more bureaucratic nature. This raw and bloody murder business isn't my speciality, is it?'

Guld's scowl deepened. 'You divine by the Deck to tally numbers? That's a new one on me, Magus.'

'Don't be a fool. What I meant was, my sorceries are in an administrative theme. Affairs of the realm, and such.' Stul Ophan looked about, his round shoulders hunching and a shudder taking him as his gaze found the covered body. 'This . . . this is foulest sorcery, the workings of a madman—'

'Wait,' Guld interjected. 'The killer's a sorceror?'

Stul nodded, his lips twitching. 'Powerful in the necromantic arts, skilled in cloaking his trail. Even the rats saw nothing – nothing that stayed in their brains, anyway—'

The rats. Reading their minds has become an art in Moll, with loot-hungry warlocks training the damn things and sending them under the streets, into the old barrows, down among the bones of a people so far dead as to be nameless in the city's memory. The thought soothed him somewhat. There was truth in the world after all, when mages and rats saw so closely eye to eye. *And thank Hood for the rat-hunters, the fearless bastards will spit at a warlock's feet if that spit was the last water on earth.*

'The pigeons?' he asked innocently.

'Sleep at night,' Stul said, throwing Guld a disgusted look. 'I only go so far. Rats, fine. Pigeons . . .' He shook his head, cleared his throat and looked for a spitoon. Finding none – naturally – he turned and spat on the cobbles. 'Anyway, the killer's found a taste for nobility—'

Guld snorted. 'That's a long stretch, Magus. A distant cousin of a distant cousin. A middling cloth merchant with no heirs—'

'Close enough. The King wants results.' Stul Ophan observed the sergeant with an expression trying for contempt. 'Your reputation's at stake, Guld.'

'Reputation?' Guld's laugh was bitter. He turned away, dismissing the mage for the moment. *Reputation? My head's on the pinch-block, and the grey man's stacking his stones. The noble families are scared. They're gnawing the King's wrinkled feet in between the sycophantic kissing. Eleven nights, eleven victims. No witnesses. The whole city's terrified – things could get out of hand. I need to find the bastard – I need him writhing on the spikes at Palace Gate . . . A sorceror, that's new – I've got my clue, finally.* He looked down at the merchant's covered body. *These dead don't talk. That should've told me something. And the street diviners, so strangely terse and nervous. A mage, powerful enough to scare the average practitioner into silence. And worse yet, a necromancer – someone who knows how to silence souls, or send them off to Hood before the steam leaves the blood.*

Stul Ophan cleared his throat a second time. 'Well,' he said, 'I'll see you tomorrow morning, then.'

Guld winced, then shook himself. 'He'll make a mistake – you're certain the killer's a man?'

'Reasonably.'

Guld's eyes fixed on the mage, making Stul Ophan take a step back. 'Reasonably? What does that mean?'

'Well, uh, it has the feel of a man, though there's something odd about it. I simply assumed he made some effort to disguise that – some simple cantrips and the like—'

'Poorly done? Does that fit with a mage who can silence souls and wipe clean the brains of rats?'

Stul Ophan frowned. 'Well, uh, no, that doesn't make much sense—'

'Think some more on it, Magus,' Guld ordered, and though only a sergeant of the City Watch, the command was answered with a swift nod.

Then the magus asked, 'What do I tell the King?'

Guld hitched his thumbs into his sword-belt. It'd been years since he'd last drawn the weapon, but he'd dearly welcome the chance to do so now. He studied the crowd, the tide of faces pushing the ring of guards into an ever tighter circle. *Could be any one of them. That wheezing beggar with the hanging mouth. Those two rat-hunters. That old woman with all the dolls at her belt – some kind of witch, seen her before, at every scene of these murders, and now she's eager to start on the next doll, the eleventh – questioned her six mornings back. Then again, she's got enough hair on her chin to be mistaken for a man. Or maybe that dark-faced stranger – armour under his fine cloak, well-made weapon at his belt – a foreigner for certain, since nobody around here uses single-edged scimitars. So, could be any one of them, come to study his handiwork by day's light, come to gloat over the city's most experienced guardsman in these sort of crimes.* 'Tell His Majesty that I now have a list of suspects.'

Stul Ophan made a sound in his throat that might have been disbelief.

Guld continued drily, 'And inform King Seljure that I found his court mage passably helpful, although I have many more questions for him, for which I anticipate the mage's fullest devotion of energies in answering my inquiries.'

'Of course,' Stul Ophan rasped. 'At your behest, Sergeant, by the King's command.' He wheeled and walked off to his awaiting carriage.

The sergeant sighed. *A list of suspects. How many mages in Lamentable Moll? A hundred? Two hundred? How many real Talents among them? How many coming and going from the trader ships? Is the killer a foreigner, or has someone local turned bad? There are delvings in high sorcery that can twist even the calmest mind. Or has a shade broken free, climbed out nasty and miserable from some battered barrow – any recent deep construction lately? Better check with the Flatteners. Shades? Not their style, though—*

The bells clanged wildly, then fell silent. Guld frowned, then recalled his order to the young corporal. *Oh damn, did that lad take me literally?*

THE MORNING SMOKE FROM THE BREAKFAST HEARTH, REEKING of fish, filled the cramped but mostly empty front room of Savory Bar. Emancipor sat at the lone round table near the back in the company of Kreege and Dully, who kept the pitchers coming as the hours rolled into afternoon. Emancipor's usual disgust with the two wharf rats diminished steadily with each refilled tankard of foamy ale. He'd even begun to follow their conversation.

'Seljure's always been wobbly on the throne,' Dully was saying, scratching at his barrel-like chest under the salt-stained jerkin, 'ever since Stygg fell to the Jheck and he balked at invading. Now we've got a horde of savages just the other side of the strait and all Seljure does is bleat empty threats.' He found a louse and held it up for examination a moment before popping it into his mouth.

'Savages ain't quite on the mark,' Kreege objected in a slow drawl, rubbing at the stubble covering his heavy jaw. His small, dark eyes narrowed. 'It's a complicated horde, them Jheck. You've got a pantheon chock full of spirits and demons and the like – and the War Chief answers to the Elders in everything but the lay of battle. Now, he might well be something special, what with all his successes – after all, Stygg fell in the span of a day and a night, and Hood knows what magery he's got all on his own – but if the Elders—'

'Ain't interested in that,' Dully cut in, waving a grease-stained hand as if shooing dock flies. 'Just be glad them Jheck can't row a straight course in the Lees. I heard they burned the Stygg galleys in the harbours – if that bit of thick-headed stupidity don't cost the War Chief his hat of feathers, then those Elders ain't got the brains of a sea-urchin. That's all I'm saying. It's Seljure who's wobbly enough to turn Lamentable Moll into easy pickings.'

'It's the nobles that's shackled the city,' Kreege insisted, 'and Seljure with it. And it don't help that his only heir's a sex-starved wanton lass determined to bed every pureblood nobleman in Moll. And then there's the priesthoods – they ain't helping things neither with all their proclamations of doom and all that tripe. So that's the problem, and it's not just Lamentable Moll's. It's every city the world over. Inbred ruling families and moaning priests – a classic case of divided power squabbling and sniping over the spoils of the common folk, with us mules stumbling under the yoke.'

Dully grumbled, 'A king with some spine is what we need, that's all.'

'That's what they said in Korel when that puffed up Captain, Mad Hilt, usurped the throne, though pretty soon no one was saying nothing about nothing, since they were all dead or worse.'

'Exception proves the rule—'

'Not in politics, it don't.'

The two old men scowled at each other, then Dully nudged Kreege and said to Emancipor, 'So, 'Mancy, looking for work again, eh?' Both dockmen grinned. 'Had yourself a run of Lad's Luck with your employers, it seems. Lady fend the poor sod fool enough to take you on – not that you ain't reliable, of course.'

Kreege's grin broadened, further displaying his uneven, rotting teeth. 'Maybe Hood's made you his Herald,' he said. 'Ever thought of that? It happens, you know. Not many diviners cracking the Deck these days, meaning there's no way to tell, really. The Lord of Death picks his own, don't he, and there ain't a damned thing to be done for it.'

'Kreege's made a point there, he has,' Dully said. 'How did your first employer go? Drowned in bed, I heard. Lungs full of water and a hand-print over the mouth. Hood's breath, what a way to go—'

Emancipor grunted, staring down at his tankard. 'Sergeant Guld nailed the truth down, Kreege. T'was assassination. Luksor was playing the wrong game with the wrong people. Guld found the killer quick enough, and the bastard slid on his hook for days before spillin' the hand at the other end of his strings.' He drank deep, in Luksor's cursed name.

Dully leaned forward, his bloodshot eyes glittering. 'But what about the next one, 'Mancy? The cutter said his heart exploded. Imagine that, and him being young enough to be your son, too.'

'And fat enough to tip a carriage if he didn't sit in the middle,' Emancipor growled back. 'I should know – I used to wedge him in and out. Your life's what you make it, I always say.' He downed the last of his ale, in the name of poor fat Septryl.

'And now Merchant Baltro,' Kreege said. 'Someone took his guts, I heard, and his tongue so the questioners couldn't make the spirit talk. Word is, the King's own magus was down there, sniffing around Guld's heels.'

His head swimming, Emancipor looked up and blinked at Kreege. 'The King's own? Really?'

Dully asked, his eyebrows lifting, 'Not nervous now, are you?'

'Baltro was of the blood,' Kreege said. He shivered. 'What was done between his legs—'

'Shut up,' Emancipor snapped. 'He was a good man in his way. It don't fair the wind to spit in the sea, remember that.'

'Another round?' Dully asked by way of mollification.

Emancipor scowled. 'Where d'you get alla coin, anyway?'

Dully smiled, picking at his teeth. 'Disposing the bodies,' he explained, pausing to belch. 'No souls, right? No trails of where they went, either. Like they was never there in the first place. So, just meat, the priests keep saying. No rites, no honouring, don't matter what the family's paid for beforehand, neither. Them priests won't touch them bodies, plain and simple.'

'It's our job,' Kreege said, 'taking 'em out to the strand.' He clacked his teeth. 'Keeping the crabs fat and tasty.'

Emancipor stared. 'You're trapping the crabs! Selling them!'

'Why not? Ain't taste any different now, do they? Three emolls to the pound – we been doing all right.'

'That's . . . horrible.'

'That's business,' Dully said. 'And you're drinking on the coin, 'Mancy.'

'Ain't you just,' Kreege added.

Emancipor rubbed at his face, which was getting numb. 'Yeah, well, I'm in mourning.'

'Hey!' Dully said, straightening. 'I seen a posting in the square. Someone looking for a manservant. If you can walk straight, you might want to head down there.'

'Wait—' Kreege began with a troubled look, but Dully jabbed his elbow into the man's side.

'It's an idea,' Dully resumed. 'That wife of yours don't like you unemployed, does she? Don't mean to pry, of course. Just being helpful, is all.'

'On the centre post?'

'Yeah.'

Hood's Breath, I'm an object of pity to these two crab-mongers. 'A manservant, eh?' He frowned. Driving carriages was good work. He liked horses better than most people. Manservant though – that meant bowing and scraping all day long. Even so . . . 'Pour me another, in Baltro's name, then I'll head down for a look.'

Dully grinned. 'That's the spirit . . . uh . . .' his face reddened. 'No reflection on Baltro's, of course.'

THE WALK DOWN TO FISHMONGER'S ROUND TOLD HIM HE'D drunk too much ale. He saw enough straight lines, but had trouble following them. By the time he reached the round, the world was swirling all around him, and when he closed his eyes it was as if his mind was endlessly falling down a dark tunnel. And somewhere in the depths waited Subly – who'd always said she'd follow him through Hood's gate if his dying left her in debt or otherwise put upon – he could almost hear her down there, giving the demons an earful. Cursing under his breath, he vowed to keep his eyes open. 'Can't die,' he muttered. 'Besides, it's jus the drink, is all. Not dying, not falling, not yet – a man needs a job, needs the coin, he's got 'sponsibilities.'

The sun had nearly set, emptying the round as the hawkers and net-menders closed up their stalls and the pigeons and seagulls walked unmolested through the day's rubbish. Even Emancipor, leaning against a wall at the edge of the round, could sense the nervous haste among the fishmongers – darkness in Lamentable Moll had found a new terror, and no one was inclined to tarry in the lengthening shadows. He wondered at his own absence of fear. The courage of ale, no doubt; that and Hood's tread having already come so near to his own life's path, somehow convinced him that nothing ill would claim him this night. 'Of course,' he mumbled, 'if I get the job then all bets are off. And, I gotta keep them eyes open, I do.'

A city guardsman watched Emancipor weave and stumble his

way to the reading post in the round's centre, near the Fountain of Beru, its trickling beard of briny froth splashing desultorily into a feather-clogged pool. Emancipor waved dismissively at the stone-faced guardsman. 'I feel safe!' he shouted. 'Hood's Herald! That's me, heh heh!' He frowned as the man made a hasty warding sign and backed away. 'A joke!' Emancipor called out. 'Hood's truth – I mean, I swear by the Sisters! Health and Plague divvy my plate – I mean, fate – come back here, man! 'Twas a jest!'

Emancipor subsided into muttering. He looked around, and found that he was alone. Not a soul in sight – they'd cleared out uncommonly fast. He shrugged and turned his attention to the tarred wooden post.

The note was on fine linen paper, solitary and nailed at chest-height. Emancipor grunted. ''Spensive paper, that. S'prised it's lasted this long.' Then he saw the ward faintly inked in the lower right-hand corner. Not a minor cantrip, like boils to the family of whoever was foolish enough to steal the note; not even something mildly nasty, like impotence or hair-loss; no, within the circular ward was a skull, deftly drawn. 'Beru's beard,' Emancipor whispered. 'Death. This damned note will outlast the post itself.'

Nervous, he stepped closer to study the words. They showed the hand of a hired scribe, and a good one at that. Sober, he could have made inferences from all these details. Drunk as he was – and knew he was – he found the effort of serious consideration too taxing. It was careless, he knew, but when faced with returning to Subly unclothed in the raiment of the employed, he had to take the chance.

One arm on the post, he leaned closer and squinted. Thankfully, the statement was short.

> Manservant required. Full time. Travel involved.
> Wage to be negotiated depending on experience.
> Call at Sorrowman's Hostel.

Sorrowman's . . . less than a block away. And 'travel', by Hood's cowl, would mean . . . well, it'd mean exactly what it meant, meaning . . . He felt a wide grin stretching his rubbery face, until it ached with sheer delight. *Coin for the wife, whilst far far away I go. School for the hairless rats, and far far away I go. Heh. Heh.*

His arm slipped from the post and the next thing he knew he was lying on the cobbles, staring up at a cloudless night sky. His nose hurt, but it was a distant pain. He sat up and looked around, feeling woozy. The round was empty except for a half-dozen urchins eyeing him from an alleymouth, all looking disappointed to see him awake.

'That's what you think,' Emancipor said as he climbed to his feet. 'I'm getting me a job, right now.' He wobbled before straightening, then plucked at his coachman's jacket and breeches – but it was too dark to see the shape they were in. Damp, of course, but that could be expected, given the heavy weave of the stiff-shouldered coat and its long, tight-cuffed sleeves. ''Spect they'll have a uniform, anyways,' he muttered. 'Tailored, maybe.' *Sorrowman's. That way.*

The journey seemed to take forever, but he eventually made out the sign of the weeping man above the entrance to a narrow, four-storey inn. Yellow light descended from the lantern hooked under the sign, revealing a doorman leaning against the door's ornate frame. A solid kout hung from the man's leather belt, and one of his beefy hands moved to rest on the weapon as he watched Emancipor's approach.

'On your way, old man,' he growled.

Emancipor stopped at the light's edge, reeling slightly. 'Got me an appointment,' he said, straightening up and thrusting out his chin.

'Not here you don't.'

'Manservant. Got the job, I do.'

The doorman scowled, lifting a hand to scratch above his ridged brow. 'Not for long, I'd say, from the look and smell of you. Mind . . .' he scratched some more, then grinned. 'You're on time, anyway. At least, I'm meaning, they're awake by now, I'd guess. Go on in and tell the scriber – he'll lead you on.'

'I'll do just that, my good man.'

The doorman opened the door and, walking carefully, Emancipor managed to navigate through the doorway without bumping the frames. He paused as the door closed behind him, blinking in the bright light coming from a half-dozen candles set on ledges opposite the cloak rack – follower of D'rek, by the look of the gilded bowl on a ledge below the candles.

He stepped closer and looked into the bowl, to see a writhing mass of white worms, faintly pink with some poor animal's blood. Emancipor gagged, hands pressing against the wall. He felt a rush of foamy, bitter ale at the back of his throat and – with nowhere else in range of his sight – he vomited into the bowl.

Through foam-flecked amber bile, the worms jerked about, as if drowning.

Reeling, Emancipor wiped at his mouth, then at the side of the bowl. He turned from the wall. The air was heady with some Stygg incense, sweet as rotting fruit – enough to mask the vomit, he hoped. Emancipor swallowed back another gag-reflex, then drew a careful, measured breath.

A voice spoke from further in and to his right. 'Yes?'

Emancipor watched as a bent, thin old man, his fingertips stained black with ink, stepped timidly into view. Upon seeing him, the scriber snapped upright, glaring. 'Has Dalg that crag-headed ox gone out of his mind?' He rushed forward. 'Out, out!' He shooed with his hands, then stopped in alarm as Emancipor said boldly, 'Mind your manners, sir! I but paused to make an offering, uh, to the Worm of Autumn. I am the manservant, if you pl'zz. Arrived punctual, as instructed. Lead me to my employer, sir, and be quick abou' it.' *Before I let heave another offering, D'rek forgive me.*

He watched the scriber's wrinkled face race through a thespian's array of emotions, ending on fearful regard, the black tip of his tongue darting back and forth over his dry lips. After a moment of this – which Emancipor watched with fascination – the scriber suddenly smiled. 'Clever me, eh? Wisely done, sir.' He tapped his nose. 'Aye. Burn knows, it's the only way I'd show up to work for them two – not that I mean ill of them, mind you that. But I'm as clever as any man, I say, and fit to stinking drunk well suits the hour, the shadow's cast from them two, and all right demeanour and the like, eh? Mind you,' he took Emancipor's arm and guided him towards the stairs that led to the rooms, 'you'll likely get fired, this being your first night and all, but even so. They're on the top floor, best rooms in the house, if you don't mind the bats under the eaves, and I'd wager it's rum to them and all.'

The climb and the lighter feeling in his stomach sobered Emancipor somewhat. By the time they reached the fourth landing, walked down the narrow hall and stopped in front of the last door on the right, he was beginning to realize that the scriber's ramble had, however confusedly, imparted something odd about his new employers – *new? Have I been hired, then? No, no recollection of that* – and he tried to think of what it might be . . . without success. He came to his mind sufficiently to claw through his grey-streaked hair while the wheezing scriber softly scratched on the door. After a moment the latch lifted and the door swung silently open.

'Kind sir,' the scriber said hastily, ducking his head, 'your manservant is here.' He bowed even further, then backed his way down the hall.

Emancipor drew a deep breath, then lifted his gaze to meet the cold regard of the man before him. A shiver rippled down his spine as he felt the full weight of those lifeless grey eyes, but somehow he managed not to flinch, nor drop his gaze, and so studied the man even as he himself was studied. The pale eyes were set far back in a chalky, angular face, the forehead high and squared at the temples, the greying hair swept back and of mariner's length – long and tied in a single tail. An iron-streaked, pointed beard jutted from the man's square, solid chin. He looked to be in his forties, and was dressed in a long, fur-trimmed morning robe – far too warm for Lamentable Moll – and had clasped his long-fingered, ringless hands in front of his silk-cord belt.

Emancipor cleared his throat. 'Most excellent sir!' he boomed. *Too loud, dammit.*

The skin tightened fractionally around the man's eyes.

In a less boisterous tone, Emancipor added, 'I am Emancipor Reese, able manservant, coachman, cook—'

'You are drunk,' the man said, his accent unlike anything Emancipor had ever heard before. 'And your nose is broken, although it appears the bleeding has slowed.'

'My humblest apologies, sir,' Emancipor managed. 'For the drink, I blame grief. For the nose, I blame a wooden post, or poss'bly the cobblestones.'

'Grief?'

'I mourn, sir, a most terr'ble personal trag'dy.'

'How unfortunate. Step inside, then, Mister Reese.'

The chambers within occupied a quarter of the top floor, oppulently fitted with two large poster-beds, both covered in twisted linen, a scriber's desk with drawers and a leather writing-pad, and a low stool before it. Bad frescos set in cheap panels adorned the walls. To the desk's left was a large walk-in wardrobe, its doors open and nothing inside. Beside it was the entrance to a private bathing area, a bead-patterned, soft-hide curtain blocking it from view. Four battered chest-high travel trunks lined one wall; only one open and revealing fine clothes of foreign style on iron hangers. There was no one else in the room, but somehow the presence of a second person remained to give proof to the tousled bed. The only truly odd thing in the room was a plate-sized piece of grey slate, lying on the nearest bed. Emancipor frowned at it, then he sighed and swung a placid smile at the man, who stood calmly by the door, which he now closed, setting the loop-lock over the latch. *A tall one. Makes bowing easier to cheat.*

'Have you any references, Mister Reese?'

'Oh yes, of course!' Emancipor found he was nodding without pause. He tried to stop, but couldn't. 'My wife, Subly. Thirty-one years—'

'I meant, your previous employer.'

'Dead.'

'Before him, then.'

'Dead.'

The man raised one thin eyebrow. 'And before him?'

'Dead.'

'And?'

'And before that I was a cockswain on the able trader, *Searime*, for twenty years doing the Stygg run down Bloodwalk Strait.'

'Ahh, and this ship and her captain?'

'Sixty fathoms down, off Ridry Shelf.'

The second eyebrow rose to join the other one. 'Quite a pedigree, Mister Reese.'

Emancipor blinked. *How did he do that, with the eyebrows?* 'Yes, sir. Fine men, all of them.'

'Do you . . . mourn these losses nightly?'

'Excuse me? Oh. No sir, I do not. The day after, kind sir. Only then. Poor Baltro was a fair man—'

'Baltro? Merchant Baltro? Was he not the most recent victim of this madman who haunts the night?'

'Indeed he was. I, sir, was the last man to see him alive.'

The man's eyebrows rose higher.

'I mean,' Emancipor added, 'except for the killer, of course.'

'Of course.'

'I've never had a complaint.'

'I gathered that, Mister Reese.' He opened his hands to gesture with one to the stool at the desk. 'Please be seated, whilst I endeavour to describe the duties expected of my manservant.'

Emancipor smiled again, then went over and sat down. 'I read there's travel involved.'

'This concerns you, Mister Reese?' The man stood at the foot of one of the beds, his hands once again clasped at his lap.

'Not at all. An incentive, sir. Now that the seas have subsided and the blood-toll is no more, well, I itch for sea-spray, a pitching deck, rolling skylines, the tip and tumble and turn – is something wrong, sir?'

The man had begun to fidget, a greyish cast coming to his

already pale face. 'No, not at all. I simply prefer travelling overland. I take it you can read, or did you hire someone?'

'Oh no, I can read, sir. I've a talent for that. I can read Moll, Theftian and Stygg – from the chart-books, sir. Our pilot, you see, had a taste for the mead—'

'Can you scribe in these languages as well, Mister Reese?'

'Aye, sir. Both scrying and scribing. Why, I can read Mell'zan!'

'Malazan?'

'No, Mell'zan. The Empire, you know.'

'Of course. Tell me, do you mind working nights and sleeping during the day? I understood you are married—'

'Suits me perfectly, sir.'

The man frowned, then nodded. 'Very good, then. The duties include arranging mundane matters related to the necessities of travel. Booking passage, negotiating with port authorities, arranging accommodation howsoever it suits our purposes, ensuring that our attire is well-maintained and scented and free of vermin, and so forth – have you done such work before, Mister Reese?'

'That, and worse – I mean, that and more, sir. I can also groom and shoe horses, r'pair tack, sew, read maps, sight by stars, tie knots, braid ropes—'

'Yes yes, very good. Now, as to the pay—'

Emancipor smiled helpfully. 'I'm dirt cheap, sir. Dirt cheap.'

The man sighed. 'With such talents? Nonsense, Mister Reese. You diminish yourself. Now, I will offer a yearly contract, depositing sufficient amount with a reputable money-holding agency, to allow for regular transferral of earnings to your estate. Your own personal needs will be accommodated free of charge whilst you accompany us. Is the annual sum of twelve hundred standard-weight silver sovereigns acceptable?'

Emancipor stared.

'Well?'

'Uh, uhm . . .'

'Fifteen hundred, then.'

'Agreed! Yes indeed. Most assur'dly, sir!' *Hood's Breath, that's more than Baltro makes – I mean, 'made'.* 'Where do I sign the contract, sir? Shall I begin work now?' Emancipor rose to his feet, waited expectantly.

The man smiled. 'Contract? If you wish. It is of no concern to me.'

'Uhm, what shall I call you, sir? Sir?'

'I am named Bauchelain. Master will suffice.'

'Of course, Master. And, uh, the other one?'

'The other one?'

'The one you travel with, Master.'

'Oh,' Bauchelain turned away, his gaze falling to rest pensively on the slab of slate. 'He is named Korbal Broach. A very unassuming man, you might say. As manservant, you answer to me, and me alone. I doubt whether Master Broach forsees a use for you.' He turned and smiled slightly, his eyes as cold as ever. 'Of course, in that I could be wrong. We'll see, I imagine, won't we? Now, I wish a meal, with meat, rare, and a dark wine, not overly sweet. You may place your order with the scriber below.'

Emancipor bowed. 'At once, Master.'

GULD STOOD ATOP DEAD SEKARAND'S CREAKING TOWER AND scanned the city, squinting to see through the miasmic woodsmoke that hung almost motionless over the rooftops. The stillness below contrasted strangely with the nightclouds over his head, tumbling, rolling on out to sea, seeming so close above him that he found he'd instinctively hunched down as he leaned on the moss-slick parapet and waited, with dread, for the lantern signal poles to be raised.

It was the call of the season, when the sky seemed to heave itself over, trapping the city in its own breath for days on end. The season of ills, plagues, rats driven into the streets by the dancing moon.

Dead Sekarand's Tower was less than a decade old yet already abandoned and known to be haunted, but Guld had little fear, since he himself had been responsible for tending and nurturing the black weeds of hoary rumour – it suited the new purpose he'd found for the dull-stoned edifice. From this almost-central vantage point, his system of signal poles could be seen in any section of Lamentable Moll.

In the days when the Mell'zan Empire had first threatened the city-states of Theft – mostly on the other coast, where the Imperial Fist Greymane had landed his invasion force, coming close to conquering the entire island before being murdered by his own troops – in the days of smoke and threatening winds, Sekarand had come to Lamentable Moll. Calling himself a High

Sorceror, he had contracted with King Seljure to aid in the city's defence, and had raised this structure as his spar of power. What followed then was confused and remained so ever since, though Guld knew more details than most. Sekarand had raised liches to keep him company within these confines, and they'd either driven him mad or murdered him outright – Sekarand had flung himself, or had been thrown, from these very merlons, down to his death on the cobbles below. Grim jokes about the High Sorceror's swift descent had run through the streets for a time. In any case, like the Mell'zans – whose presence on Theft remained in but a single, downtrodden port on the northwest coast with half a regiment of jaded marines – Sekarand had been a promise unfulfilled.

Guld had used the tower for three years now. He'd seen a few shades, all of whom vowed service to a lich who dwelt under the tower's foundations, but apart from proferring this tidbit of information, they'd said little and had never threatened him, and the nature of their service to the lich remained a mystery.

It had been Guld who'd asked them to moan and howl occasionally, keeping the plunderers and explorers at bay. They'd complied with tireless dedication.

The clouds felt heavy overhead as Guld waited – as if bloated with blood. The sergeant stood unmoving, expecting at any moment the first drops of *something* to come spattering against his face.

After a while, he sensed a presence beside him and slowly turned to find a shade hovering near the trapdoor.

Clothed in wispy rags, ghostly limbs sporting knotted strips of sailcloth, twine and faded silk – all that held it to this mortal world – its black-pit eyes, set in a pallid face, were fixed on the sergeant.

Guld sensed, with sudden alarm, that the shade had been but moments from launching itself at his back. *One shove, and over I'd go . . .*

Discovered, the ghostly figure now slumped, grumbling to itself.

'Pleased with the weather?' Guld asked, fighting down a chill shiver.

'An air,' the shade rasped, 'to smother sound and scent. Dull the vision. Yet it dances unseen.'

'How so?'

'Among the Warrens, this air dances bright. My master, my lord, lich of liches, supreme ruler, He Who Awakened All Groggy after centuries of slumber but is now Bursting With Wit, my master, then, sends me – me, humourless serf, humble savant of social injustices, injustices that persist no doubt to this day, me, then, I come with a warning by his insistent command.'

'A warning? Is this weather fed by sorcery?'

'A hunter stalks the dark.'

'I know,' Guld growled. 'What else,' he asked without expecting a comprehensible answer, 'do you sense about him?'

'My master, my lord, lich of—'

'Your master,' Guld interrupted, 'what of him?'

'—liches, supreme ruler, He Who—'

'Enough of the titles!'

'—Awakened All Groggy after—'

'Shall I call on an exorcist, Shade?'

'If you'd not so rudely interrupted I'd be done by now!' the ghost snapped. 'My *master*, then, has no desire to be among the hunted. There.'

Guld scowled. 'Just how nasty is this killer? Never mind, you've answered me, haven't you? At the moment, I can't stop him, whoever he is. If he chooses to ferret out your master, well, I can only wish the lich luck.'

'Amusing,' the shade grumbled, then slowly vanished.

Amusing? The shades of this tower are damned odd, even for shades. In any case, keeping mulling, Guld. Lamentable Moll's known for its sorcerors, its diviners and readers, its warlocks and well-sounders, seers and the like, but it's mostly small fish – nobody's ever claimed Theft to be an island of high civilization. In Korel it's said a demon prince runs a merchant company, and in the old city-swamps of the lowbeds the undead are as common

*as midges. Glad I don't live in Korel. What was I thinking about?
Oh, yes, suspects . . .*

Nothing else of note marked the next hour. The fourth bell
after midnight came and went. Even so, Guld was not surprised
a short time later when three wavering lights rose in panicked
haste above the dark buildings in a nearby quarter. *The twelfth.
Unending, each night . . .* Maybe Stul Ophan had been right – the
beacons rose from the estate district, from the nobility's pinched,
bloodless heart.

He spun from the merlon and took a step to the trapdoor, then
stopped, the shock of rain against his brow sending a superstitious
chill through his bones. A moment later he shook himself. *Not
blood. Just water, nothing more. Nothing more.* He pulled up the
heavy wooden door with an angry wrench, and quickly plunged
down into the darkness below.

The shades set up a howl all the way down, and this time Guld
knew that their gelid moans, ringing from the stone walls on all
sides, had nothing to do with keeping thieves and adventurers at
bay.

A N HOUR BEFORE DAWN, BAUCHELAIN INSTRUCTED EMANCIPOR to ready his bed. Of the other man – Korbal Broach – there'd been no sign, which did not seem to perturb Bauchelain, who'd spent the night inscribing sigils and signs on the piece of slate. Hours, hours on end at the desk, the man hunched over the grey stone. Etching and scribing, muttering under his breath, and consulting from a half-dozen leather-bound books – each worth a year's wage in paper alone.

Emancipor, hung-over and dead tired, puttered here and there in the room, once he'd had the remains of the supper removed, tidying up as best he could. He found in Bauchelain's travel chest a finely made hauberk of black-iron chain, long-sleeved and knee-length, which he oiled from a kit, using spare wire to repair old damage – cut and crushed links – the coat had known battle, and so too the man who owned it. And yet to look at him, as Emancipor often did from the corner of his eye, it was hard to believe Bauchelain had ever been a soldier. He scribed and mumbled and squinted and occasionally poked out his tongue as he worked over the slate. Like an artist, or an alchemist, or a sorceror.

A damned strange way to pass the night, Emancipor concluded. He bit back on his curiosity, which grew more tempered with his suspicions that the man indeed was a practitioner in the dark arts. *The less gleaned the better, I always say.*

He finished with the mail coat and, grunting under its slippery weight, returned it to its perch. As he adjusted the inside-padded shoulders on the heavy hanger, he noticed a long, flat box positioned below the coat-hooks. It had a latch, but was otherwise unlocked. He removed it, grunting again at its weight, and set it on the spare bed. A glance over at Bauchelain assured him that his master was taking no heed, so Emancipor unlatched the lid and lifted it away to reveal a dismantled crossbow, a dozen iron-shod quarrels and a pair of mail gauntlets open at the palm and the finger-tips.

His memory swept him back to his youth, on the battlefield that would in legend be known as Estbanor's Grief, where the rag-tag militias of Theft – before each city found its own king – had thrown back an invading army from Korel. Among the Korelri legions were soldiers who carried Mell'zan weapons – each superbly made and superior to anything local. This was such a weapon, made by a master smith, constructed entirely of hard-ened, tempered iron – maybe even the famous D'Avorian Steel – even the stock was metal. 'Hood's Breath,' Emancipor whispered, running his fingers over the pieces.

''Ware the heads,' Bauchelain murmured, having come up to stand behind Emancipor. 'They kill at a touch, if blood be drawn.'

Emancipor's hand recoiled. 'Poison?'

'You think me an assassin, Mister Reese?'

Emancipor turned and met the man's amused gaze.

'In my days,' Bauchelain said, 'I've been many things . . . but poisoner is not among them. They are invested.'

'You're a sorceror?'

Bauchelain's lips quirked into a smile. 'Many people call them-selves that. Do you follow a god, Mister Reese?'

'My wife swears by 'em – I mean, uh, she prays to a few, Master.'

'And you?'

Emancipor shrugged. 'The devout die too, don't they? Clove to an ascendant just doubles the funeral costs, 'sfar as I can see, and that's all. Mind, I've prayed fierce on occasion – maybe it saved my skin, but maybe it was just my cast to slip Hood's shadow so far . . .'

Bauchelain's gaze softened slightly, lost its focus. 'So far . . .' he said, as if the words were profound. Then he clapped his man-servant on the shoulder and returned to his desk. 'A long life is yours, Mister Reese. I see no shadow's shadow, and the face of your death is a distant one.'

'The face?' Emancipor licked his lips, which had become uncommonly dry. 'You, uh, you divined my moment of death?'

'As near as one can,' Bauchelain replied. 'Some veils are not easily torn aside. But I think I have as much as needed.' He paused, then added, 'Even so, the weapon needs no cleaning. You may return it to its trunk.'

Not just a sorceror, then. A Hood-stained, death-delving necromancer. Damn you, Subly, the things I do . . . He replaced the lid and set the latches. 'Master?'

'Hmm?' Bauchelain was busy over his slab again.

'My face at death – did you see it truly?'

'Your visage? Yes, as I said.'

'Was it, was it a face of fear?'

'No, surprisingly. It seems you die laughing.'

'**D**IE LAUGHING,' EMANCIPOR MUTTERED AS HE STUMBLED HIS way down the empty, dark streets, seeing only his soft, Subly-warmed bed hovering in his mind's eye. 'That's likely a damned lie, I'd say, unless I quit – get as far away from that death-dealer as I can. Queen of Dreams, what a mess I'm in. It's the Lad o' Luck for certain, not the Lady. It's the push, not the pull. I was drunk – too drunk to sniff it all out, and then it was too late. He's seen my death, too. He has me. I can't quit. He'll send something after me – a ghoul, or a k'niptrill, or some other damned spectre – to tear my heart out, and Subly'd be cursing the blood-stained sheets down at Beater's Rock an' all the lye she'd have to buy and that'd be a curse to my name even then, with me dead and gone and the brats fighting o'er my new boots and—'

He stopped with a grunt as he walked clean into another man, whose body felt as solid as a bale of hides, and who – as Emancipor stepped back in alarm – was as big as a half-blooded Trell. 'M'pardon, sir,' Emancipor said, ducking his head.

The man raised a black-mailed arm, at the end of which was a massive, flat, pale and soft-looking – almost delicate – hand.

Emancipor took another step back as the air between them seemed to crackle and something tugged hard at his guts.

Then the hand twitched, the fingers fluttered, and the arm slowly dropped back down. A soft giggle came from under the stranger's hood. 'Sweet fate, he's marked for me,' he said in a high, quavering voice.

'I said my pardon, sir,' Emancipor said again. He realized he was in the Estate District, having gone by the shortest route between Sorrowman's and his house – damned stupid, what with blood-hungry private guards patrolling the nobles' quarter, determined to catch the mad killer for their masters, and the rewards to follow. 'If you'll let me pass, sir,' Emancipor said, moving to step past. There was no one else about, and dawn was still a quarter-bell away.

The stranger giggled again, then said, 'Such a mark, saving. You felt the chill, then?'

Damned strange accent. 'It's a hot enough night,' he mumbled as he hurried by. The stranger let him go, but Emancipor felt cold eyes on his back as he walked down the street.

A moment later he was surprised to see a cloaked figure hurrying its way down the other pavement – small, feminine. Then he was further startled by the passage of an armoured man, rustling and softly clanking, moving along on the woman's trail. *Hood's Herald, the sun's not even up yet!*

He suddenly felt very tired. Somewhere ahead, he now saw, was a commotion of some kind. He saw lantern lights, heard shouting, then a woman's scream. He hesitated, then took a side route that'd take him around the scene and back on to more familiar ground.

Emancipor felt clammy under his clothes, as if he'd just brushed . . . something unpleasant. He shook himself. 'Better get used to it, working nights and all. Anyway, I was safe enough – no chance of laughing this damned night, that's for sure.'`

'A MESSY ONE,' THE CHALK-FACED GUARD MUTTERED, WIPING across his mouth with the back of his hand.

Guld nodded. It was the worst he'd seen yet. Young Lordson Hoom, ninth-removed from the throne's own blood, had died ignobly, with most of his insides strewn and smeared halfway down the alley.

And yet no one had heard a sound. The sergeant had come upon the scene less than a quarter-bell after the two patrol guards had themselves stumbled on to it. The blood and bits of flesh weren't yet cold.

Guld had sent off the tracking dogs. He'd dispatched his corporal to the palace with two messages – one to the king, and the other – far less softly worded – to Magus Stul Ophan. With the exception of his squad detachment and a lone terrified horse still hitched to the Lordson's overturned carriage – *overturned. Hood's breath!* – there was only one other person present at the scene, and that presence had Guld deeply, profoundly, worried.

He finally turned his gaze from the carriage to study the woman. *Princess Sharn. King Seljure's only child. His heir, and, if the rumours are true, a real dark piece of work in her own right.*

Though it would mean trouble later, Guld had insisted on detaining the royal personage. After all, it'd been her screaming that had drawn the patrol, and the question of what the princess was doing out in the city well after the night's fourth bell – with no guard, not even her maid in waiting – needed answering.

His eyes narrowed on the young girl. She was wrapped in a voluminous cloak, hooded with her face hidden in shadows. She'd regained her composure with alarming ease. Guld scowled, then approached her. He jerked his head to the two guardsmen flanking the princess, and they moved away.

'Highness,' Guld began, 'your calm is an impressive example of royal blood. Frankly, I'm awed.'

She acknowledged this with a slight tilt of her head.

Guld rubbed at his jaw, glancing away for a moment, then swung upon her an intense professional expression. 'I am also relieved, for it means I can question you here and now, whilst your memory remains fresh, unclouded—'

'You are presumptuous,' the princess said in a light, bored tone.

He ignored that. 'It's clear you and Lordson Hoom were involved in a clandestine relationship. Only this time, either you came later, or he came early. For you, then, a pull of the Lady. For the lad, a push of the Lord. I can imagine your relief, Princess, not to mention your father's – who will have been duly informed by now.' He paused at hearing her quickly drawn breath. 'So, what I need to know is what you saw, precisely, upon arriving. Did you see anyone else? Did you hear anything? Smell anything?'

'No,' she answered. 'Hoomy was . . . was already, uh, like that,' she gestured towards the alley behind Guld.

'Hoomy?'

'Lordson Hoom, I mean.'

'Tell me, Princess, where is your handmaid? I can't believe you would come here entirely alone. She'd be your messenger in this affair, obviously, since I imagine the secret love notes flew fast and often—'

'How dare you—'

'Save that for your cowering underlings,' Guld snapped. 'Answer me!'

'Do nothing of the sort!' a voice commanded behind the sergeant.

He turned to see Magus Stul Ophan pushing his way past a

line of guards at the alleymouth. It was nearing dawn, and the fat man's arrival was peculiarly accompanied by the day's first birdsong. 'Highness,' Stul said, inclining his head, 'your father the King wishes to see you immediately. You may take my carriage.' Stul turned a dagger glare on Guld. 'The sergeant is, I believe, done with you.'

Both men stepped back as Princess Sharn hurried past and quickly disappeared inside the carriage. As soon as the door closed and the driver flicked the horses into motion, Guld rounded on the Magus. 'Now, I gather that Lordson Hoom was anything but an appropriate hay-roller for the precious princess, and I can imagine that Seljure wants to bury any *royal* involvement in what's happened here – but if you ever again step between me and my investigation, Ophan, I'll leave what's left of you for the crabs. Understood?'

The Magus went red, then white. He spluttered, 'The King's command, Guld—'

'And if I'd found *him* standing here over the lad's mangled corpse, I'd be no less direct in my questioning. The king is one man – his fear is nothing compared to the city's fear. And you can tell him, if he wants anything left to rule, he'd best stay out of my way and let me do my job. Gods, man, can't you feel the panic?'

'I can! Burn's Blood, I damned well share it!'

Guld took a handful of Stul Ophan's brocaded cloak and pulled the man to the alley. 'Take a long look, Magus. This was managed in silence – neither estate to each side awoke – even the garden hounds remained silent. Tell me, what did this?' He released Stul Ophan's cloak and stepped back.

The air turned icy around the magus as he hastily cast a series of cantrips. 'A spell of silence, Sergeant,' he rasped. 'The lad screamed all right, gods how he screamed. And the air itself was closed, folded in on itself. High sorcery, Guld, the highest. No smell could escape to afright the dogs on the other sides of these walls—'

'And the carriage? It has the look of having been rammed, as if by a mad bull. Scry the horse, dammit!'

Stul Ophan staggered up to the quivering, lathered animal. As he reached up one hand the horse reared back, eyes rolling, ears flattening against its skull. The magus swore. 'Driven mad! Its heart races but it cannot move. It will be dead within the hour—'

'But, what did it see? What image remains behind its eyes?'

'Obliterated,' Stul Ophan said. 'Wiped clean.'

They both turned at the fast-approaching sound of shod hooves on the cobblestones. An armoured rider appeared, boldly pushing his white charger past the guards – *Hood, what's the point of having a cordon of guards?* The newcomer wore a white fur-lined cloak, a white-enamelled iron helm and a coat of silver mail. The pommel at the end of his broadsword looked to be a single polished opal.

Guld cursed under his breath, then called out to the rider. 'What brings you here, Mortal Sword?'

The man reined in. He removed his helmet to reveal a narrow, scarred face and close-set eyes that glittered black. Those eyes now turned to the lantern-lit scene in the alley. 'The foulest of deeds,' he rasped, his voice thin and ragged – the story went that a Drek assassin's dagger had come near to opening the man's throat a dozen years back – but Tulgord Vise, Mortal Sword to the Sisters, had survived – while the assassin hadn't.

'This is not a religious matter,' Guld said, 'though I thank you for your vow to scour the nights until the killer is found—'

'Found, sir? Carved into pieces, this I have sworn. And what do you, cynical unbeliever, know of matters of faith? Do you not smell the stench of Hood in this? You, Magus, can you deny the truth of my words?'

Stul Ophan shrugged. 'A necromancer – most certainly, Mortal Sword, but that doesn't perforce mean a worshipper of the God of Death. Indeed, the priesthood disavows necromancy. After all, those dark arts are an assault on the Warren of the Dead—'

'Political convenience, that disavowal. You are a spineless, mewling fool, Ophan. I have crossed swords with Hood's Herald, or do you forget?'

Guld noted one of his guardsmen flinch at that. 'Tulgord Vise,' the sergeant said, 'Death was not the goal here – hasn't been all along.'

'What do you mean, sir?'

'I mean the killer is . . . collecting—'

'Collecting?'

'Parts.'

'Parts?'

'Organs, to be more precise. Ones generally considered vital to life, Mortal Sword. Their removal results in death as a matter of course. Do you see the distinction?'

Tulgord Vise leaned on the horn of his saddle. 'Semantics are not among the games I play, sir. If only organs are required, why then the destruction of souls?'

Guld turned to the magus. 'Destruction, Stul Ophan?'

The man shrugged uneasily. 'Or . . . theft, Sergeant, which is of course more difficult . . .'

'But why steal souls, if destroying them more easily serves the purpose of ensuring your inability to question them?'

'I don't know.'

Tulgord Vise settled back in his saddle, one gauntleted hand resting on his sword. 'Do not impede me, sir,' he said to Guld. 'My blade shall deliver what is just.'

'Better the madman writhe on the hooks,' Guld replied, 'unless you feel sufficient to the task of quelling a city's blood-lust.'

This silenced the Mortal Sword, if only briefly. 'They will sit well with my deed, sir—'

'It won't be enough, Mortal Sword. Better still if we drag him through every street, but it's not up to me. In any case,' Guld added, stepping forward, 'it's you who'd best stay out of my way. Interfere with me at your peril, Mortal Sword.'

Tulgord Vise half-drew his weapon before Stul Ophan leapt close and stilled the man's arm.

'Tulgord, 'tis precipitous!' the magus bleated.

'Remove your feeble grip, swine!'

'Look about you, sir. I beg you!'

The Mortal Sword glanced around, then slowly resheathed his weapon. Clearly, unlike Stul Ophan, he hadn't heard the locking of six crossbows, but the weapons were trained on him now, and the expressions on the faces of Guld's squad left no doubt as to their intent.

The sergeant cleared his throat. 'This is the twelfth night in a row, Mortal Sword. It has, I believe, become very personal to my men. We want the killer, and we'll have him. So again, stay out of my way, sir. I seek no insult to you or your honour, but draw your blade again and you'll be dropped like a rabid dog.'

Tulgord Vise kicked Stul Ophan away, then wheeled his mount. 'You mock the gods, sir, and for that your soul will pay.' He put spurs to the charger's flanks and rode off.

The moment was closed by the sudden collapse of the carriage horse, followed immediately by the heavy snap of quarrels released in the animal's direction. Guld winced as the six bolts buried themselves in the horse's body.

Dammit, those fingers itched, didn't they. He swung a sour look on his sheepish men.

Stul Ophan occupied the embarrassed moment by straightening his clothing. Then he said without looking up, 'Your killer's a foreigner, Sergeant. No one in Lamentable Moll is of this high order in necromancy, including me.'

Guld acknowledged his thanks with a nod.

'I'll report to the king,' the magus said as his own carriage returned, 'to the effect that you've narrowed your list of suspects, Sergeant. And I shall add my opinion that, barring interference, you're close to your quarry.'

'I hope you're right,' Guld said in a moment of honest doubt that clearly startled Stul Ophan, who simply nodded then walked to his carriage.

Guld waited until the man left, then singled out one of his guards and pulled him to one side. He studied the young man's face. 'Death's Herald crossed your trail, then?'

'Sir?'

'I saw you react to Vise's words. Of course, he meant someone else in that sordid role, since it's a claim he's made for twenty years. But what did you hear in those words?'

'A superstition, Sergeant. A drunken old man, earlier this night, down in the wharf district – he called himself that, is all. Was nothing, in truth—'

'What was the man doing?'

'Reading a posted notice in Fishmonger's Round, I think. It's still there, warded, I heard.'

'Likely nothing to it, then.'

'As the gods decree, sir.'

Guld narrowed his gaze, then grunted. 'Fair enough. Once I've done reporting to the King, let's take a look at this notice.'

'Yes, sir.'

At this moment the dogger returned with his hounds. 'It's a mess,' he reported. 'By their tuck they found a woman's trail, or a man's, or both, or neither. One, or two, then a third, heavy I'd say, that last one, with brine and sword-oil, or so the dogs danced, anyway.'

Guld studied the six hounds on their limp leashes, their heads hanging, their tongues lolling. 'Those trails. Where did they all lead?'

'Lost them down in the wharfs – y'got rotting clams and fish guts to contend with, eh? Or else the trails were magicked. My children here all closed in on a sack of rotting fish – not like 'em, I say, not like 'em at all.'

'From the smell, your hounds did more than just close in on that sack of rotting fish.'

The dogger frowned. 'We thought we might do better hiding our scent, sir.'

Guld stepped closer to the man, then flinched back. *Hood take me, wasn't just the dogs that rolled in those fish!* He stared at the dogger.

The man looked away, licking his lips, then yawning.

SUBLY'S VOICE CAME FROM THE MAIN ROOM. 'PIGEONS! THEY'RE roosting over our heads, in the eaves, in the drain pipes – why haven't you done anything about it, Emancipor? And now . . . and now, oh, Soliel forfend!'

It was a voice that could penetrate every corner of their house. A voice from which there was no domestic escape. 'But soon . . .' Emancipor whispered, knowing his mood was miserable from lack of sleep and too much drink the night before, knowing he was being unfair to his poor wife, knowing all these things but unable to stop the dark torrent of his thoughts. He paused to examine in the tin mirror the blur of his lined face and the bloodshot eyes, before setting the blade once again to his whiskers.

The brats whined from their loft, their scratching so loud he could hear every scrape of grubby nails against flesh. They'd been sent home, both with the mange. Their mother was . . . mortified. There'd be need for an alchemist – at great expense – but the damage was done. The foul-smelling skin mould that was the curse of dogs and lowly street urchins had invaded their home, befouling their position, their prestige, mocking their pride. A bowl-full of gold coins in Soliel's temple could not reverse the disaster. And for Subly the cause was clear—

'The pigeons, Emancipor! I want them out! You hear me?'

She'd been in a good enough mood earlier in the day, doing a poor job of hiding her shock at his finding work so swiftly, and an even poorer job of disguising the avaricious glint that came into her eyes when he explained the financial arrangements that had already been made. For these rewards, Subly had yet to take the broom to him, driving him out into the muddy, garbage-strewn, slate-filled backyard to deal with the pigeons. She'd even allowed him an extra hour of sleep before wailing in horror at their children's ignoble return from the tutor's.

They could afford the alhemist, now. They could even afford to move closer to the school, into a finer neighbourhood, full of proper people thus far spared Subly's dramatic life.

He told himself he shouldn't be so mean – after all, she'd stood by him all these years. 'Like a mountain . . .' And she'd had her own past, dark and messy and tainted with blood. And she'd done her share of suffering since, though not so much as to prevent her begetting two whelps during the years he'd mostly spent at sea. Emancipor paused again in his shaving to scowl. That had always nibbled at his insides, especially since neither child looked much like him. But he'd done his part raising them, so in a way it didn't matter. Their contempt for him was truly and surely sufficient proof of his fatherhood, no matter the blood's mix.

Emancipor washed the crusty suds from his face. Maybe to-night he'd meet the other man, the mysterious Korbal Broach. And he'd have his new uniform measured, and his travelling kit assembled.

'I want the traps set, Emancipor Reese! Before you leave, you hear me?'

'Yes, dear!'

'You'll stop at the alchemist's?'

He rose from the stool and reached to the bed-post for his coat. 'Which one? N'sarmin? Tralp Younger?'

'Tralp, of course, you oaf!'

Add another two silver crowns to the cost, then. She's already getting comfortable with the new state of affairs . . .

'Set the traps! Hood's Herald visit those damned pigeons!'

Emancipor frowned. *Hood's Herald. Something, yesterday . . .*

He shook his head and shrugged. 'Curse of the ale,' he muttered, as he turned to the hanging covering the bedroom entrance. 'Dear Subly . . . The mountain that roars . . . but soon, so very soon . . .'

THE KING HAD SHOWN HIM FEAR. IN ELDER DAYS THAT WOULD have condemned Guld to the assassin's knife. But Seljure was an old man, now – older than his years. His Highness had found tremulous uncertainty his bed-mate, now that the concubines had been sent away. The king's tight-skinned, snaked-eyed advisors remained, of course, but even they hadn't been present for Guld's report. Even so, if they caught a sniff – the king had shown his fear, not just of the killer in the city, but of the dark storm brewing in Stygg and the rumbles from the Korelri Compact to the south. The king had . . . babbled. To a simple sergeant of the guard. And Guld now knew more about the precious Princess Sharn than he'd care to.

He shrugged to himself as he strode down the narrow, winding and barrow-humped Street of Ills on his way to Fishmonger's Round. Twilight had descended on Lamentable Moll in every way, it seemed. In any case, he'd done his duty, made his report to King Seljure; he received the expected instructions to quell the rumours of the royal involvement. Lordson Hoom's father, a landholder of some clout, had been taken care of – with a chestful of coin and promises, no doubt, and Guld had returned to the city's quiet, tense streets.

He'd left the corporal standing guard over the posting, even though the death ward made the notice's theft highly unlikely. Guld had been forced to await the audience with Seljure for most of the day, and now the sun was low in the sky over the bay. News of the noble son's murder had deepened the fearful pall over the city; already the shops were closing up, the streets emptying, because tonight there would be hired killers out – shadowy extensions of noble wrath – indiscriminate with a vengeance. Tonight, anyone foolish enough to remain on the streets without good cause (or a bristling squad of bodyguards) was likely to get his entrails pulled out, if not worse.

Guld turned a corner and approached the Round. His corporal – standing nervously with a hand on his shortsword – was the only occupant left, save one skinny dog, a bedraggled crow perched atop the post and a dozen seagulls squabbling over something in the sewer trench.

A breeze had come in from the sea, only marginally cooler than the turgid, sweltering heat in the city. Guld wiped sweat from his upper lip and walked up to his corporal.

'Anyone take the measure of you, lad?'

The young man shook his head. 'No, sir. I've been here all day, sir.'

Guld grunted. 'Sorry, I was delayed at the king's palace. Feet tired?'

'Yes, sir.'

'Well then, let's exercise them – you have the address from the notice?'

'Yes, sir. And I heard from a rat-hunter that there's two of them, foreigners, who came in on the *Mist Rider* . . .'

'Go on.'

The corporal shifted weight. 'Uh, well, the *Mist Rider* last called out of Korel and has since picked up cargo after unloading some iron, and left for Mare this morning. Oh, and the foreigners hired their manservant.'

'Oh?'

'Yes, sir, and he was the coachman for Merchant Baltro, sir. Imagine that.'

Guld scowled. 'All right, lad, let's go then.'

'Yes, sir. Sorrowman's Hostel. It's not far.'

DALG THE DOORMAN GRINNED KNOWINGLY AT GULD. 'AIN'T s'prised you come, Sergeant, ain't s'prised at all. Come to see Obler, eh? Only he's retired. Ain't lending money no more, least not as I can see, and—'

Guld cut in, 'You have a pair of guests. Foreigners.'

O-Oh, yes, them. Odd pair.'

'What's odd about them?'

The doorman frowned and scratched his head. 'Well,' he said. 'You know. Odd. One of 'em never leaves the room, eh?'

'And the other one?'

'Not so often neither, and hardly at all now that they got their manservant. Oh, they don't visit nobody and nobody visits them, and they eat in their room, too.'

Guld nodded. 'So, are they both in right now?'

'Yes, sir.'

The sergeant left the corporal with the doorman and entered Sorrowman's. He was immediately confronted by the hostelier, who approached with an offerings bowl and a cloth in his hands. He quickly set the bowl on a ledge and tucked the cloth into his belt. 'Guardsman, can I help you?'

Guld watched the man's long, blackened fingers begin weaving a nervous pattern as they clasped and unclasped at the hostelier's lap. 'Obler, isn't it? Keeping honest these days?'

The man blanched. 'Oh yes indeed, Guardsman. For years! Run this establishment, y'see, and do scribing on the side.

53

I'm respectable now, sir. Upstanding and all, sir.' Obler's eyes darted.

'I want to speak to your two foreign guests, Obler.'

'Oh! Well, I'd best get them, then.'

'I'll go with you.'

'Oh! Very well, follow me, sir, if you will.'

They headed up the narrow, heavily-carpeted stairs, strode down the hallway. Obler knocked on the door. They waited a moment, then an old man's voice spoke from the other side.

'What is it, Obler?'

The scriber leaned close to Guld. 'That's Reese,' he hissed. 'The manservant.' He then called, 'A guardsman to speak with your masters, Reese. Open, if you please.'

Guld glared at Obler. 'Next time,' he rasped, 'just get them to open the damned door.' He could hear the murmurs of conversation from within, and he reached up a hand to more forcefully pound on the door when it suddenly opened and the manservant quickly slipped out into the hallway, then shut the door once again behind him.

Emancipor's eyes widened as he looked up and recognized the sergeant.

'Emancipor Reese,' Guld drawled. 'I questioned you not two days ago, and now here you are again. How strange.'

'A man needs work,' Reese grumbled. 'Nothing more to it.'

'Did I say there was?'

'You said "strange", but it's nothing strange about it, 'cepting you coming here.'

Huh, the old bastard's got a point. 'I wish to speak with your masters. You may announce me now, or whatever it is they want you to do.'

'Ah, well, Sergeant. My master regrets to inform you he's not receiving guests this evening, as he is at a crucial juncture in his research—'

'I'm not here as a guest, old man. Either announce me or step aside. I will speak to the men within.'

'There's but one within,' Reese said. 'Master Bauchelain is a scholar, Sergeant. He wishes no distractions—'

Guld growled and tried to push Reese aside, but the old man planted his feet and stood his ground. The sergeant was surprised at Reese's deceptive strength until he saw the old sword-scars on his right forearm. *Damned veteran. I hate dealing with veterans – they don't buckle.* Guld stepped back, placing a hand on his sword. 'You've done more than should be expected, Reese, protecting your master's wish for privacy. But I'm a sergeant of the City Watch, and this is an official visit. If you impede me further, you'll end up in the stock, Reese.' Guld felt his body tense as Reese's lined face darkened dangerously. *Damned veteran.* 'Don't make this messy. Don't.'

'If I let you in, Sergeant—' Reese's voice was like gravel shifting in the surf, 'I'll likely get fired. A man needs to work. I need this job, sir. I ain't had the best of luck, as you know. I need this job, and I mean to keep it. If you've questions, maybe I can answer 'em, maybe I can't, but I won't let you pass.'

'Hood's breath,' Guld sighed, taking another step back. He turned to Obler, who had begun whimpering and throwing futile gestures at the two men. 'Get my corporal, Obler. He's out front. Tell him: double-time, weapon out. Understood?'

'Oh! I implore you—'

'Now!' The scriber scurried down the hall. Guld swung back to Reese, who looked resigned. The sergeant spoke quietly, 'My corporal, Reese, will make a lot of noise coming up here. You'll be disarmed and restrained. Loudly. You'll have done all you could. No master worth his salt will find cause to fire you. Do it my way, Reese, and you'll not get arrested. Or killed. Otherwise, we'll work through you – we'll take our time, until your breath is short and you're done, then we'll cut you down. Well, which way is it to be?'

Reese sagged. 'All right, you bastard.'

They heard the corporal's heavy boots on the stairs, the clatter of his scabbard as it struck the railing spokes, then his gasps as he appeared at the landing, his blade held out in front of him, his face flushed. The lad's eyes widened upon seeing his sergeant and the manservant standing calmly watching him, then he ran forward as Guld waved him on.

Guld turned back to Reese. 'All right,' he whispered, 'make it sound convincing.' He reached out and grasped Reese by the coat's brocaded collar. The old man bellowed, throwing a boot back to hammer the door, rattling it in its frame. Guld pulled Reese to one side and pushed him up against the wall. The corporal arrived.

'Your sword to the bastard's neck!' Guld ordered, and the corporal complied with undue zeal, nearly slitting Reese's throat until Guld pulled the lad's arm back in alarm.

At that moment the door opened. The man in the threshold took in the scene in the hallway with one lazy, cool glance, then met Guld's stare. 'Release my servant, sir,' he said softly.

Guld felt a chill race along his veins. *This one's for real.* The sergeant gestured at his corporal. 'Step back, lad.' The guard, confused, did as he was told. 'Sheathe,' Guld commanded. The sword slid into its scabbard with a rasp and click.

'That's more agreeable,' the foreigner said. 'Please come in, Sergeant, since you seem so eager to meet me. Emancipor, join us, please.'

Guld nodded to his corporal. 'Wait out here, lad.'

'Yes, sir.'

The three men entered the room, Reese closing the door and dropping the latch.

Guld looked around. A desk cluttered with . . . slabs of slate; the remains of a breakfast on a chair, recently finished. *Odd, it's near sunset.* Two slept-in beds, travel trunks, only one open and revealing a city-dweller's clothes, a coat of mail – a weapon box beneath it – and a false backing. The other three trunks were securely locked. Guld took a step closer to the desk, eyeing the slate. 'I don't recognize those runes,' he said, turning to the austere man. 'Where are you from?'

'A distant land, Sergeant. Its name would, alas, mean nothing to you.'

'You have a facility for languages,' Guld noted.

The man raised an eyebrow. 'Passing only. I understand my accent is, in fact, pronounced.'

'How long since you learned Theftian?'

'That is this language's name? I thought it was Mollian.'

'Theft is the island. Moll is a city on it. I asked you a question, sir.'

'It's an important one, then? Very well, about three weeks. During our passage from Korel, I hired one of the crewmen to instruct me – a native of this island. In any case, the language is clearly related to Korelri.'

'You are a sorceror, sir.'

The man assented with a slight nod. 'I am named Bauchelain.'

'And your travelling companion?'

'Korbal Broach, a freed eunuch, sir.'

'A eunuch?'

Bauchelain nodded again. 'An unfortunate practice among the people from whom he hails, done to all male slaves. For obvious reasons, Korbal Broach desires solitude, peace and quiet.'

'Where is he, then? In one of the trunks?'

Bauchelain smiled. 'I did not say *shy*, did I, Sergeant? No, he remains outside the city, as crowds disturb him.'

'Where?'

'Precisely? I cannot be sure. He . . . wanders.'

Guld looked down at the slate slabs. 'What are these?'

'Imperfect efforts, Sergeant. The local slate possesses some intriguing mineral properties – no doubt the reason why the ancient tomb-builders used them – there is within them a natural energy. I am seeking to harness it towards . . . order.'

'Do you intend to stay in Moll long?'

Bauchelain shrugged. 'That will depend on whether I succeed in my efforts. Of course,' he smiled slightly, 'even my patience has limits.'

Guld heard the implicit warning and ignored it. 'How do you contact your friend, the eunuch . . .' *Dammit, why does that bother me? Moll's own history has its eras of slavery and castration . . . so why in Hood's name is my skin crawling?*

Bauchelain shrugged again. 'A simple cantrip of communication. He will come to the locale appointed for rendezvous, punctually.'

'Are you a necromancer, Bauchelain?' Casually asked, but Guld turned to gauge the man's reaction. There was none but faint amusement.

'That is a fell endeavour, Sergeant. I have no interest in delving into Hood's Warren—'

'Is it Hood's, then? Some say it's the very opposite.'

'Many conjectures abound on the subject. I myself concur with the sage Kulp Elder's theory that necromancy occupies the threshold of Hood's Warren – the in-between of life and death, if you will. A necromancer might well know more, but it's not in his or her nature to expound on the subject. Practitioners of the Death Arts are, of course, very secretive.'

Guld nodded. He walked slowly to the door. 'Your manservant's a stubborn man, Bauchelain. He was prepared to give his life, protecting your privacy.'

'Had I known,' Bauchelain said, glancing over at Reese, 'I would have added a cautioning provision to my request, Sergeant, regarding those who do not take "no" for an answer.'

Guld grunted. 'Good idea. You almost lost yourself a good man.'

'That would have been unfortunate indeed. Thank you for your concern. Is that all you wish of me?'

'For now,' Guld said. He stopped at the door. 'You've paid for this room in advance?'

'Until week's end, Sergeant. Why?'

He opened the door, hiding his wry grimace. *Suddenly dense, are we?* 'Good evening, sir.' He stepped out into the hallway, closing the door. The corporal and Obler waited outside, their eyes wide and fixed on the sergeant's face. Guld headed down the hallway. Both men followed.

'He says they've paid for the week,' Guld said to Obler.

The hostelier nodded. 'Aye, sir.'

'Four more days.'

'Aye.'

'Corporal?'

'Yes, sir?'

'Remain outside this building until you're relieved. Obler, is there a back door?'

'Aye, but it's thrice-bolted.'

'Meaning?'

The scriber tapped below his left eye and grinned. 'All very loud to draw back. Wakes me up, sir, every time.'

'Used lately?'

'No, sir. Not in weeks, sir. Not since before they arrived.'

'So this Korbal Broach left by the front door?'

Obler paused at the landing. 'Which one be him, sir?'

'The eunuch – the one who's out right now.'

'One's out right now? You're certain, sir? I ain't seen but the one of them out of that room since they arrived, sir, and that be the one you just seen, sir. That other one, he's in there, sir, 'cause he ain't never left.'

Guld's frown deepened. 'You're mistaken, Obler.'

But the scriber just shook his head.

'Well, does the man eat?'

'Uh, no sir, he don't.'

The frown became a scowl.

Obler's eyes darted and he licked his lips. 'Come to think on it, sir, that's kind of odd. Unless they share the meals, sir. Fasting, like.'

Guld moved on down the steps, the corporal on his heels. 'The eunuch,' he said over his shoulder to Obler, who crowded behind the corporal, 'what did he look like?'

'Big, sir. Huge. Didn't say anything I don't think. Just smiled a lot, sir. Clammy as a dead whale, sir, that's how he looked. Never knowed he was a eunuch, but now that you've said it, it's plain. Aye, a eunuch.'

'HAVE SOME WINE,' BAUCHELAIN SAID, POURING TWO GOBLETS full and handing one to Reese, who took it gratefully.
'I'm sorry, Master—'

'Not at all. As the guard implied, it would have been unfortunate – and undesired – if you had come to any harm.' He turned an inquisitive gaze on the old man. 'Why so stubborn? You seem a wise man, Mister Reese – to assault and defy a sergeant of the Watch . . .'

'Well, I didn't want to fail you, Master. I, uh, I like this job.'

'You feared losing it? Do not be concerned on that account, Mister Reese. We find you ideal.'

Emancipor looked around. *We?*

'And besides,' the sorceror continued, sipping his wine, 'I have foreseen a long acquaintance between us, Mister Reese.'

'Oh? Oh.'

'Although your mind still holds its mysteries.'

'It does, Master?'

'Mmhmm. For example, your wife of thirty years . . .'

'Subly? Well, I gripe a lot, Master, 'tis true, but she's stayed by me all this time, and sometimes she's been all I had to hold on to, sir, if you understand me. I love her dearly—'

'I know. It's not that, Mister Reese. In your mind I can hear her voice, yet I cannot find an image – I cannot see her within you, and that is what I find so peculiar . . .'

They stared at each other over their gold cups, neither blinking, for a long moment, then Bauchelain downed the last of his wine, cleared his throat and turned away.

'I have work for you tomorrow, Mister Reese.'

'Master?'

'And . . .' Bauchelain refilled his goblet. 'Book us passage. Westward, as far as a ship will take us.'

Emancipor's eyes narrowed. 'Yes, Master. Should I get a refund from Obler?'

'No, leave that be. But I want us out of Moll in two days hence. Is this likely?'

''Tis the turning of the season, Master. I can guarantee it.'

'Excellent. Oh, and Mister Reese?'

'Yes, Master?'

'Be circumspect.'

'Of course, Master.'

'You've met this sergeant before, Mister Reese?'

Emancipor nodded. 'Twice. Once, a year back, when my employer was assassinated, and then when Merchant Baltro was murdered.'

Bauchelain nodded thoughtfully. 'He seems a sharp man.'

'In every way, Master. He's famous. The King himself commands that Sergeant Guld conduct investigations. Certain ones, that is. Murder, mostly. Guld's never failed.'

'I take it he is the man investigating this night-killer haunting your city.'

'Yes, sir, he is.'

Bauchelain smiled. 'Well, then, I suppose it was a matter of course that we, as foreigners, be sought out and questioned.'

'I'd guess, Master.' Reese made his tone flat.

'Even so,' Bauchelain continued, his gaze on the wine in his goblet. 'I am a private man, and so dislike official . . . attention. Hence my decision to leave early, Mister Reese. I would not wish to unduly alarm the sergeant, however . . .'

'He'll not hear a word, Master.'

'Excellent. Now, take to your bed here – I'll need you sharp for your efforts tomorrow.'

'Yes, Master. Thank you, Master.' Emancipor went to the bed and laid down on it. *Unduly alarm Guld. Of course. Who me, a necromancer? Really, sir. Huh.* He was exhausted, but he didn't expect to sleep well. *Not well at all.*

GULD STEPPED THROUGH THE ENTRANCE TO SQUINT'S. HE paused in the unlit threshold, eyes already smarting with the thick, heavy wood smoke layering the crowded, low-ceilinged main room, a murky tide of noise washing over him.

The soldier he'd sent to trail the foreigner emerged from the press and stepped close. 'He's at the back, sir. We can get a better look at 'im from the bar.'

'Lead on,' Guld grunted.

Voices fell away to either side as the sergeant and his guardsman pushed their way to the long, sagging bar running the length of one side, voices that then rose again behind them with evident relief. Squint's rated among the seediest establishments in Lamentable Moll. Had he wished – and had he another thirty guardsmen – Guld could have arrested everyone present, just on principle.

They reached the bar. The young soldier turned and gestured towards the tables at the back. 'There, sir.'

Seated alone with his back to the rear wall was a grey-hooded figure, face hidden in shadows. The grey cloak covering his shoulders was threadbare. From Guld's position the man's right leg was visible from the knee down, moccasin-clad, a large hunting knife sheathed alongside the calf. The man's lean, long-fingered hands, wrapped around a tankard, were deeply tanned and scarred. An unstrung longbow leaned against the wall behind him.

Frowning, Guld stepped forward, but was brought up short by the guardsman's hand. 'No, not him. That one.'

'Ah.' *Was wondering about the sudden change of attire . . .* The foreigner he'd noted at the last two murder scenes sat at the table next to the hooded man. Still armoured, his back to the room, he was eating noisily – for even at six paces away and through the reverberating cacophony of the denizens, his lip-smacking, grunting and snorting was audible. 'Wait here, soldier,' Guld ordered, then made his way towards the man.

A local was sharing the foreigner's table, was talking nonstop. '—so I says to myself, self I says, "this ain't my house! Least, I don't think it is!" The roof, y'see, started at barely my chest, and I ain't a tall man as you can see. Were you here for the rains? Two weeks back? A deluge! So, anyway, what happened? Well, the house'd been sitting atop a barrow – no surprise there, not in Lamentable Moll, right? But a drain had blocked, and the water carved another way down to the sea – right through the barrow under us! The whole damned thing slumped, taking the house down with it! And if that wasn't bad enough, there was my wife, in bed, but not alone! Oh no! Not my beloved, treacherous Mully! Four – count 'em, *four* – damned ghosts was in there wi'er. Minor ones, of course – that's all y'ever get from those barrows – but powerful enough to tickle and poke and nudge and stroke and my, wasn't they having fun with moaning Mully! And she whimperin' and beggin' f'more! "More!" she cries. "More!"—'

'Enough,' Guld growled.

The local looked up and nodded. 'That's what I said! I said—'

'Be quiet!' the sergeant snapped. 'Find another table. Now.'

The foreigner had glanced up at Guld's interruption, then had resumed his meal.

'Uh,' the local stammered, pushing his chair back. 'OK. Right away. I hear you, Sergeant Guld – oh yes, I know you. Seen you. Hundreds of times – no, I wasn't doing nothing illegal, nothing y'could prove anyway—'

'Get out right now,' Guld said, 'or I will dispense with the need

64

to prove anything, and throw you in the stocks for a week or three.'

'I'm getting out. Here, see, here I go—'

Guld watched the man slip into the crowd, then sighed and slowly settled down in the vacated chair beside the foreigner. 'I have a few questions for you,' he said in a low voice.

The foreigner belched, then grunted and continued eating.

'Where are you from? And why are you so damned interested in murder scenes?'

The foreigner snorted and shook his head, still not meeting Guld's eyes. 'Just seeing the sights, Sergeant,' he said, his accent harsh.

'Moll's not much, but it's got more to offer than alleys with dismembered corpses.'

The man paused. 'Does it now?'

'Unless, of course,' Guld resumed, 'killing is what you do.'

The foreigner collected the last of his bread and began soaking up the broth in his bowl. 'If it's what I do, Sergeant, I don't do it that way.'

'If that's what you do,' Guld retorted, 'then what are you doing here?'

'Passing through.'

'So you'll be leaving tomorrow.'

The foreigner shrugged. 'Could be.'

'Where are you staying?'

The man finally turned a broad smile on Guld. 'That guard you've got following me should know.'

The sergeant narrowed his gaze. 'He reports to me regularly. If I don't hear from him at the appointed time, I am personally coming looking for you.'

'As you like.'

Guld rose. 'You've left a piece of bread,' he observed.

'For the gods.'

'What if they're not hungry?'

'They're always hungry, Sergeant.'

'Y'LOOK HORRIBLE, 'MANCY,' KREEGE SAID, WITH A GRIN, AS Emancipor slumped down at the table. 'Subly keepin' you awake at night, old man?' Kreege winked broadly at Dully who sat opposite him. 'Y'ask me, she looks to be a woman of, uh, considerable appetites . . .'

'I wasn't asking you,' Emancipor growled, glaring down at his mug of dark ale, 'and why should I? It's not like I don't know, is it?'

''Course not!' Dully loudly agreed.

'Hey,' Kreege said, leaning back, 'you ain't picked up none of that mange your squeakers come down with, have you?'

'No.'

'Glad to hear,' Kreege sighed. 'Had that once. Horrible. Gods forbid, the stuff behind your ears—'

'No more a that,' Dully growled.

Emancipor drank deep, then leaned forward on the table. 'I need a ship. Sailing out tonight or tomorrow morning.'

Dully's brows rose. He met Kreege's eyes, then both men edged closer. 'Well,' Dully muttered, 'that ain't too hard.'

'He's right,' Kreege nodded. 'Easy pickings. Though, it all depends on what exactly you're looking for. Like, if you want circumspect, you don't want the *Barnsider*, since that's Captain Pummel and he's an upright-by-the-ledger sort. '

'And if you're looking for fast and seaworthy,' Dully said, 'you don't want *Troughbucket*, since she's been shipping bad and

Cap'n Turb's owing half the lenders in Moll, including Obler, so's he can't get the repairs done.'

'*Swarmfly* might be a good bet but I heard the rats chased the whole damn crew off and there's no telling when or if they'll try storming her.' Kreege frowned, then shook his head. 'Maybe not so easy after all, come to think of it.'

Dully raised a stubby finger. 'Hold on. There's one. The *Suncurl*.'

Kreege choked on a mouthful of beer and the next few moments passed as Emancipor and Dully watched the man hack and gag and choke, his face turning purple before he finally managed to draw a clean breath.

Emancipor turned to Dully. 'The *Suncurl*, you said? Don't know that one—'

'Come in from Stratem,' Dully explained with a casual shrug. 'Needed some re-fitting here. Me and Kreege did some off-loading, then swung them a good price on iron nails.'

Kreege, now recovered enough to speak, cleared his throat and said, 'Yeah, Dully's got a good notion there. A good-looking ship, a trough-runner for sure. Captain's very quiet – Hood, the whole crew's a quiet, private bunch. The *Suncurl*. Perfect for your needs, 'Mancy, whatever your needs might be. She's at the Trader's Dock, just back down off the rollers and sitting pretty.'

Emancipor finished his ale, then rose. He was exhausted, his thoughts seeming to swim behind a thick fog. 'Thanks. I'll head straight there. See you.'

'See you 'Mancy, and don't mention it. Hey, did Subly have any luck at the alchemist's?'

Funny, I don't recall telling 'em about all that. Must have, though. Kreege dotes on our youngest lad – guess it's a natural concern. Guess he's just a nice, caring man, is Kreege. 'She did well enough,' Emancipor replied as he stepped away from the table and turned towards the door. 'Thanks for asking.'

'No problem, 'Mancy. Glad to hear it.'

'Me too,' Dully added. 'See you, 'Mancy.'

SERGEANT GULD MADE HIS WAY DOWN DOLL STREET, SEVENTY-seven winding paces through a tortured alley draped in shadow. Brushing his shoulders on either side, with restless clattering, were hundreds of wooden, bone, rag and feathered dolls, each hanging by the neck from shop overhangs on hairy strands of seaweed twine. Shell, studded or painted eyes seemed to follow his passage, as if every ghastly puppet and marionette was demon-possessed. At the very least, Guld well knew, some of them were. Doll Street did not rank among his favourite haunts in Lamentable Moll. If human eyes tracked him, they were hidden in the chill gloom of the shop interiors.

As luck would have it, Mercy Blackpug's closet of a shop was at the far dead-end, leaning against a warehouse wall and facing on to the heaved-cobble alley. A row of leather-bound, bestial and bristly dolls depended from the jutting overhang. Misshapen faces grinned beneath strands of oily hair, onyx eyes glittering. Drawing closer, Guld's gaze narrowed on the dolls. Not leather, after all, rather, something more like pigskin, poorly tanned and wrinkled around the stitches.

Hood knows who buys these things.

A deep melodic voice sang out from beneath the overhang, 'Buy a doll for your young tikes? Every child should know terror, and are not my little ones terrible?'

Guld pushed his way through the miniature gallows row. 'Where's the old woman?' he demanded.

The dark, exquisite face within its blanket shawl cocked to one side. Startling blue eyes regarded him curiously. 'Old woman, soldier?'

'The one who's said to own this shop,' Guld replied. 'The one selling these dolls and other equally ugly . . . things. The one seen at every scene of murder this last fortnight. Mercy Blackpug.'

The woman's laugh was low. 'But *I* am Mercy Blackpug. You must be referring to my sister, Mince. She takes my wares to market.'

'Your sister? That hag? Do you think me a fool?'

The woman began filling a hookah. Her long-fingered hands moving in the darkness made Guld think of seasnakes. 'Different lifestyles,' she murmured, 'alas. Mince eats no meat, no fish. Only vegetables. And herbs. She drinks no alcohol. She smokes no durhang, nor my own favourite, rust-leaf. She is celibate, an early-riser, asleep with the sunset. She jogs the cliff-trail out to More-Pity Point and back every day, no matter the weather. She is but a year older than me. Thirty-six.'

Smoke plumed, billowed to fill the shack with its swirling haze. 'I, on the other hand,' Mercy continued, 'imbibe all manner of vices, much to her disgust. In any case, my dear, I take it you are not here to sample my . . . wares.'

I'll have to think about that. Dammit, do not get distracted! 'I want to know the nature of Mince's interest in the murders. Where is she?'

'Probably down at the docks, haranguing the sailors.'

'About what?'

'They are an offense to wellness. Mince would reform them—'

'Hold on, she's not the woman who petitions the king every week?'

'The very same. My sister would be pleased to see Lamentable Moll a bastion of pure, righteous behaviour. Offences punishable by death, of course. This rust-leaf is flavoured with essence of mint, would you care to try?'

'No.' *Not now. Maybe later. Yes, later—* 'No, I said!'

Her blue eyes widened. 'Was I insisting?'

'Sorry. No, you weren't.'

'My sister likely attends murder scenes in search of converts. She preys on fear, as you might imagine.'

'So why is it she tolerates you? Enough to try and sell your dolls at market?'

Mercy laughed. 'You of all people should know that the king's spikes are rarely . . . unadorned. Lamentable Moll breeds criminals faster than rats, faster even than the king can hang them up.'

Guld glanced at a doll hanging close to him. *Not pigskin, then.*

Mercy drew on her mouthpiece, then continued, 'The skin of criminals. My sister finds the irony delicious.'

Sudden nausea threatened the sergeant. He stared down at the woman, aghast.

She gave him a broad, white smile that seemed to sizzle right through him. She said, 'Mostly relatives of the dead, my customers. Mementos of the departed. Who can fathom the human mind?'

'I may be back,' Guld managed, stepping outside.

'Who indeed?' she laughed. 'Until later, then, Sergeant.'

He staggered up the alley, struggling to calm his thoughts. A voice cackled from the shadows to his right. ''Ware my sister, young man!'

Guld wheeled.

Mince's crunched-leather face grinned humourlessly at him from between two hanging dolls. She had few teeth left, worn down to stumpy pegs. 'She will be the death of you!' the hag rasped. 'She is a pit! A whirlpool of licentiousness! A temptress. A knower of Moll's most secret and vice-ridden lairs – you would not believe the extent of her business interests!'

Guld's eyes thinned. 'Lairs, you said? Tell me, Mince, would she also know details of who frequents such places?'

'She knows all, does my evil sister! Except how to take care of herself! Ill health stalks her, as yet unseen, but as sure as

Hood himself! Soon, you shall see! Soon, unless she mends her ways!'

The sergeant glanced back down the alley. *No reason to delay, is there? Not at all. I need to question Mercy. In detail. May take hours, but there's nothing to be done for it.*

'Do not succumb!' Mince hissed.

Ignoring the hag, Guld began marching back down Doll Street.

KNOLL BARROW WAS BY FAR THE LARGEST AND THE ONLY grassy barrow in Lamentable Moll. It had been riven through countless times, and had the unique quality of containing absolutely nothing. Boulders, gravel and potsherds were all that the endless looters and antiquarians unearthed.

Guld found the city's two pre-eminent rat-hunters picnicking atop the Knoll. They had built a small fire over which they roasted skinned rats. A dusty bottle of fine wine waited to one side, beside a clay jar with a sealed lid.

Birklas Punth and Blather Roe were not quite typical among Moll's professional rat-hunters. Nevertheless, the sergeant had on occasion made use of their vast knowledge of every conceivable facet of the city's underworld, and had found them of sufficient value to tolerate their peculiarities.

'Such a serious regard!' Birklas observed with a fluttering wave of greasy fingers as Guld ascended the barrow. 'Why is it, I wonder, that the lowborn are so often seen maundering, nay, burdened unto buckling with the *seriousness* of their hapless lot? Is it then the sole task of the pure blooded denizens of fair Moll to while away the days – and indeed the nights – with unfeigned slovenity?'

'And what's so pure about your blood, Punth?' Guld growled as he reached the two men.

'Singular intent, poor sergeant, is the most cleansing of

72

endeavours. Witness here before you amiable myself, and, at my side, himself. We two are *most* singular.'

Both men wore little more than rags, apart from large, floppy, leather hats – Birklas' dyed a sun-faded magenta and Blather's a mottled yellow. Countless rat-tails hung from their twine belts, and encircling their wrists and ankles were more rat-tails, these ones braided in ingenious patterns.

Blather Roe reached for the jar and pried open the lid with a blood-stained dagger. 'You've come jutht in time, Thergeant. The ratth are almotht roathted and the pickled pinkeeth offer uth a perfect appetither. Pleath, theat yourthelf at our thides.'

'And I,' Birklas added, 'shall pour the vintage, whilst my partner fishes out some of those pickled pinkies.'

The vinegar had made the baby hairless rats pinker than was natural, a detail strangely adding to his horror as Guld watched Blather drawing one forth and raising it to his mouth. The pinky vanished between his lips with a sucking sound. The man swallowed, then sighed.

'A fine beginning,' Birklas observed. 'Shucked like an oyster, true evidence of cultured breeding.'

Guld scowled. 'Cultured breeding? Do you mean Blather, or the rats?'

'Oh, tho very droll, Thergeant,' Blather Roe tittered. 'Join uth, pleath!'

'No thanks, I've already eaten.'

Birklas turned to his partner. 'Can you not discern, friend, that Sergeant Guld here is sorely disposed? Dreadful murders every night! The bells peal! The rats scurry hither and tither, and even Whitemane himself hides in his deepest cove. Aye, something foul stalks fair Moll, and here is its chief hunter, come to us in need of assistance.'

Blather drew back. 'Motht thertainly I wath cognithant of the thergeant'th therious plight! I wath but being courteouth!'

'No more arguing about civility,' the sergeant growled. 'I've heard you talk about Whitemane a hundred times and I want to know once and for all, does he really exist?'

'Thertainly!'

'Indisputably, Sergeant.'

Guld fixed his gaze on Birklas. 'And he's a Soletaken?'

'Aye, he is. An unprepossessing man, when in that shape. But once he's veered, the most intimidating of rats. A clever and vicious tyrant, Ruler of the Furred Kingdom, Slayer of All Challengers, Fornicator of the Highest—'

'Yes yes, all that. And you're saying he's hiding from our murderer?'

'Burrowed deep, Sergeant. Quivering—'

'I see. Should I then assume Whitemane has met the killer?'

Birklas shrugged. 'Perhaps he has. More likely his runners have, or his junction guards, or his rooftop peepers—'

'But not hith food tathters,' Blather cut in.

'No,' Birklas solemnly agreed. 'Not his food tasters indeed. Blather, how are his food tasters doing?'

Blather Roe prodded the skewered rats. 'Done, I would thay.'

'Excellent! Now, Sergeant, is there anything else we can do for you?'

'Maybe. The princess and Lordson Hoom.'

Birklas' eyebrows lifted. 'Oh dear, not a conversation to accompany supper . . .'

Guld squatted down. 'I can wait.'

Dead Sekarand's tower creaked in the offshore breeze that had grown steadily since the sun had set. Guld wrapped his cloak around his shoulders, exhaustion more than the wind making him chilled. Below, the day's haze of wood smoke had been stripped away. Oil-glow and candle-light spotted the sides of the tenements like muddy stars at Guld's feet, as if they were all mortals could achieve to mirror the bristling night sky.

Guld heard a scuffing at the stairway, then Stul Ophan's grunt as the magus climbed on to the platform. 'Burn's uneasy rest, Guld,' the old man gasped. 'A simple rendezvous on a street corner would have done me better.'

The sergeant leaned on a merlon and looked down on the wharf district. 'I may have the man, Stul,' he said.

The magus stopped cursing. From behind Guld, Stul Ophan said, 'How certain are you? When will you make the arrest?'

'I haven't worked that detail out yet. Am I certain? Well, my gut's still in knots – something I've missed, but it may still point to the same man, once I've worked the unease loose.'

'What do you wish of me?'

Guld turned. Stul Ophan stood near the trapdoor, a silk cloth in one hand with which he blotted his brow. The magus shrugged feebly. 'I'm not the best with heights, Sergeant. You'll forgive me if I remain here, though it relieves me naught with the whole edifice swaying as it is.'

Guld opened his mouth to say something, then scowled and said instead, 'You live in a damned tower!'

Ophan shrugged again. 'It's . . . expected of me. Isn't it? I reside on the main floor, mostly.'

The sergeant studied the man a moment longer, then sighed. 'I was thinking of the hounds. The ones I sent on the trails leading from Lordson Hoom's murder. A man, maybe two men – one a warrior, or a veteran – the other unknown. And a woman's scent as well, or two women, or none . . .'

'If the hounds danced to a woman's scent, Guld, how could there be none?'

'Good question. Can you attempt an answer? Before you do, let me say there *was* a woman who fled the scene that night, but she's not the killer.'

Stul Ophan frowned, mopped his forehead. 'I don't understand.'

Guld grimaced. 'Recall your own discoveries, Magus. And your uncertainties. Answer me this: a man is not a man, and might be mistaken for a woman – if sorcerous paths are the means of investigation – or even if a hound finds the scent. Assume your efforts to ascertain the killer's gender were *not* confused – that, as with the hounds, your answer was a true one. How could that be?'

'A man not a man? Mistaken for a woman, even by hounds? Sergeant, there is no answer to be culled from such confusion. We were deliberately misled—'

'No. It was more a matter of the murderer's indifference – a past knowledge that such detection efforts would, inevitably, yield confusion. Like a demon's riddle, Stul Ophan. The answer is too simple. Do not think so hard.'

The magus scowled. 'You mock me, Guld.'

Guld turned back to gaze down on the city. 'What, Stul Ophan, would be the mark of a eunuch?'

He heard the air slowly hiss through the man's teeth.

'You are right, Sergeant. A demon's riddle indeed. You've found the killer.'

'I know him,' Guld corrected. 'I've not *found* him.' His gaze narrowed as he looked down at the Noble Quarter. 'But I think,' he said, 'someone else has. The knot begins to unravel.'

'What do you mean?'

'I mean, she's on the move,' Guld said, as he watched lantern after lantern light up the rooftops, each marking a path taken by the one mystery that remained in this game. The sergeant spun and raced to the stairs. 'Go home, Magus,' he said. 'The night's work begins in earnest.'

HE'D MADE HIS INQUIRIES, FOLLOWING HIS AUDIENCE WITH the king. He'd asked enough questions, delivering the right kind of pressure when necessary, and had harvested enough details to put things together. Lordson Hoom's unpleasant appetites included a taste for blood, the application of pain. It was what had drawn him and Princess Sharn together. It was what had made – for both the Lord and for Seljure – the union unattractive. Damned frightening, in fact.

There'd been no maid in waiting at her side last night, because the girl had already been sent off, close on the killer's trail. Hoomy had been revealed as a mere acolyte in those twisted arts of flesh and pain. The killer had shown the princess just how far – how wonderfully far – things could be taken. A brush of promise on Sharn's trembling lips, and now she thirsted for more.

The maid in waiting had done her job well. Guld's man had reported her return at dawn; and now she and the princess were on their way, and they'd lead Guld and his men to the quarry.

He exited the tower's gaping gateway and moved quickly down the streets. Sharn was making a terrible mistake. The last thing Guld wanted to do was to arrive too late – although it'd serve to deliver a message to the king: *impede my investigation at your peril, Sire. You should've let me question her.* But the satisfaction of that wasn't worth a young woman's life – likely the lives of two young women, since the maid in waiting was likely to share Sharn's fate.

He'd worked out their route from the succession of lights revealed by his men, and arrived with, he guessed, minutes to spare, at the mouth of an alley opening on to Fishmonger's Round. A battered, partly slumped barrow marked the alleymouth. Guld crouched on the broken slate and recovered his breath.

The Round was empty, the post black and unadorned, save for the fiercely flapping notice, which had yet to be removed by Bauchelain. Atop the post sat a crow, asleep, rocking with the gusting salt-breeze. A dog loped across the cobblestones to lap at Beru's Fount. Guld remained in the shadows. He slowly unsheathed his longsword, and fervently hoped that his squad had managed to stay on the trail, which they should have picked up outside the palace.

A lone knot of uncertainty remained for the sergeant. The eunuch had managed to leave Sorrowman's unseen. There were sorceries that could achieve that, of course. A possibility that troubled Guld.

He stiffened as he saw a cloaked woman arrive from the street to his right. *The handmaiden. Damn, a brave lass.* He watched as she cautiously approached the wood post in the Round's centre. *There to await him? That makes no sense – I can't imagine the girl actually spoke to the eunuch – it would've been enough to simply ascertain his daily hiding place. No, this makes no sense at all.* He thought to voice a shout, to run out there, but instead remained motionless behind the slight mound, as a second robed figure – the princess – appeared, following the maid with langourous, appallingly confident strides.

The maid had stopped in front of the post, and seemed to be regarding its height as if about to supplicate herself before it. Sharn was about ten paces away and closing.

Atop the post, the crow bestirred itself.

Guld's eyes widened with sudden understanding. He opened his mouth to bellow out a warning, then something hard and heavy hammered the base of his skull. Groaning, he sagged, fighting waves of blackness. Close, yet seeming from a great distance, he heard a deep voice whisper at his side.

'Apologies, Sergeant. This is but one, and I want them both. We need to wait. We need the blood, for only then will Korbal Broach be vulnerable – enough to call for help. And then my long hunt ends . . .'

Guld was unable to resist as the man beside him, massive and dark and armoured – *the foreigner with the scimitar* – pried the sword from the sergeant's numbed fingers. The man had a heavy iron crossbow resting on his left forearm, a rune-crowded quarrel in place and nocked. 'Don't worry,' the man whispered in his appalling and barbaric accent, 'you'll get what's left of 'em both, enough to appease the mob. But now leave me to my business. You have no idea what you face – be glad for that.'

Guld managed to lift his head. The scene spinning before his eyes, he could only half-discern what was happening at the post. The crow had spread its wings, then it drifted down towards the handmaid. There was a blur and a cold ripple and the crow became a man, a huge, chain-armoured, bald-headed man, who looked down on the maid. She said something and he giggled in reply. He raised a hand, gestured delicately and the girl buckled, gurgling, then flew limp and sprawling to one side with blood spraying on to the cobbles.

Princess Sharn groaned as if in ecstacy.

The eunuch slowly approached her.

Beside Guld, the hunter raised his weapon weapon and took careful aim.

'Shoot,' Guld managed to hiss. 'Shoot, damn you!'

He heard creaking sounds come from the hunter, and turned to see the man's face darken, as if with great strain. 'What in Hood's name is the matter with you?' Guld tried to push himself upright, but the pain lancing through his head was too much. He could only stare in dawning realization as the hunter strained with all his might, yet could not move a muscle.

A cool, calm voice spoke behind them. 'Steck Marynd, you are a stubborn one, aren't you? You are welcome to struggle all you like, but I assure you that, although you cannot see it, the demon holding you fast exercises but a modest effort in restraining you.

Gods,' Bauchelain continued as he stepped around both men, 'what a wasted life, this maniacal pursuit. How many years since that unfortunate crossing of our paths? Far too many indeed. I suggest you retire, thankful that I've spared your life, once again – but, I add, for the last time. 'Tis not mercy that stays my hands, sir. But indifference, alas. You are, after all, naught but a minor irritation. Well,' he paused, then raised his voice to the eunuch even as the monstrosity began a sorcerous gesture of death in front of the princess. 'Korbal Broach! Leave off the damsel, old friend. Her poor maid will suffice this night, surely?'

Korbal Broach hesitated, then cocked his head in Bauchelain's direction. 'Twice touched, this one, Bauchelain,' he said in a reedy thing voice. 'She belonged to last night, yet deprived was I, humble servant to life.'

'The Lady pulled, then,' Bauchelain said easily, walking up to his companion. 'Give her that.'

The eunuch pouted. 'You would deprive me of begetting, again, Bauchelain?'

'I think you have enough for now,' the man replied. 'Besides, detecting a hastening of events, I have dispatched our man-servant to the docks – after imposing a long slumber on the corporal outside Sorrowman's, of course. In any case, vast coin is even now being spent on our behalf, and so our departure is imminent.'

'But Bauchelain,' Korbal Broach said softly, 'all who neared my trail are assembled. We could silence them each one, and the city would remain ours for many more weeks. Even the sergeant's squad has been taken care of – who now could endanger our efforts? Kill the sergeant, kill Steck Marynd, kill the princess, and 'lo, we are at ease once again.'

'In a city plunged into violent chaos.' Bauchelain shook his head. 'Steck's death is not to be by our hand this night, Korbal. He will live many years yet, unfortunately. As for the sergeant, I admit to sufficient respect to warrant him a grave threat – should the princess die tonight—'

'Then kill him. 'Tis easily solved.'

'Not so,' Bauchelain answered smoothly. 'Less than an hour past, the Mortal Sword, Tulgord Vise, swore a blood-vow, consecrated by the High Priestess of the Sisters. It seems our entourage of pursuers has grown by one, and like Steck Marynd, the goddess-charged fool will not relent in his hunt. So, let us not add Sergeant Guld to the train. The Mortal Sword, blooded by the Sisters, even now defies my wards, and approaches.'

'Kill him.'

Bauchelain shook his head. 'Best to wait a year or two, when the power of the ritual has faded somewhat. I've no wish to stain my clothes—' He turned as the clash of horse hoofs sounded from down a side street. 'Oh dear, it seems we've tarried too long as it is . . .'

Tulgord Vise had broken through the wards. The thundering charge of his warhorse fast approached from beyond the humped barrow that rose like a tiny hummock where the street opened on to the Round.

Bauchelain sighed. 'The Mortal Sword's sudden gift of power is . . . formidable.' He raised a hand. 'Alas, he forgot to bless his horse.' A gesture. On the other side of the barrow there was a bestial scream, then a terrible crashing sound followed by a solid crunch. The stones of the barrow seemed to bulge momentarily in the low torchlight, then settled once more in a haze of dust. 'It will,' Bauchelain spoke, 'be some time before the Mortal Sword regains his senses, sufficient, that is, to extricate his head and shoulders from the barrow.' He swung back to Korbal Broach. 'My friend, we've outstayed our welcome. Our manservant lays out the coin – our baggage is being carted to our transport. It is time, Korbal, we must move on.'

At that moment something white and the size of a fat cat darted from the shattered barrow. Spying it, Bauchelain murmured, 'Oh, I like the look of that.' He gestured once more.

An ethereal demon rose hulking and massive in the white rat's path. A taloned hand snapped down. The rat – *Whitemane*, Guld realized, *it must be* – had time for a single piteous squeal before it vanished into the demon's fanged maw.

'Get that out of your mouth right now!' Bauchelain roared, stepping forward.

The towering demon flinched, shoulders hunching.

'Spit!'

The demon spat out a mangled, red-smeared lump of fur that bounced once on the cobbles then lay still.

'Korbal, examine the unfortunate Soletaken, if you please.'

The eunuch sniffed in the rat's direction, then shrugged. 'It will live.'

'Excellent.' Bauchelain addressed the demon once more, 'Fortunate for you, Kenyl'rah. Now, gather up the hapless thing and return to my trunk—'

'Not tho fatht!' a voice cried from one side.

Guld managed to turn his head and saw Blather Roe and Birklas Punth standing on the other side of the fountain, their hats pulled low. Both held their long-shafted rat-stickers leaning over a shoulder.

'And who might you two be?' Bauchelain inquired.

'Kill them,' Korbal Broach whined. 'I don't like them. They make me nervous.'

'Remain calm, my friend,' Bauchelain cautioned. 'While I share your unease, I am certain some amiable arrangement can be achieved.'

Guld stared at the two floppy-hatted men. *They're just rat hunters – why all this anxiety?*

Birklas was eyeing the Kenyl'rah demon with distaste. 'Dreadful apparition, begone!'

The demon wilted, wavered, then vanished.

On the cobbles Whitemane suddenly lifted its head, glanced about, then scurried for the shadows.

'That was unkind of you,' Bauchelain complained. 'I dislike having my servants dismissed by anyone other than myself.'

Birklas shrugged. 'Moll may indeed be a modest city, Wizard, but only in outward appearance. It has its games, and its players, and we like things the way they are. You and your necromantic friend have . . . upset things.'

'Thingth,' Blather added, 'that don't like being upthet.'

'They smell of a barrow,' Korbal Broach said.

Bauchelain slowly nodded. 'Indeed, they do. Yet this city's barrows are so . . . insignificant, I cannot imagine . . .'

'Wards are not eternal,' Birklas murmured. 'Although, I will grant you, it took us some time to find our way out of the Knoll. Only to find we had been preceded by almost every efficacious spirit and being once interred alongside us in the lesser barrows. They used the rats, you see. Blather and I, however, did not. In any case, enough of all this. Consider yourselves expelled from Lamentable Moll.'

Bauchelain shrugged. 'Acceptable. We were just leaving in any case.'

'Good,' Blather smiled.

Slowly recovering, Guld leaned against a wall and pushed himself to his feet. 'Damn you, Bauchelain—'

The sorceror turned in surprise. 'Whatever for, Sergeant?'

'My men. That's earned my own blood-vow—'

'Nonsense. They are not slain. They wander confused. Nothing more. This I swear.'

'If you lie, Mage, you'd best kill me now, for I—'

'I do not, Sergeant. And proof of that is found in my letting you live.'

'He speaks true,' Birklas said to Guld. 'As I intimated earlier, we will tolerate only so much.'

Bauchelain laid a hand on Korbal Broach's shoulder. 'Let's be on, friend. We can join our able manservant at the docks.'

Waves of pain half-blinding him, Guld watched the two men stride off.

Princess Sharn seemed to shake herself awake. Her face white as the moon, she stared after them as well. Then she hissed in outrage, 'He meant to kill me!'

'He's a damned eunuch,' Guld rasped. 'What charms would you have offered him? He doesn't even need to shave.'

Steck Marynd groaned, then slumped to the cobbles, his crossbow clattering but not discharging. Guld glanced down to see the man unconscious, a slightly stupid smile on his features.

Birklas Punth and Blather Roe offered Guld elegant tips of their hats, then sauntered off.

The sergeant took a step away from the wall, tottered, but managed to stay upright. Blood flowed down around his neck. He heard distant shouts. His men were finally on the way. Guld sighed, his eyes falling in the handmaiden. Her body lay in a spreading pool. He watched a mongrel dog trot purposefully in her direction. The sergeant's stomach lurched. 'Madness,' he whispered. 'All madness!'

A hacking hiss sounded from the shadows further down the alley, then a rasping voice sang out, *'See what comes of a life of vice?'*

EMANCIPOR REESE AWOKE GROGGILY, AND FOUND HIMSELF staring at the four travel trunks strapped to the wall in front of him. Creaking sounds inundated him, and the cot he laid on pitched and rolled under him.

The Suncurl. I remember now. Hood, what an awful night!

He slowly sat up. The ship climbed and fell – they were in the Troughs, beyond Moll Bay and in the Tithe Strait. The air was hot and damp in the close cabin. *Barely time to send her word. She'll manage, might even be relieved once she's calmed down some.* He looked around. The other two berths were empty.

Emancipor glared at the trunks. *Damn, but they'd been heavy. Come close to breaking the cart's axle.* Of course, Bauchelain's second trunk had held a huge wrapped piece of slate – the man had taken it out, and set it on the floor. On its flat surface was an intricate scribed pattern. He blinked down at it, then frowned. There had been a sound, he suddenly recalled, a sound odd enough to awaken him. Something was slapping around in one of Korbal Broach's trunks. Something had come loose.

Emancipor climbed to his feet. He unstrapped the retainers, examined the lock. The key was in it. He unlocked the latch and pulled back the trunk's heavy lid.

There were no words to describe the horror of what he saw within. Gagging, Emancipor slammed the lid back, then, his hands fumbling, he re-attached the retaining straps.

The cabin was suddenly too small. He needed air. He needed
. . . to get away.

Emancipor staggered to the door, then out into the aisle and up
the weathered, slat-bleached steps. He found himself amidships.
Bauchelain stood near the prow, seemingly unaffected by the
Suncurl's pitching and yawning. Crewmen scrambled around both
the necromancer and Reese – you sweated blood in the Troughs.

Gaping like a beached fish, Emancipor worked his way to
Bauchelain's side.

'You seem peaked, Mister Reese,' the mage observed. 'I have
some efficacious tinctures . . .'

Emancipor shook his head, gasping as he leaned on the rail.

'I'd have thought,' Bauchelain continued, 'that you'd not be inclined towards seasickness, Mister Reese.'

'The, uh, the first day, master. My legs will find me soon
enough.'

'Ahh, I see. Did you peruse my handiwork?'

Emancipor blanched.

'The slate, Mister Reese.'

'Oh, yes Master.'

'I indulge Korbal's ceaseless efforts to beget,' Bauchelain said.
'And so devise . . . platforms, if you will. The inscribed circle
preserves and, if need be, provides sustenance. It never fails that,
in such endeavours, I learn something new. And so we are all
rewarded. Are you all right, Mister Reese?'

But Emancipor did not answer. He stared unseeing at the
swelling grey waves that kept rising like a wall towards him
with each plummet of the bow, and trembled without feeling
the thundering repercussion through the ship's hull. *Begetting?
Oh, the gods forgive!* What lay within the trunk, heaped and
throbbing and twitching, sewn one organ to another, each alive
and no doubt retaining souls in a torturous prison from which
escape was impossible – what lived there in Korbal Broach's
trunk . . . only to a mind twisted beyond sanity could such a . . . *a
monstrosity* be deemed a child. The eunuch's dreams of begetting
yielded only nightmares.

'Does not this crisp, clean air revive one's spirit?' Bauchelain said, breathing deep. 'I am always . . . rejuvenated with the resumption of our wandering, our explorations of this world. 'Tis a good thing, the appeasement agreed with the Storm Riders. Passage on the seas should not cost more than a jar or two of blood – we can all agree on that, I'm sure. Now then, Mister Reese, allow me to treat you for this unfortunate illness of yours. My past efforts in dissection and vivisection have determined the cause of the malady – to be found in, of all places, the inside of your ears. As an alchemist of some skill, I have some talent in addressing this sensitivity from which you suffer. I assure you . . .'

Oh, Subly . . .

'Daylight is such a remarkable thing, isn't it, Mister Reese? The gods know, I see so little of it. Oh, and there's Korbal . . .'

Emancipor turned to where Bauchelain was pointing. There, in their wake, flew a single crow amidst a dozen wheeling seagulls. The black bird dipped and glided on the wind like a torn piece of darkness.

'He's tireless, is Korbal Broach,' Bauchelain said, smiling fondly.

Tireless. Oh.

'I should warn you, Mister Reese. I have sensed something awry with this ship. The captain, she seems disinclined to provide details as to our destination, and then there's the oddity of the nails, Mister Reese, the nails holding this ship together . . .'

He went on, but Emancipor had stopped listening. *Destination? Damn you, Bauchelain – you say westward, as far as anyone'd go. So I done what you said, damn you. And now, here I am . . . trapped.* Beyond Tithe Strait lay the open sea, stretching . . . *stretching away, for gods-damned forever, Bauchelain! That's the ocean out there, dammit!*

'Mister Reese?'

'Yeah?'

'Do you anticipate this journey to last very long?'

Forever, you bastard. 'Months,' he snapped, his jaws grinding together.

'Oh my. This could prove . . . unpleasant. It's the nails, you see, Mister Reese . . . they may affect my scribed circle. As I was saying, the iron's aspected, in some mysterious manner. My concern is that Korbal's child might well escape . . .'

Emancipor clamped his mouth shut. He felt a tooth crack.

His laughter, when it burst out, set off the seagulls astern. Their wild, echoing cackling ended abruptly. Sailors shouted. Emancipor fell to his knees, unable to stop, barely able to breathe.

'Unfortunate,' Bauchelain murmured. 'Even so, I had no idea seagulls burned so readily. Korbal so dislikes loud noises, Mister Reese. I do hope you succeed in restraining your odd mirth, soon. As soon as possible, Mister Reese. Korbal is looking agitated, very agitated indeed.'

THE LEES OF
LAUGHTER'S END

WEST OF THEFT, THE TITHE STRAIT OPENS OUT INTO THE
Wastes. A vast stretch of ocean through which naught
but the adventurous and the foolhardy dared brave
the treacherous, dubious sea-lanes as far as the Red Road of
Laughter's End, and from there, onwards to the islands of the
Seguleh and the southern coast of Genabackis, where the lands
of Lamatath offered sordid refuge for pirates, wastrels, the rare
trader and the ubiquitous pilgrim ships of the Fallen God.

What launched the free-ship *Suncurl* out from the sheltered
waters of Korel and Theft was a matter known only to Captain
Sater and, might be, her First Mate, Ably Druther. Such currents
of curiosity, as might lead one to speculate on said matters, could
reach out and grasp a soul fierce as a riptide, so Bena's mother
warned in her whispering, rattling way, and Bena was not one to
clap ears in stubborn countenance to such stern advice.

Not while her mother remained with her, to be certain, never
silent for long with that wave-rolling and wind-sighing voice, the
'waring whistles, wry hoots and mocking moans as true and as
familiar as any music of the heart. Why, her hoary hair danced in
the wind still, reaching out to brush Bena's young, smooth and – it
was said well below – tantalizing features as Bena crouched in her
usual perch in the crow's nest, her maiden's eyes thinned as she
studied the western Wastes with its white-furled waves and not
another sail in sight, waiting as was her mordant responsibility

to first spy the darkening of the waters, the grim blood-dark seas that marked Laughter's End.

A full week out now from Lamentable Moll's cramped little harbour, and at night Bena listened to the hands below muttering their growing fears, decrying the endless creak of the nails in the berths and bulkheads, the strange voices rising from the hold and from behind the strongroom's solid oak door – when all knew that there was naught behind it but the captain's own gear and the crew's stowage of rum, with the captain alone holding the fang-toothed key to the enormous iron lock. And in answer to all these goings on, with surety blood had been let over the side in the darkest bell every night since, each hand spilling into the cup their precious three drops from a stippled thumb.

Had some curse clambered aboard in Lamentable Moll? Mael knew, there was nothing good arriving in the guise of the passengers they had taken on there. A highborn toff with a spiked beard and cold, empty eyes. A rarely seen eunuch, the highborn's companion, and as their manservant none other than 'Mancy the Luckless, who – she had learned – had swum from more wrecks than the Storm Riders themselves, or so it sounded. *Fare begone these wretched guests*, Bena's mother muttered again and again whenever *Suncurl* pulled a peg or two to correct course, and Bena would huddle down as the mast tucked and tilted, heaved and dipped, tipping the wicker basket of the crow's nest hard over so that she could look up and, on occasion, see the bend of waves.

Wayward as the wind 'ere, beloved daughter, them guests, and see yon again that crow, oh fluttering black wing in our wake, why, nary a strip of bleached coral for fifty leagues since the Shingles yet the be-demon spawn bobs and slides dark as a re-gret! Look yee that crow, darling, and make no nest 'ere for one as that!

Oh, Bena had not heard her mother moan so in all the time that they'd shared this nest, and so, with a gentle caress, Bena reached out a hand to stroke her mother's wispy hair, only a few strands coming away from the parched, salted scalp above the shrunken, sightless eye sockets.

Huddle me come for company this night, darling daughter, for ahead soon runs the blood-dark seas of Laughter's End, when the nails shall speak their dread words. Hold ever, sweet child, to our tiny home here high above – we'll suck down the last snot of those gull eggs and pray for rain to slack our throats and lo, you will cry in delight to see me swell into ripeness once more, my darling.

Huddle me come for company this night!

And now, far to the west, Bena saw as her mother had said she would see. The vein of blood. Laughter's End. She tilted back her head and loosed a piercing cry to announce to those below the long-awaited sighting. Then added a second cry, *bless the begging, if you would, send up another bucket of vittles and the rum ration, please yee, before night is birthed! And*, she added to herself, *yee all die.*

As the wordless animal cry from Bena Younger in the crow's nest faded, First Mate Ably Druther clambered up on to the aft deck and stood beside his captain. 'Only a day late for the blood-dark,' he said, 'and given this buffeting wind that's been pushing us round, that's not too bad.'

Hands on the wheel, Captain Sater said nothing.

After a moment, Ably continued, 'Them dhenrabi are still in our wake. Expect they're heading for the red road just like us.' When he still received no reply or comment, he edged closer and in a low voice asked, 'Think they're still after us?'

Her expression tightened. 'Ably Druther, ask that again and I'll cut your tongue from your mouth.'

He flinched, then tugged at his beard. 'Apologies, Captain. It's a bit of the nerves, y'see—'

'Be quiet.'

'Yes, sir.'

He stood at her side in what he hoped and came to believe was companionable silence, until he was comfortable enough to decide that some other subject was acceptable. 'Sooner we get 'Mancy off this ship, the better. Ill luck squats in that man's lap, according to the hands we brought on in Lamentable Moll. Why, even back on the Mare Lanes I heard tales of—'

'Give me your knife,' Captain Sater ordered.

'Captain?'

'I don't want your blood on mine.'

'Sorry, Captain! I figured—'

'You figured, yes, and that is the problem. It's always the problem, in fact.'

'But this thing 'bout 'Mancy—'

'Is irrelevant and stupid besides. I'd order the crew to stop talking about it, if that'd work. Better to sew all their mouths shut and be done with it.' Her tone dropped dangerously. 'We know nothing about the Mare Lanes, Ably. Never been there. It was bad enough you blabbering in Lamentable Moll that we'd hailed from Stratem, which was as good as pissing on a tree-stump for the ones on our trail. Now, listen to me, Ably. Carefully, because I will not repeat this. For all we know, they've hired themselves a fleet of Mare raiders, meaning we've got a lot worse tracking our wake than a few dozen bull dhenrabi looking to mate. Just one word that the Mare might be looking for us is enough to start a mutiny. I hear anything like that from you again and I will cut your throat where you stand. Can I be any clearer?'

'No, Captain. As clear as can be. We ain't never been to the Mare Lanes—'

'Correct.'

'Only the three who came with us keep talking about them lanes and our run through 'em.'

'No. They don't. I know them well. Better than you. They're not saying a word, so if the knowledge is out, it's because of you.'

Ably Druther was now sweating in earnest, and tugging frantically at his beard. 'I might've made mention, once. But careless then and I ain't careless no more, Captain, I swear it.'

'Careless once and the rest don't matter.'

'Sorry, Captain. Maybe I can make it seem like I'm a liar. You know, lotsa tall tales and the like, exaggerations and worse. Why, I know one story – from Swamp Thick, that nobody'll believe!'

'They might not,' she replied slowly, 'except everything you've ever heard about Swamp Thick happens to be true. I should know, since I was bodyguard to the Factor there for a time. No, Ably, never mind trying the liar's route – your problem is not just that you talk too much, it's that you're stupid besides. In fact, it's a damned wonder you're still alive, especially since my three friends have had to listen to you night after night. Even if I don't murder you, they probably will, and that could make things complicated, since I'd have to execute one or all of my oldest companions, for killing an officer. So, all things considered, I should probably demote you right now.'

'Please, Captain, talk to them! Tell them I won't say another thing ever again, about anything! By Mael's own spit, I swear it, Captain!'

'Ably Druther, if you weren't the only one of us who actually knows which end of a ship points where we're going, you'd be long gone. Now, get out of my sight.'

'Aye, sir!'

'COOK'S A POET,' SAID BIRDS MOTTLE AS SHE SAT DOWN OPPO-
site her friend.

Heck Urse nodded amiably, but said nothing as he was
stuffing his mouth with food. Few others around in the galley,
which was how Heck, Birds and Gust Hubb preferred it. Gust
had yet to arrive, which left the two of them and only one other
and that one was on his own bench, staring down at his bowl
of grub as if trying to read in the jumbled mash his future or
something. Which wasn't a thing a man like 'Mancy the Luckless
should be doing, as far as Heck was concerned.

But never mind him. They'd been months now on this damned
stolen ship, and while things had been a little rough at the start, it
had settled out some – all the way until the harbour of Lamentable
Moll. But now, Heck had come to realize, things were getting
rough all over again. 'Mancy the Luckless was the least of their
worries. The damned ship was haunted. No other possible explanation. Haunted. As bad as the Catacombs of Toll's City, voices
and wraiths and whisps and creaks and crackles and shuffles –
no, wasn't rats neither, since no one could recall seeing a rat since
Moll. And when rats jumped off a ship, well, that was bad as
things could get, or nearly almost, by Heck's reckoning.

Rough at the start, aye, for Sater and the three of them here now
no different from any other salts. But none of them were. Salts,
that is. Not Sater, whose captaincy had been in Toll's City palace
guard – before the Night of Chants, anyway. And not Heck, nor

Birds nor Gust, all of whom had been sentries at the city's southeast corner gate that fateful night. The fifth in their motley group, Ably Druther, they'd picked up at Toll's Landing, but only because he knew stuff about sailing and he'd had the runner they'd needed to cut loose of the Stratem mainland. And he was handy enough with that cutlass so that stealing the *Suncurl* had proved a whole lot easier than it probably should have been.

Ably Druther. Just the name made Heck scowl over his empty bowl. 'Liabilities,' he muttered.

And Birds Mottle nodded. 'Captain's own word, aye. And this is where we are, Heck, sure as the clock-lock chunks on. Wonder,' she added, 'if those dhenrabi are hungry.'

But Heck shook his head. 'Word is they don't eat during mating season, which is why all those sharks are staying close instead of whirling away so fast they break the waves like they was trying to fly. The males will fight once we're well along the Red Road, and the sharks will get fat. So I'm told.'

Birds Mottle scratched at her short hair and squinted with her bad eye, which was what she did when struck by some unpleasant thought. 'I ain't never hated the sea more than I do now. It's like we're trapped here, as good as in any prison, and day after day the view don't change one bit. And with all the creepy sounds we're hearing . . .' She shivered, then made the Chanter Sign with her left hand, 'it's no wonder we're all having nightmares.'

Heck leaned forward. 'Birds, best keep that signing to yourself.'

'Oh. Sorry.'

'Chances are,' Heck said by way of mollification, since he loved Birds with all his heart, 'nobody here has heard of the Chanters. But best be safe anyway, since we don't none of us want to be . . . liabilities.'

'You got that right, Heck.'

'Besides, I found us a good answer to those damned nightmares. I got us switched over to night watch.'

'You did?' That bad eye squinted even tighter.

'What's wrong?' Heck asked. 'Don't it make more sense – after all, sleeping during the day and the nightmares won't be nearly so bad, right?'

'I'd wager the ones you traded with are dancing on the boom right now, Heck. You shoulda come to me first, so I could put some reason in your head. Night watch, Heck, means maybe coming face to face with what's scaring the runnels outa us.'

Heck Urse paled, then made the Chanter Sign. 'Gods below! Maybe I can switch it back—'

Birds snorted.

Sagging, Heck stared down at his bowl.

At that moment the third Stratem deserter, Gust Hubb, bolted into the narrow galley, his eyes wild and so wide the whites were showing on all sides. One hand was clamped over one ear and there was blood running down that hand. His pale fly-away hair waved about like a frenzied aura. He stared at Heck and Birds for a moment, his mouth working, until words came out: '*When I was sleeping! Someone cut off my ear!*'

S EATED A SHORT DISTANCE AWAY, EMANCIPOR REESE, 'MANCY
the Luckless, was jolted from his contemplation of myriad
peculiarities by the sailor's panicked entrance. Sure enough,
once one of the others managed to get Gust to pull his hand away,
the ear was missing. Deftly sliced clean off leaving a trickling
streak of red and peeled-back skin, and how the man had slept
through that was a true mystery.

Likely drunk on tipped-in illegal spirits and the victim of some
feud in the crew's berths, Emancipor concluded, returning his
attention to the bowl of food before him. 'Cook's a poet,' one
of the swabs had said, before wolfing the stuff down. Madness.
He had sailed plenty of ships and had weathered the fare of a
legion of cooks, and this was by far the worst he had ever tasted.
Indeed, it was virtually inedible, and would be in truth if not for
the copious amounts of durhang he had taken to stuffing into his
pipe along with the usual rustleaf. Durhang had a way of making
one ravenous, sufficient to overcome the dreadful misflavours of
such malodorous staples. Saving that, Emancipor would now be
nothing but scrawn and bone, as his wife Subly was wont to say
whenever any of their spawn came down with worms and some
pronouncement was required – although she was wont to say it
with a tinge of envy in her tone, given her girth. 'Scrawn and
bone, by the blessed mounds!'

He might even be missing her right now. Even the urchins of
questionable seed. But such emotions seemed as distant and left

102

behind as the harbour of Lamentable Moll. Less than a hazy smear on the horizon, aye, and let's have another bowl of durhang.

Listening in on the conversation of the swabs – before the arrival of their one-eared companion unleashed a flurry of shock, concern and then nervous speculation – had left Emancipor the vague sense that something was indeed awry with those three. Never mind the adamant opinions of the rest of the crew that these sailors knew a ship like a mole knows a treetop, and that maybe Captain Sater knew even less, and if not for the First Mate they'd have all long ago run aground or into some dhenrabi's giant maw. No, there was even more to it, and if only Emancipor could pull the thick webs from his thoughts, why, he might have an idea or two.

Eager hunger beckoned, however, slowly transforming this bowl of consumptive goat spume into a delectable culinary treasure, and before long he too was cramming the horrid stuff down his throat.

The bowl rocked and he leaned back, startled to find his meal suddenly done. And here he was, licking his fingers, pushing the ends of his moustache down into his mouth to suck loose whatever gobs had clung there, then probing past his lower lip with a still urgent tongue. He looked around, furtively, to see who might have witnessed this frantic, beastly behaviour, but the three swabs had left – rather quickly, he recalled, to seek out the ship's medic. Emancipor was alone.

Sighing, he rose from the bench, collected the wooden bowl and, dropping it into the saltwater cask near the hatch, made his way on to the mid-deck.

A bucket of food was being hoisted up to the crow's nest atop the mainmast, and Emancipor looked up, squinting in the glare. They all said she was pretty, the daughter, that is. But maybe mute – hence the eerie cries wafting down every now and then. And as for Bena Elder, why, a squall witch, she was, and had not come down, not even showed her prune face since before Moll – and life was better for it, aye. Well, strain as he might, he couldn't see anyone up there.

Still, a nice thought to think the young one was pretty.

Smiling, he made his way aft. It was good to smile these days, wasn't it. Belly pleasantly full and mostly quiescent. Fair sky over-head and a decent wind caressing easy swells on the sea. Subly far away and the imps with worms crawling out of every orifice just as far away, as, well, as Subly herself. Murdered employers and crazed killers and – oh, right, some of that, alas, was not so far away as any sane man might prefer.

Worthy reminder, aye. He found himself standing braced to the roll and pitch near the aft rail, pushing rustleaf in his pipe bowl, his blurry vision struggling to focus on the black-shrouded figure hunched against the stern rail. On the fat, pale fingers working with precision on the hook and the weighted line. On the round, pallid face, a sharp red tongue tip visible jutting up over the flabby upper lip, and those lank, low-lidded eyes, the lids and lashes fluttering in the breeze.

Focusing, aye.

As Korbal Broach worked the severed ear on to the barbed iron hook.

Then flung it over the side and began letting out loops of line.

THE NAILS CREAKED WITH THE COMING OF NIGHT, AND THOSE creaks were the language of the dead. There had been much to discuss, plans to foment, ambitions to explore, but now, at last, the voices grew in urgency and excitement. Trapped in the nails for so long now, but release was coming.

The red road that was Laughter's End beckoned, and wave by wave the thunder of cloven swells rumbling along the timbers of the hull, wave by wave, they drew yet closer to the grim vein, the currents of Mael's very own blood.

The Elder God of the Sea bled, as was the way of all things Elder. And where there was blood, there was power.

As night opened its mouth and darkness yawned, the iron nails bound to the ship *Suncurl*, nails that had once resided in the wood of sarcophagi in the barrows of Lamentable Moll, began a most eager, a most hungry chorus.

Even the dead, it is said, can sing songs of freedom.

'IF YOU WOULD, EMANCIPOR REESE, EXTRACT MY CHAIN ARMOUR. Scour, stain and oil. If I recall, no repairs are necessary beyond these simple ablutions, and given your present condition, this is fortuitous indeed.'

Emancipor stood just inside the cabin door, blinking at his master.

Bauchelain's regard remained steady. 'You may now heave yourself into motion, Mister Reese.'

'Uh, of course, Master. Armour, you said. Why, I can do that.'

'Very good.'

Emancipor rubbed at the back of his neck. 'Korbal Broach is fishing.'

'Is he now? Well, as I understand, he has acquired a sudden need for shark cartilage.'

'Why, do his knees hurt?'

'Excuse me?'

'Squall witches swear by it, sir.'

'Ah. I believe, in Korbal Broach's case, he has in mind some experimental applications.'

'Oh.'

'Mister Reese.'

'Master?'

'My armour – no, wait a moment.' Bauchelain rose from where he sat on the edge of his bed. 'I believe we have arrived at something of a crisis in our relationship, Mister Reese.'

'Sir? You're firing me?'

'I trust it need not come to that,' the tall, pale-skinned man said, adjusting his brocaded cloak, then reaching up to stroke his pointy beard. 'This voyage has, alas, seen a marked degradation in your skills, Mister Reese. It is common knowledge that excessive use of durhang has the effect of diminished capacities, of chronic ennui, and the obliteration of all ambition in the user. Your brain, in short, has begun to atrophy. You proceed in your waking period through an unmitigated state of numb stupidity; whilst your sleeping periods are occasioned by an inability to achieve the deeper levels of sleep necessary for rest and rejuvenation. This has, alas, made you both useless and boring.'

'Yes sir.'

'Accordingly, for your own good and – more importantly – mine, I am forced to confiscate your supply of durhang for the duration of this voyage and, if necessary, from now on.'

'Oh, sir, that would be bad.'

A single eyebrow arched. 'Bad, Mister Reese?'

'Yes, Master. Bad. It's my nerves, you see. My nerves. They aren't what they used to be.'

'And what is it, Mister Reese, that so assails your nerves?'

Well now, that was the question, wasn't it? The one all the durhang was letting Emancipor avoid, and now here was his master demanding a most sordid level of sobriety, in which all escape was denied him. Suddenly mute, Emancipor pointed at a massive wooden trunk set against one wall.

Bauchelain frowned. 'Korbal Broach's child? Why, Mister Reese, this is silly. Has it ever escaped? Indeed, have you not seen it but once, and that at the very beginning of this voyage? Furthermore, have you no faith in the bindings and wards I have set upon that modest homunculus? Paranoia, I should add here, is a common affliction among durhang abusers.'

'Master, every night, I can hear it. Burbling, moaning, gurgling.'

'Proper mouths and vocal tracts do not rate much importance in Korbal's estimation. Such noises are entirely natural given the creature's physical constraints. Besides,' and all at once Bauchelain's tone hardened, 'we will ever have guests in our company, many of them far less pleasant that my companion's quaint assemblage of organs and body parts as now resides in that chest. I was under the assumption, Mister Reese, that you accepted this commission in fullest understanding of such matters. After all, my principal hobby is the conjuring of demons. While my companion, Korbal Broach, explores the mysteries of life and death and all that lies in between. Is it not a given that we will all experience a plethora of peculiarities during the course of our adventures? Indeed, would you have it any other way?'

To that, Emancipor Reese found no possible reply. He stared, gaping, his eyes locked with Bauchelain's.

Until the sorceror turned away, with the faintest of sighs. 'In any case, Mister Reese, the child should not be the source of your disquiet. I believe I spoke of this matter with you before – shortly upon our standing down for the open seas, in fact. This ship was in Moll Harbour for both re-supply and repairs, in addition to taking on new crew. Of these purposes, it is the repairs that are relevant to our impending situation.'

Pausing, Bauchelain walked to the stern port and leaned both hands on the frame as he bent to peer through the lead glass. 'Ah, dusk approaches, Mister Reese. And in moments we shall be in the throes of Laughter's End. Iron nails, Mister Reese. Purchased in Lamentable Moll.'

Emancipor frowned. Now, mention of that stirred something in his head. The voices of two friends in a bar. Kreege and Dully, aye, the scroungers. *Nails. Iron nails . . .*

Bauchelain glanced back at Emancipor. 'Tell me, Mister Reese, since you are a native of Lamentable Moll: what, precisely, is a *Jhorligg?*'

HECK URSE KNEW HE SHOULD BE SLEEPING, RIGHT UP UNTIL the bell sounded the night watch, but his mind was a maelstrom of anxieties, terrors and niggling worries. It was understandable, wasn't it, that the shift over of duties from day to night would require some awkward adjustments, a stuttering transition, aye. And while Birds Mottle seemed able to plunge into deep slumber at a moment's beckoning, well, she'd been in the auxiliary of the Chanter garrison at Toll's City, hadn't she? Close to a real soldier as any of them. As for Gust Hubb, truly the man's luck was impressive. Imagine, losing an ear just like that and there was the ship's cutter pushing into his hands a bottle of d'bayang nectar and a mouthful of that you could sleep through Burn's own bowel movement no matter how many mountains fell over.

Alas, poor Heck Urse still had both ears, and none of a soldier's talent for sleeping anytime anywhere. So here he stumped about, restless and wobbly as a whiskerless cat. And there at the stern rail dead ahead was one of the guests, the fatter one that nobody ever saw except when they did and that wasn't common at all, except there he was, all cloaked in black and the hood drawn up.

Heck thought to wheel about, but then he'd be passing right by the captain again and once without a comment or command was lucky enough but twice was damned unlikely. Instead, and with a deep settling breath, Heck made his way to the rail beside the eerie man. 'Near t'dusk, sir, an' a calm night looks ahead, I'd say.'

The hooded head tilted slightly and Heck felt rather than saw those fishy eyes fixing on him. Repressing a sudden shiver, the swab leaned on the rail. 'Ah, runnin' out a line, I see. Angry waters 'ere about, so I'm told. Sharks and dhenrabi. Makes fishin' a bit of a risk – you ever notice, did you, sir, that sailors nearly never fish? Just the passengers and the like. Odd, isn't it? I'd warrant it's t'do with the likelihood of us feedin' those fishes some day, which is a crawly thought indeed.'

'Sharks,' the man said in a high, thin voice.

Heck blinked, then frowned. 'What's that? You fishin' for sharks? Oh, I sure 'preciate a sense of humour, I do. Sharks, ha. Looking to snag a big one, too, are ya? Like, maybe, one of those gold-backs that's as long as the *Suncurl* itself. Why, that'd be a fight or two, eh? You could lay bets who'd pull who aboard!' And he laughed, and kept laughing.

As long as his courage allowed, anyway, under that silent study from the shadowed face.

'Hah hah . . . hah . . . hah.'

Light was fading. The man reeled out a few more loops of line.

Heck scratched at his stubbly jaw. 'Sharks like meaty bait,' he said. 'Bloody bait. We ain't had fresh meat aboard since two days outa Moll. Whatcha using, sir? Had a nibble yet?'

The man sighed. 'No. Yes, you say true. Bait needs to be bloodier.'

'That it would, sir.'

'And, perhaps, more substantial.'

'Aye, I'd so wager. And a good-sized hook, too, why, a gaff-hook, in fact.'

'Yes. Excellent notion. Here, hold this.'

Heck found himself holding the bundle of line, feeling the thrum of waves and depths as the trailing bait was tugged in steady rhythm. He turned to advise the guest that he was about to go on watch, but the man had wandered off.

He stood, wondering what to do. If the bell sounded and the fool wasn't back by then, why, he'd be in trouble, would Heck Urse.

Boots sounded behind him and with relief he turned. 'Glad you're back, sir – oh, Captain!'

'What in Hood's name are you doing, Heck?'

'Uh, holding this line, sir.'

'You are fishing.'

'No sir! I mean, it was one of the guests! The fat one, he was fishing and he asked me to hold this until he got back, and I never had no chance to say I couldn't, cause of the night watch and all, so here I am, sir, stuck.'

'You damned idiot, Heck. Tie it off in the rail. Then go wake up Birds and Gust, the sun's nearly down.'

'Aye, Captain!'

'LAST ONE I HEARD OF WAS ABOUT TWENTY YEARS AGO, WHEN I was upland in Theft so I never saw it for myself,' Emancipor said, cursing his sudden sobriety which probably came from whatever Bauchelain had slipped into the tea he was now drinking. 'They caught up to it down under the docks. The tide was out, you see – if it'd made water they'd have never got it and not a fisher boat would dare the bay for months, maybe years. Took twenty strong soldiers to kill it with spears and axes and the like, and even then only four walked away from the scrap.'

'A formidable creature then,' Bauchelain mused from behind steepled hands.

'Aye, and this one was only half a day old. They grow fast, you see, from eating their mothers.'

'Eating their mothers?'

Emancipor glowered down at his tea. 'No one knows for sure, but the tale is like this. Jhorligg seeds swim the waters, like little worms. And if one finds a young woman in her time of bleeding – a conch diver or pearl swimmer or net crawler – why, that worm slides right on in, steals the womb, aye. And she gets big and big fast and then bigger still, and she starts eating enough for three grown men and keeps eating for six, seven months, until her skin itself starts to split. And then, usually on a moonless night, the Jhorligg rips its way free, straight through the belly, and eats the woman right there and then. Eats her all up, bones and all. Then down it races, for the water.'

'Curious,' Bauchelain conceded, 'yet not as unlikely or bizarre as one might think. Parasites abound, and the majority of them dwell in water, both salt and fresh. Finding means of entry into hosts via any available orifice.'

'Jhorligg just ain't beasts,' Emancipor said. 'Nearly as smart as us, it's said. They deliberately swim into nets and then curl up tight, until they're pulled aboard, then they tear loose and murder every fisher in the boat, eat them all. Some even use weapons, swords and the like lost overboard or thrown to the spirits of the sea. But Master, Jhorligg live in the shallows, coastal waters only. Never open sea. Never out here.'

'Reasonable,' murmured Bauchelain. 'Too much competition in these waters, not to mention the risk of becoming prey. Now, Mister Reese, what you describe is a wholly marine creature that navigates on land only at birth, in the manner of turtles and dhenrabi. Yet is quite capable of lithe endeavours on a fisher boat's deck. By this, we must assume that it can survive out of water as necessity demands. But, I wonder, for how long?'

Emancipor shrugged. 'It's said they look like lizards, but long and able to stand on their hind legs. Got a long sinewy tail, and two clawed arms, though it's said their bite is worst of all – can pull a man's head right off and crunch the skull like eggshell . . .' He trailed off then, as Bauchelain had slowly leaned forward, eyes piercing.

'A most interesting description.'

'Not the word I'd use, Master.'

Bauchelain leaned back. 'No, I imagine not. Thank you, Mister Reese. I trust your senses have returned to you?'

'Aye, Master.'

'Good, set to my armour, then, and quickly.'

'Quickly, Master?'

'Indeed. We are about to find ourselves on the red road, Mister Reese. Tonight,' he added as he rose, rubbing his hands together, 'shall prove most fascinating. When you are done with the armour, hone my sword – the red-bladed one, if you please.'

Armour? Sword? Emancipor felt his insides grow watery with burgeoning terror, as he only now became aware of the veritable cacophony of sounds emanating on all sides. Groaning timbers, the squeal of joins and click of shifting nails, the strange moans of things thumping alongside the hull, then slithering under to come round to the other side.

Suncurl pitched drunkenly, and darkness took the sky beyond the lead glass porthole.

And somewhere down below, in the hold, someone screamed.

BENA YOUNGER HEARD THE TERRIBLE SHRIEK AND COWERED lower in the crow's nest.

Oh yes, my darling daughter, the night begins! Many are the terrible secrets of Laughter's End, an' could we fly wi' wings of black now's the time to leave the nest, dearie! But who in this world can flee their terrors? Hands o'er the eyes, ye see, and voices t'drown out all sordid griefs, an' the mind has wings of its own, aye so beware the final flight! Into the abyss wi' all flesh left behind!

The stars swirled strange overhead and the *Suncurl* wallowed as if the wind had gasped its last. Black waves licked the hull.

But we are safe, darling, 'ere above the squalid fates. Like queens we are. Goddesses!

As yet another scream railed from the darkness below, Bena Younger realized that she did not feel like a queen, or a goddess, and this reach of mast and the nets of cordage creaking almost within reach did not seem nearly high enough for whatever horrors were unveiling themselves beneath the deck of the *Suncurl*.

While beside her, Bena Elder crooned and moaned on, with hair standing on end and fluttering about, brushing her daughter's face like the wings of moths.

'WHO WAS DOING THAT SCREAMING?' HECK URSE DEMANDED, reaching his lantern as far ahead as he could, the shadows dancing about the hull of the creaking ship, the rough, damp timbers of the ceiling brushing the top of his head. He peered into the gloom of the hold, sweat beading cold on his skin.

Others were awake now, but few had ventured beyond crowding the hatch leading from the crew's berths, and Urse recalled – with a sneer diffident in its bravado – seeing all those white rolling eyes, mouths open, round and dark like the tiny pocks in cliff walls where swifts nested. *Cowards!*

Well, they hadn't been soldiers, had they? Not a one of them, aye, so it was natural they'd look to Heck and Gust and Birds Mottle, not that any of them was quite free with their professions. No, such things came by obvious, in this hard confidence and the like when things were fast swirling down into some dark ugly pit. So here he stood, crowded by Birds and Gust both, with lantern in one hand and shortswords at the belts of the two soldiers at his back, Hood bless 'em.

'Briv's gone missing,' Gust Hubb said, interrupting his endless praying to deliver this detail in a strained, squeaking voice. 'Said he was coming down 'ere for a cask a something.'

'Briv. Cook's helper?' asked Birds Mottle.

'No, Carpenter's helper.'

'Was he named Briv too then?'

'He was, and so's the rope braider, named Briv.'

Heck cut into this stupid conversation. 'So Briv's gone missing, right.'

'Carpenter's helper, Briv, aye.'

'And he went down 'ere, right?'

'Don't know,' Gust Hubb said. 'I suppose he did if that was his screaming, but we don't know for sure now, do we? Could be one of the other Brivs doing the screaming, for all we know.'

Heck turned round to glare at his one-eared companion. 'Why would one of the other Brivs be screaming, Gust?'

'I wasn't saying one was, Heck. I was saying we don't know where Briv did the screaming, if any of 'em.'

'Why does it have to be one of the Brivs doing the screaming?' Heck demanded, his voice rising in frustration.

Gust and Birds exchanged a glance, then Birds shrugged. 'No reason, love.'

'Unless,' said Gust, 'all three was going for the same cask!'

'That's not the question at all!' Birds retorted. 'What's a carpenter's helper doing getting a cask of any kind? That's the question! Cook's helper, sure, makes sense. Even the rope braider, if'n he was looking—'

'She,' cut in Gust.

'The Briv who braids ropes is a "she"?'

'Aye.'

'Well, my point was, you get wax in casks, right? And pitch, too, so there's no problem Briv the braider coming down here—'

'Listen to you two!' Heck Urse snapped. 'It doesn't matter which Briv—'

There were shouts from the hatch above.

Gust snorted. 'They found Briv!'

'But which Briv?' Birds demanded.

'It doesn't matter!' Heck shrieked. Then took a deep breath of the fetid air and calmed down. 'The point is, nobody's missing, right? So who did that screaming we heard down 'ere?'

Gust rolled his eyes, then said, 'Well, that's what we're down here trying to find out, Heck. So stop wasting time and let's get on with it!'

Heck Urse edged forward, pushing the lantern still further ahead.

'Besides,' Gust resumed in a lower tone, 'I heard a rumour that Briv the braider isn't Briv at all. It's Gorbo, who likes to dress up like a girl.'

Heck turned again and glared at Gust.

Who shrugged. 'Not too surprising, there's one of those on every ship—'

'And where did you hear that?' Heck demanded.

'Well, it's just a guess, mind. But a damned good one, I'd wager.'

'You know what I wish?' Heck said. 'I wish whoever cut off your ear hadn't cut off your ear at all.'

'Me too—'

'I wish it'd been your tongue, Gust Hubb.'

'That's not a nice thing to say, Heck. I wasn't wishing no one cut off any part of *you*, you know. It still hurts, too. Stings fierce, especially now I'm sweating so much. Stings, Heck, how'd you like that? And then there's the swishing sounds. Swishing and swishing—'

'I'm going to go to the head,' Heck said.

'What, now? Couldn't you have done that—'

'It's up there, fool! I'm going to check it, all right?'

Gust shrugged. 'Fine by me, I suppose. Just make sure you wash your hands.'

'THAT SCREAM WASN'T NO JHORLIGG,' EMANCIPOR REESE asserted, licking suddenly dry lips.

Bauchelain, still adjusting the sleeves of his chain armour, glanced over and raised one brow. 'Mister Reese, that was a death cry.'

'Don't tell me Korbal Broach has—'

'Assuredly not. We are too far from land for Mister Broach to predate on this crew. That would, obviously, be most unwise, for who would sail the ship?' Bauchelain drew on his black chain gauntlets and held both hands out for Emancipor to tighten the leather straps on the wrists. 'A most piteous cry,' the necromancer murmured. 'All foreseen, of course.'

'Them nails, Master?'

A sharp nod. 'It is never advisable to loose the spirits of the dead, to wrest them from their places of rest.'

'It's kind of comforting to think that there are such things as places of rest, Master.'

'Oh, I apologize, Mister Reese. Such places do not exist, not even for the dead. I was being lazy in my use of cliché. Rather, to be correct, their places of eternal imprisonment.'

'Oh.'

'Naturally, spirits delight in unexpected freedom, and are quick to imagine outrageous possibilities and opportunities, most of which are sadly false, little more than delusions.' He walked over to his sword and slid the dark-bladed weapon from its scabbard.

'This is what makes certain mortals so . . . useful. Korbal Broach well comprehends such rogue spirits.'

'Then why are you all get up for a fight, Master?'

Bauchelain paused, eyed Emancipor for a long moment, then he turned to the door. 'We have guests.'

Emancipor jumped.

'No need for panic, Mister Reese. To the door please, invite them in.'

'Yes, sir.'

He lifted the latch then stumbled back as Captain Sater, followed by the First Mate, walked in. The woman was pale but otherwise expressionless, whilst Ably Druther looked like he'd been chewing spiny urchins. He stabbed a bent finger at Emancipor and hissed, 'It's all your fault, Luckless!'

'Quiet!' snapped Captain Sater, her grey eyes fixing on Bauchelain. 'Enough dissembling. You are a sorceror.'

'More a conjuror,' Bauchelain replied, 'and I was not aware of dissembling, Captain.'

'He's a stinking mage,' Ably Druther said in a half-snarl. 'Probbly his fault, too! Feed 'em to the dhenrabi, Captain, and we'll make the Cape of No Hope with no trouble in between— By the Stormriders!' he suddenly gasped, only now seeing Bauchelain's martial fittings. Ably backed up to the cabin door, one hand closing on the shortsword at his belt.

Captain Sater swung round to glare at her First Mate. 'Get down below, Druther. See what our lads have found in the hold – Hood's breath, see if they're even still alive. Go! Out!'

Ably Druther bared his crooked teeth at Bauchelain, then bolted.

Sater's sigh was shaky as she turned back to the conjuror. 'What plagues this ship? It seems the air itself is thick with terror – all because of a single scream. Listen to the hull – we seem moments from bursting apart. Explain this! And why in Hood's name are you armed as if for battle?'

'Mister Reese,' said Bauchelain in a low voice, 'pour us some wine, please—'

'I'm not interested in wine!'

Bauchelain frowned at Sater, then said, 'Pour me some wine, Mister Reese.'

Emancipor went to the trunk where his master kept his supply of dusty crocks, bottles and flasks. As he crouched to rummage through the collection, seeking something innocuous, Bauchelain resumed speaking to the captain.

'Panic is a common affliction when spirits awaken, Captain Sater. Like pollen in the air, or seeds of terror that find root in every undefended mortal mind. I urge you to mindfulness, lest horror devour your reason.'

'So that scream was just some mindless terror?'

Emancipor could almost see the faint smile that must have accompanied Bauchelain's next words. 'I see the notion of loosed spirits is insufficient to assail you, Captain, and I am impressed. Clearly you have an array of past experiences steadying your nerves. Indeed, I am relieved by your comportment under the circumstances. In any case, that scream announced the most horrible death of one of your crew.'

There was silence then behind Emancipor and he lifted into view a bottle of black, bubbly glass, only to recoil upon seeing the thick glassy stamp of a skull on the body and a clatter of long bones girdling the short neck. He hastily returned it, reached for another.

'Spirits,' said Captain Sater in a cold, dead tone, 'rarely possess the ability to slay a living soul.'

'Very true, Captain. There are, of course, exceptions. There is also the matter of the Red Road, Laughter's End and its lively current. A most foul conspiracy of events, alas. To be more certain of what has awakened below, I must speak with my companion, Korbal Broach—'

'Another damned sorceror.'

'An enchanter, of sorts.'

'Where is he, then? Not long ago he was on deck but then he vanished – I was expecting to find the creepy eunuch down here with you.'

Emancipor found another bottle, the murky green glass devoid of scary stamps. Twisting round, he held it up to the lantern light and saw nothing untoward swimming in the dark liquid within. Satisfied, he collected a goblet, plucked loose the stopper and poured his master a full serving. Then paused and, with great caution, sniffed.

Aye, that's wine all right. Relieved, he straightened and delivered it into Bauchelain's left, metal-wrapped hand, even as the conjuror said, in a light manner, 'Captain Sater, I advise you to refrain from voicing such gruff . . . attributions in your description of Korbal Broach. As Mister Reese can attest, my companion's affability is surely as much a victim of bloody detachment as was his—'

'All right all right, the man's a damned crab in a corner. You didn't answer me – where's he gone to?'

'Well,' Bauchelain paused and downed a mouthful of the wine, 'given his expertise, I would imagine he has . . .' And the conjuror's sudden, inexplicable pause stretched on, five, seven, ten heartbeats, before he slowly turned to face Emancipor. An odd fire growing in his normally icy eyes, the glisten of minute beads of sweat now on his brow and twinkling in his beard and trimmed moustache. 'Mister Reese.' Bauchelain's voice sounded half-strangled. 'You have returned the bottle to my trunk?'

'Uh, yes, Master. You want more?'

Trembling hand now, there, the one gripping the goblet. A peculiar, jerking step closer and Bauchelain was pushing the sword into Emancipor's hands. 'Take this, quickly.'

'Master?'

'A dark green bottle, Mister Reese? Unadorned glass, elongated, bulbous neck?'

'Aye, that's the one—'

'Next time,' Bauchelain gasped, his face flushing – delivering a hue never before seen by Emancipor – no, not ever on his master's normally pallid, corpulent visage. 'Next time, Mister Reese, any of the skull-stamped bottles—'

'But Master—'

'Bloodwine, Mister Reese, a most deadly vintage – the shape

of the neck is the warning.' He was now tugging at his chain hauberk, seemingly in pain somewhere below his gut. 'The warning – oh gods! Even a Toblakai maiden would smile! Get out of here, Mister Reese – get out of here!'

Captain Sater was staring, uncomprehending.

Taking the sword with him, Emancipor Reese rushed to the door and tugged it open. As he crossed the threshold Sater made to follow, but Bauchelain moved in a blur, one hand grasping her by the neck.

'*Not you, woman.*'

That grating, almost bestial voice was unrecognizable.

Sater was scrabbling for her own sword – but Emancipor heard the savage tearing of leather and buckles even as the woman uttered a faint squeal . . .

And oh, Emancipor plunged out into the corridor, slamming the door behind him.

Thumps from the cabin, the scraping of boots, another muted cry.

Emancipor Reese licked his lips – yes, he was doing a lot of that, wasn't he? *Bloodwine, where have I heard that name before? Toblakai, said Master. Them giants, the barbaric ones. Tree sap, aye, mixed with wine and that's fair enough, isn't it?*

Rhythmic creaking and pounding now. Womanly gasps and manly grunts.

Emancipor blinked down at the sword in his hands. The overlong, near two-handed grip. The rounded silver and onyx pommel, well-weighted and gleaming as if wet.

Desperate cries moaning through the door's solid oak.

He thought back to that bottle's neck, then looked down at the sword's handle and pommel once more. *Oh. One mouthful? Just the one? Gods below!*

'**Y**OU HEAR THAT?'

Birds Mottle squinted over at Gust Hubb. 'Hear what?'

'Water. Rushing – I think we're holed!'

'No we aren't – feel it – we'd be sluggish, Mael's tongue, we'd be knee deep down here. We ain't holed, Gust, we ain't nothing so shut that trap of yours!'

They were whispering, since both understood that whispering was a good thing, what with Heck Urse creeping ever closer to the head in his search of whoever had done that scream and maybe finding what was left of the poor fool or even worse, nothing at all except maybe smears of sticky stuff that stank like wet iron.

'I hear water, Birds, I'd swear it. A rush, and clicks and moaning – gods, it's driving me mad!'

'Be quiet, damn you!'

'And look at these nails – these new ones – look how they're sweating red—'

'It's rusty water—'

'No it ain't—'

'Enough – look, Heck's at the head.'

That did what was needed in silencing Gust Hubb, apart from his fast breathing right there beside her as they crouched on the centre gangway running the length of the keel. Both strained their eyes at that wavering pool of lantern light fifteen paces ahead. They watched as the black, warped door was angled open.

Then Heck Urse's silhouette blotted out the glow.

'Look!' hissed Gust. 'He's going in!'

'Brave man,' Birds Mottle muttered, shaking her head. 'I shoulda married him.'

'He ain't that brave,' said Gust.

She slowly drew her knife and faced him. 'What did you just say?'

Gust Hubb caught nothing of that dangerous tone, simply nodding ahead. 'Look, he's just peeking in.'

'Oh, right.' She sheathed her knife.

Heck leaned back and shut the head's door, then, drawing his lantern back round, hurried back to where they waited.

'Nothing,' he said. 'No one and nothing there.'

Gust Hubb yelped and clapped a hand to the bandaged wound on the side of his head.

Heck and Birds stared at him.

'Something nipped me!'

'Something nipped what, exactly?' Heck asked. 'It's a ghost ear now, Gust Hubb. It ain't there, remember?'

'I'd swear . . .'

'Your imagination,' Birds Mottle said. Then she turned back to Heck Urse. 'So what do we do now?'

Someone was coming up the walkway and they turned to see Ably Druther clambering closer.

'We did a search and all, sir,' Heck said as the First Mate arrived. 'Didn't find nothing and no signs neither.'

Ably crouched, drawing them all into a huddle. 'Listen, the whole damned crew is awake and eyes are rolling every which way – finding nothing won't work—'

'They do a count?' Heck asked. 'Who's missing?'

'Rope braider Briv.'

'Sure it was her?'

'That's what I was told. The short one with the orange hair and the stubbly legs—'

'Was Gorbo there?'

Ably Druther nodded.

Heck and Birds exchanged a glance. 'You sure of that?' the former asked.

Ably Druther scowled. 'Aye, he was the one reporting Briv missing.'

Birds Mottle snorted. 'Was he now?'

'I just said he was.'

'And nobody else missing?'

'Well, just that fat passenger, the one always fishing.'

'Ow!' Gust Hubb clapped a hand on to the bandage again.

'What's your problem?' Ably Druther demanded. 'What's with the side of your head?'

'Didn't hear?' Birds asked, then continued, 'Someone went and chopped off his ear – when he was sleeping, if you can believe that. And now it's a ghost ear.'

'You can hear ghosts?'

The three ex-soldiers stared at the First Mate for a moment, then Heck Urse said, 'That he can, only sometimes they take bites.'

'What a horrible thing!' Ably Druther straightened and began backing away, fading with every step from the pool of lantern light.

Which was probably why none of the ex-soldiers crouched on the walkway actually saw whatever it was that rose up behind the First Mate and bit off his head.

L IKE A BLOT ON THE TURGID SEAS, THE DECK OF THE *SUNCURL* WAS A stain far below Bena Younger and her cackling mother. Edges blurred, the blackness itself the only proof that the ship existed at all, as the swirling thrusts of spume on the seas broke and rolled out to the sides, blooms of crimson-tinged luminescence cavorting away into the night.

Sails flapped as the *Suncurl* drifted as if indifferent to the wind, nudged along on the currents of the Red Road. No one visible at the wheel. Only shadows caught in the rat-lines and rigging. No lantern swinging beneath the prow to light the way.

Close round the hatch to the hold huddled most of the crew. Reams of sand had been spread in a futilely protective circle, encompassing the hapless sailors, a detail that loosed hacking laughter from Bena Elder's gaping mouth.

Overhead, the fitful wind shredded rifts through the thin shrouds of grey cloud, yet whatever world those rents revealed was naught but soulless darkness, bereft of stars.

Laughter's End exuded lifeless sighs into this turning, alien night sky, and Bena Younger crouched down, knees drawn up, arms wrapping them close against her chest, shivering in waves of blind, despairing terror.

Whilst her mother's desiccated head nodded in rhythmic reassurance, and she sang on in her crooning way. *Lust and death this night, the murderous charade of love and treasures plundered! Oh, utopian circumstance as like a philosophe's wet aspiration – yes, all the dancers pause as if pinned through their free feet by dread spikes of reason! Exalted music of procreation! The Luckless fool has perchance undone us all – must we bless the sackless madman and his lurking lurker in the locked trunk? But no, warded indeed is that child – by none other than the one lost to all cogency!*

You and me, beloved, we shall survive this night, oh yes. Bena Elder promises! Safe from all hungry harm. Your dearest, loving mother is swelled to all decent proportions, for such are these exuding sighs that travel the Red Road, the whispered promise of rightful majesty accorded all things maternal, one hopes, and hopes, yes.

Cry not, daughter. Warm yourself in your mother's unrelenting embrace – you are safe from the world. Safe and safer still. Virgin is your blood, virgin is your child mind, virgin yes, is the power of your soul – your sweetest kiss, yes, upon which the only one who truly loves you feeds, persists, endures.

You are mine ever and ever, even this night, and so I shall prove to all, no matter how hoary and dismal and desperate the challenge from below!

Let me sip each whimper from your lips, daughter. My strength grows!

ONE SCREAM. A SUDDEN WIDENING OF THE EYES, A FAINT primordial shiver. The soul tenses, crouches, awaits a repetition, for it is in repetition alone that a face is painted on to the dark unknown, a face indeed frightened, frightening, wracked with pain, or – and so one wishes – in bright, startled delight. But alas, this latter entreaty is yielded up so rarely, for such are grim truths unveiled, one beneath another and seemingly without end.

One scream. Breath held, heart stilled. What comes?

Now, an eruption of screams. From three throats. Well that is indeed . . . different.

The hammer and thump, the wild pitching of inadequate light from somewhere down below. Boots on slick wood, the screams growing ravaged as tender tissue splits to the torrent of sound. And this, then, is the place and the moment when all totters on the knife-edge, precipice yawning, wind howling oblivion's flinty echo – does madness arrive? Unleashing misdirected violence and random calamity? Vague figures charging into one another, mouth-stretched faces crushed under heel, shapes pitching over the rail, bones snapping, blood gushing, grimy fingers digging into eyes – oh, so much is uttered by the fates to the chant of remorseless madness.

A deep, reverberating shout – nothing more would have been needed – a commanding voice to tug souls back from the brink.

If only one was there, among that huddle of crew, of the fortitude and iron spine to seize that one moment of salvation.

But terror had swum the night's sultry currents, seeping into flesh and mind, and now, in the wake of that terrible shrieking from below, chaos blossomed.

Life, as Bauchelain would well note – were he of any mind to voice comment – was ever prone to stupidity and, in logical consequence, atrocious self-destruction.

Of course, he was too busy spilling an endless flood of seed into a barely sensate and in no way resisting Captain Sater down in his cabin, and this, as all well know, is the pinnacle of all human virtue, glory and exaltation.

IN WILD WHIRLING LANTERN LIGHT ABLY DRUTHER'S HEADLESS corpse continued kicking even as blood gushed from the ragged nightmare that was his neck. His hands waved and twitched about as if strung to belligerent puppets. Birds Mottle, Gust Hubb and Heck Urse had collectively recoiled along the gangway towards the head – not Ably's, which had vanished, but the one at the bow – and in the process their feet had tangled, precipitating all three in a shrieking tumble down along one side of the mouldy hull, and there they thrashed, with Heck still holding the lantern high, in suddenly sodden clothes pungent with the reek of urine and, in Gust's case, something worse.

If the slayer now sought their souls, the harvest would have been virtually effortless. But nothing descended upon them, and apart from their screams, and the thumping of Ably's boots – and now, it must be added, the panicked thunder of feet from the deck overhead – there was no slithery, slurping rush to where they struggled and clawed, no hissing descent of slavering fangs.

Despite this, terror held the three ex-soldiers by their throats, especially when Ably Druther sat up, then twisted on to his hands and knees and jerkily regained his feet. Blood wept down his torso front and back, triggering in Heck's mind a dismayed revulsion that the man didn't even have the decency to use a napkin. Hands groping, Ably Druther took a step closer.

That step pitched him from the walkway and the trio of shrieks redoubled as the headless First Mate plunged down on to them.

Fingers snagged whatever they caught, and Gust wailed as his other ear was torn away from the side of his head, a blessing of symmetry if nothing else, but now terrible crunching, crackling sounds surged into his brain to war with the endless swishing of water.

Flailing, he scrabbled free from the corpse's reach, landing face first into the crevice between raised gangway and hull, only to find his gaping mouth suddenly filled with oily fur, squirming as he instinctively bit down even while gagging. A piteous squeal from the rat that ended on an altogether too high note, as if bladders of air had been disastrously squeezed and fluids most foul filled Gust Hubb's mouth.

His stomach revolted with spectacular effect, propelling the mangled rat a man's length out on to a tumbling landing on the walkway, where it came to rest on its back, tiny legs in the air, blood-wet slivery tongue lolling down one side of its open mouth.

Heck Urse, in the meantime, was being choked to death by a headless First Mate – who clearly wanted a head and any one would do. As a result, he forgot all about the risks of holding the lantern, electing in his extremity to use it as a weapon. In this, instinct failed him, since such a weapon was in truth likely only effective against the back of his assailant's head. A head that wasn't there. The hard, hot bronze of the lantern's oil-filled body cracked Urse in the face, igniting his beard and breaking his nose. Blinded, he flung the lantern away, spreading a flaring sheet of burning oil in its wake.

This elongated sheet of fire landed in between Bird Mottle's legs, as she was at that moment sitting up. As heat rushed for her nether parts, she kicked, lunging backward, to land skidding on the dead rat, all the way to the head which met her own with a solid crunch. Eyes pitching upwards, she sagged unconscious.

Blood having extinguished his smouldering beard, Heck now had both hands on the lone hand squeezing his neck, and he began breaking fingers one by one. From Ably Druther came a series of anal gasps of, presumably, pain. And finally Heck Urse was able to twist free, clambering on to the First Mate's back, where he pounded down with futile abandon.

Gust Hubb loomed into view, his earless head ghastly in the flickering fire light, vomit slicking his chin to mingle with the blood streaming down both jaw-lines. Bulging eyes fixed on Heck Urse.

'Kill it! Kill it! Kill it!'

'I'm trying, you damned fool!' Heck retorted. 'Get me a sword! A spike! Get me ropes, damn you!'

Gust Hubb scrambled past on the walkway. 'Get it yourself! I ain't staying down here – no way – and I ain't ever coming down here again!'

Cursing, Heck reached for his knife. Still straddling the struggling body of Ably Druther, he twisted round and hamstrung the First Mate, one side, then the other. 'Try walking now!' he snarled, then giggled, pushing himself back on to the walkway, yelping at the still-licking flames, then crabbing towards Birds Mottle.

'Wake up, love! We gotta get out of here – *wake up!*'

The third hard slap to the side of her face brought a flutter to her lids, then her eyes snapped open and she stared up at him, momentarily uncomprehending.

But Heck couldn't wait, and he began pulling Birds to her feet. 'Come on, sweet. There's a demon or something down here – Gust's already bolted, the bastard – come on, let's go.'

She looked at him blankly. 'The ship's on fire. That's not good.'

'We'll get the crew down here, every damned one of them, to put it out.'

'Good. Yes. It's not good if everything catches fire.'

'No, darling, that it ain't. Here, watch your step . . .'

WITH HECK URSE DRAGGING A MUMBLING BIRDS MOTTLE up the steep steps to the deck above, the headless corpse of Ably Druther was left more or less on its own, attempting to regain its feet but, alas, its legs had stopped working. Dejected, the First Mate sat down on the walkway, forearms resting on thighs and hands hanging down.

The spark of life could leap unfathomed distances, could erupt in places most unexpected, could indeed scurry along tracks of muscle and nerve, like a squirrel with a chopped tail. And sometimes, when even the life itself has fled, the spark remains. For a little while.

Once seated, Ably Druther ceased all movement, beyond a fainting slumping of the shoulders that quickly settled. Even the blood draining from various wounds finally slowed, the last drops thick and long.

Of the dread slayer, there was no sign.

The flames, which had been climbing the tarred hull, predictably eager, suddenly flickered, then guttered out.

And soft footsteps sounded, down the walkway from the head. Large, almost hulking, a figure wearing a full-length hauberk of black chain that slithered in the gloom. Bald pate a dull grey, thick-fingered hands reaching down as the figure crouched above the crushed body of the rat.

A soft whimper escaped Korbal Broach's flabby lips.

The very last rat aboard *Suncurl*. His most cherished, if

temporary, servant. Witness to the monstrosity that had slain the First Mate with such perfunctory delight. And well *of course* the victim's head was missing. That made perfect sense, after all.

Korbal Broach paused, cocking a suitably attached ear.

The panic above seemed to have dwindled. Perhaps the crew had abandoned ship, and oh, that would be regrettable. Surely neither the captain nor Bauchelain would permit such a thing. Did not Bauchelain know how Korbal so cherished these myriad pulses of sordid, not-especially-healthy lives? A harvest promised him, yes, once they were no longer necessary. *Promised.*

Why, Korbal Broach might have to pursue them, if truly they had fled—

A rasping cackle from the darkness – somewhere far down towards the stern.

Korbal Broach frowned. 'Rude,' he murmured, 'to have so interrupted my precious thoughts. So rude.'

The cackle crumbled into a rasp, and a voice drifted out. '*You.*'

'Yes,' Korbal Broach replied.

'*No, it can't be.*'

'But it is.'

'*You must die.*'

'So I must. One day.'

'*Soon.*'

'No.'

'*I will kill you. Devour your round head. Taste the bitter sweetness of your round cheeks. Lap the blood in its round pool beneath you.*'

'No.'

'*Come closer.*'

'I can do that,' Korbal Broach replied, straightening and walking towards the stern. He passed beneath the grainy rectangle of lesser darkness that was the still undogged hatch. And in his mailed hand was a crescent-bladed short-handled axe that seemed to be sweating oily grit. Gleaming most evil.

'*That cannot hurt me.*'

'Yes, no pain. But I have no wish to hurt you.' And Korbal Broach giggled. 'I will chop you up. No pain. Just pieces. I want your pieces.'

'*Bold mortal. We shall indeed test one another . . . but not right now.*'

Korbal Broach halted. The demon, he knew, was gone. Disappointed, he slipped the handle of the axe under his belt. He sniffed the air. Tasted the darkness. Listened to the slurp and swirl of water beyond the hull. Then, scratching his behind, he turned and began climbing the steps.

He never reached the top. But then, he had never intended to.

A T THE RUSH OF CHAOTIC COMMOTION ON THE MID-DECK OF *Suncurl* immediately following the screams from below, Emancipor Reese crouched down in the doorway of the cabin hatch, stared out at the shrieking, hair-tearing, biting, clawing mob of sailors thrashing this way and that. Bodies plummeting over the rail. More screams rising up unabated from the hold's hatch. And he muttered, 'Not again.'

This was how the world circled round itself, curly as a pubic hair, plucked and flung wayward on whatever wind happened by as the breeches were tugged down and coolness prickled forever hidden places – as hidden as the other side of the moon, aye – and life spun out of control again and yet again, even as scenes repeated themselves, ghastly and uncanny – why, he half expected to hear the crunch of wood against rocks and ice, the squeal of horses drowning below decks, the staggering figures their faces blurring past in a smear of blood and disordered features. As the wind howled as if flinging darkness itself in all directions, a mad night's fit of murderous destruction.

But that, he reassured himself, was long ago. Another ship. Another life.

As for this, well.

Adjusting his grip on Bauchelain's oversized sword, Emancipor Reese straightened and ascended the steps on to the deck. He raised the weapon high. Then bellowed, *'Sailors abide! Abide! Abide for orders, damn you all!'*

Stentorian roars, as invariably erupted from officers in charge of things and the people working those things, could, if the fates so decreed, reach through to that tiny walnut-sized knob of civil intelligence that could be found in the brains of most sailors; could, with the Lady's blessing and Mael's drawn breath, shock into obedience those figurative nuts, and so deliver order and attentiveness—

'It's 'Mancy the Luckless! He's to blame! Get him!'
'Aw shit.'

GUST HUBB, HAPLESS IN HIS EARLESSNESS, POKED HIS MANGLED head up from the hatch and, eyes bugging, was witness to a frenzied rush upon that manservant so aptly nicknamed the Luckless. Who happened to be holding an enormous sword which he began waving dangerously in an effort to hold back the snarling sailors. A belaying pin knocked the weapon from 'Mancy's hands and Gust saw the weapon cartwheel through the air – straight for him.

Bleating, Gust Hubb lunged back, and fire exploded between his eyes. Blood spurting everywhere as he brought his hands up to where his nose used to be, only to find two spraying, frothing holes. He fell to one side and rolled away from the hatch. The terrible smell of cold iron flooded up into his brain, overwhelming even the pain. This, commingled with the endless rush of water – which he now felt streaming from his half-blinded eyes – and some faint creaking from somewhere else, was all too much for his assailed senses and blessed oblivion swept in to engulf him in the black tide of peace.

For now.

Heck Urse, pulling Birds Mottle up into view, glanced over to see Gust lying motionless on the deck, his head resting in a pool of blood. Anger surged, white hot. He dragged Birds over the lip of the hatch and left her there, tugging free his short sword that only a while earlier he had forgotten was even there.

A score of sailors jostled around something at the base of the mainmast, lines rippling, then they were hoisting a limp body upwards, scraping against the mast, arms dangling. 'Mancy the Luckless, beaten senseless and maybe worse, tied by one ankle, climbing skyward in ragged jerks.

'What in Hood's name are you doing?' Heck roared, advancing on the mob.

A woman named Mipple, her hair looking like a long-abandoned vulture nest, snapped her head round and bared stained teeth at him. 'Luckless! Tryin' to kill us all! We's sacrificing him to Mael!'

'Atop the mainmast? You fools, let him down!'

'No!' cried another sailor, waving a belaying pin and strutting about as if in charge.

Heck scowled at the man, trying to recall his name. 'Wister, is it?'

'You ain't a man o'the seas, Heck Urse – and don't go tryin' to tell us different! Look at you, you're a damned soldier, a deserter!'

''Mancy ain't got—'

'He cut off your friend's nose!'

Heck stopped, his scowl deepening. He wiped the blood from his own nose, heard a click. 'He did?'

'Aye, with that big sword – the one jammed in the rail there – see the blood on the blade? That's Gust's blood!'

A chorus confirmed these details, heads nodding on all sides, manly sideways spits to punctuate Wister's assertions.

Heck slid his sword back into its scabbard. 'Well then, hoist away!'

*D*ARLING DAUGHTER, WHAT COMES? LISTEN TO THE SCRAPE *and bump, the creak and groan! Petard lofted the raving demon comes! No senses fired, reason's candle snuffed, make ready my sweetness, and together we shall slit its throat wide and loose a rain of blood upon the fools below!*

The crow's nest pitched in gentle, vaguely circular motion, as all headway had been surrendered and *Suncurl* waddled in the swells, slowly edging crossways along the Red Road of Laughter's End. Figures still ran here and there below, as cries for the captain finally arose, then came the horrifying news of First Mate Ably Druther's brutal murder in the hold – by some beast unknown. A beast that could, Bena Younger heard, vanish into thin air. Panic was born anew on the deck below.

Trembling, she now found herself listening, breath held, as something bulky was being slowly hauled up the mast. All the way up, if her mother spoke true. A demon. Bena gripped ever tighter the small knife in her hand. Slit its throat, yes. With Mother's help.

Listen! Almost here!

SHEATHED IN SWEAT, BAUCHELAIN ROLLED OFF CAPTAIN SATER.
She moaned, then said, 'Some mouthful.'

He blinked away the sting in his eyes and regarded her. 'Most dire consequences follow imbibing Toblakai Bloodwine. I most humbly apologize, Captain.'

'Done with me, then?'

'I believe so.'

Armour, straps, fittings and underclothes were scattered all about the cabin. The lantern wick was dimming, oozing shadows into the corners, the light that remained singularly lurid. Somewhere near by liquid dripped, a detail neither was anxious to pursue.

Sater sat up. 'Do you hear something?'

'That depends.'

'On deck – and we're drifting – no one's at the wheel!'

As his gaze travelled over the captain's bared chest – he'd torn away her blouse in the first frenzied moments – the ample mounds swinging faintly then lunging as she reached for a scrap of clothing, Bauchelain felt a stirring once more. Grimacing, he looked away. 'We were to discuss this fell night,' he said, finding his quilted under-padding – one sleeve torn away at the seams – and pulling it on over his head. Pausing then to slick back his iron-hued hair.

'Ghosts,' she snarled, rising to draw up her leggings, wincing with each tug.

'Not this time,' he replied, combing through his beard. 'A lich.'

Sater stopped, stared across at him. 'How in Hood's name did a lich get aboard my ship?'

'The nails, and perhaps something else. Korbal Broach no doubt knows more.'

'And I'm sure I asked – earlier – where is he?'

'He walks the warrens, I expect. Likely hunting the creature through the maze of Hood's realm. A great risk, I might add. The Lord of Death holds no precious fondness for Korbal Broach.'

She squinted. 'Hood knows your friend . . . *personally*?'

'Gods are easily irritated.' Bauchelain lifted his hauberk, the chain flowing around his hands. 'I must retrieve my sword. Should the lich stride in truth into our realm, here on this ship, well, we shall face a challenge indeed.'

'Challenge?'

'Yes, in staying alive.'

'It wasn't us!' she suddenly shouted.

Bauchelain paused, frowned at her. 'You are hunted.' Then he nodded. 'As we suspected. What follows in our wake, Captain?'

'How should I know?'

'Describe your crime.'

'That's got nothing to do with anything. It wasn't even a crime. Not really. More like . . . opportunism.'

'Ah, a sort of temptation to which one yields, casting aside all fear of consequences.'

'Exactly.'

'A momentary failing of ethics.'

'Just so.'

'Expedience winning its war with duty.'

'So would we argue, yes—'

'A defence based on the weakness of nature belongs to un-tutored children and dogs that bite, Captain. You and your cohorts are all adults and if you relinquished your honour then fierce punishment is righteous and deserves a vast audience, a mob, if you will, expressing their most civilized glee over the cruel misery of your fate.'

Her mouth hung open for a moment longer, then she reached for her sword and swiftly clasped the belt on to her pleasantly curved hips. 'You're one to talk.'

'Whatever do you mean?'

'Temptation and dogs that bite and all that. Damn you, I can barely walk. Do you imagine I take kindly to rape? I even tried for my knife but you twisted my wrist—'

'It is well known that Bloodwine – even in minute traces on my lips, or in my mouth – will effect a complementary lust in the victim. Rape ceased as a relevant notion—'

'Doesn't matter when it ceased being whatever, Bauchelain! It's not like I consented, is it? Now for Hood's sake get your armour on – the weight just might hold you down – so I can start thinking straight – and don't worry, I won't cut your throat until we're out of all this.'

'I did apologize,' Bauchelain said. 'Impulses beyond my control—'

'Better you grabbed your manservant—'

'Since I am not inclined that way I would have murdered him, Captain.'

'We're not done with this.'

'I dearly hope we are.'

She marched to the door and flung it open, then paused at the threshold. 'Wizard, can we kill this lich?'

Bauchelain shrugged.

'Oh, would that I could kill *you* right now.'

He shrugged again.

AS SOON AS THE CABIN LATCH DROPPED BACK DOWN AND THE thump of the captain's boots hurried away, Bauchelain turned in time to see Korbal Broach stride out from a suddenly blurry back wall.

'Silly woman,' the eunuch said in his reedy voice, heading towards his trunk. 'Could she know the true absence of sexual pleasure—'

'Silly? Not at all. From shock to shame to indignation. She is right to feel offended, at me and at her own eager response. I am now considering a scholarly treatise on the ethical context of Bloodwine. Member emboldened by chemical means, desire like a flood, overwhelming all higher functions, this is a recipe for procreative and indeed non-procreative mayhem. It is a great relief to my sensibilities to know how rare Bloodwine is. Imagine a ready supply, available to all humans the world over. Why, they'd be dancing in the streets, brimming with false pride and worse, egregious smugness. As for the women, why, pursued endlessly by men they would swiftly lose their organizational talents, thus plunging civilization into a hedonistic headlong collapse of swollen proportions – rather, sizeable proportions – oh, never mind. Clearly, I will need to edit with caution and diligence.'

Korbal Broach knelt in front of his trunk and flipped back the lid. Wards dispersed with minute breaking sounds, as of glass tinkling.

Bauchelain frowned down at his friend's broad back. 'Humbling, the way you do that.'

'Ah!' cried Korbal Broach as he leaned forward and stared down at his seething, slurping, burbling creation. 'Life!'

'Is it hungry?'

'Oh yes, hungry, yes.'

'Alas,' observed Bauchelain, coming up to stand beside his companion and looking down at the monstrosity throbbing in its gloomy cave, a score of beady eyes glittering up at him. 'Would that it could do more than heave incrementally in pursuit of prey. Why, a snail could flee it with nary shortness of breath and—'

'No more,' sighed Korbal Broach. 'Pleasant past-time. I harvested all the rats on board, yes?'

'So you did, and I wondered at that.'

'Child is now propelled by a flurry of feet.'

Bauchelain's brows rose. 'You have melded rat appendages to your offspring?'

'Feet, limbs, jaws, eyes and spines and tails, yes. Child now has many, many mouths. Sharp teeth. A snivel of noses, a perk of ears, a slither of tails.'

'Nonetheless, who would condescend to being gnawed to death?'

'Child will grow, clasping all to itself and so become more agile, larger, ever more hungry.'

'I see. Is there a limit to its girth, then?'

Korbal Broach looked up and smiled.

'I see,' Bauchelain said again. 'Is it your intent to set your child in pursuit of the lich? Into the warrens?'

'Hunt,' the eunuch said, nodding. 'My child, freed to hunt!' He licked his thick lips.

'This will delight the crew.'

'For a time,' and Korbal Broach giggled.

'Well, I shall leave you to it, then, whilst I set out to find my sword – for the time when your child flushes our unwelcome guest.'

But Korbal Broach was already mumbling rituals of sorcery, lost in his own, no doubt pleasant, world.

EMANCIPOR REESE OPENED HIS EYES AND FOUND HIMSELF staring up at the horrid, desiccated visage of an ancient, toothless, nearly skinless woman.

'Aunt Nupsy?'

From somewhere nearby a thin voice cackled, then said in a rasping tone, 'I have you now, demon. Slit your throat. Cut out your tongue. Twist your nose. Pluck your brows. Oh, pain delivered to start tears in your eyes and blood everywhere else! Agony and nerves afire! Who's Aunt Nupsy?'

Emancipor set his hand against the dead face hovering in front of him and pushed the corpse away. It toppled to one side, folding in a clatter against a wicker wall.

'I'll get you for that! See this knife? An engagement with your navel! Hard about and cut your sheets, snip at the wrists and over the side – all hands on deck! Husbands are a waste of time so don't even think it! I bet she hated you.'

Bruises, knobby bumps on the brow, gritty blood on the tongue, maybe a bruised rib or three, throbbing nose. Emancipor Reese tried to recall what had happened, tried to figure out where he was. Darkness above, a faint ethereal glow from the grey-haired corpse, swaying, creaking sounds on all sides, the moan of the wind. And someone talking. He twisted round on to one elbow.

A scrawny wide-eyed child huddled against a curved wicker wall, clutching a knife in her small, chapped hands. 'Don't hurt me,' she said in a mousy squeak. Then added, in that wise rasp he'd heard earlier, 'She's not for you, oh no, demon! My teeth will leap at your throat! One by one! See that knife in my daughter's hands? It has drunk the life from a thousand foes!'

There was a rope tied round one of his ankles, the skin beneath terribly abraded. All his joints ached, leading him to a certain theory of what had occurred. 'I'm in the damned crow's nest. They strung me up, the bastards.' He squinted across at the girl. 'You're Bena Younger.'

She flinched back.

'Easy there, I won't be hurtin' you. I'm Emancipor Reese—'

''Mancy the Luckless.'

'Some things a man can't live down, no matter how lucky he is.'

A cackle. 'Lucky?'

'Gainfully employed, aye. Secure income, civil masters – why my wife must be dancing on the mound in our backyard, back in Lamentable Moll. My children worm-free at last and with clean, evenly waxed teeth and all the other modern conveniences. Aye, my ill-luck is long past, as dead as most of the people I knew back then. Why—'

'Shut up. The nails, fool, have twisted free. Spirits unleashed, wailing spectres and wraiths, yet one has risen, yes, above all the others. Clawed hands snatching. Souls grasped – oh hear their shrieks in the ether! Grasped, devoured, and the one grows. Power folded in, and in, layer upon layer, grim armour defying banishment – sweet in its multitude of nostrils the scent of mortal life, oh how it now hunts, to take all into its fang-filled, slavering, black-gummed and unpleasantly-smelling mouth! Lo, I hear skull bones crunching, even now!'

'You addled, child? What is this old hag's voice that comes so wrongly from your young lips?'

Bena Younger blinked. 'Mother,' she whispered, nodding to-wards the corpse. 'She speaks, she warns you, yes – why look upon me so strange? Why ignore her terrible glare so fixed upon you, sir? Bena Elder warns us – there is one below! Most terrible, oh, we have nowhere to go!'

Grunting, Emancipor Reese sat up and began loosening the knot at his ankle. 'You've that right, Bena Younger. Nowhere at all.' He knew to tread now with great care with the hapless girl, whose mind had so clearly snapped, imprisoned up here in this wicker basket with a mother who was weeks dead at the very least. The gulf of loneliness, of abandonment, had proved too deep, and into the cauldron of madness she had gone.

Bena Elder reappeared in the manner of suddenly bared teeth on her daughter's face. 'Everyone shall die. Except me and my daughter – when the one comes, scaling the mast, and reaches so sure into this nest, it shall be *your* throat it shall grasp, Luckless. And we shall watch as it drags you over the edge. We shall hear the snap and crunch of your bones, the gurgle of your blood, the squishy plop of your eyeballs—'

'Think it won't smell you two up here? Your daughter for certain, her life blood, the heat of her breath – all a tender lodestone to an undead—'

'I shall protect her! Hide her! In my embrace, yes!'

Emancipor struggled to his feet, leaned against the basket edge. 'Might work. I wish you both the Lady's tug. As for me, I'm going back down—'

'You mustn't! Hear them down there! Insanity! And the one stalks, drinking deep on terror—'

And, as if to confirm the horror of all Bena Elder described, more shrieks from below. Renewed, redoubled, repeated. Nether, despairing, primal.

The mast and crow's nest rocked as if buffeted by a giant's fist. Sharp, splintering sounds. They heard a yard slide from rings then crash on to the deck below.

'Hood's breath!' Emancipor gasped, clutching the edge, then twisting round and squinting downwards. Shadows flitted here and there across the deck, more nightmarish than real. A body was sprawled near the hatch. There was no sign of what had struck the base of the main mast, but Emancipor could make out white lines to mark the splitting further down, almost luminescent against the tarred wood. 'Something hit us down there, maybe even at the step down in the hold.' He glanced back to warn Bena Younger of the risk, caught a blurred sight of a knife pommel, flashing for his head.

White light!

It's the bells, Subly! Can't you hear the damned bells?

Oh, wife, what did I do now?

BEAUTIFUL, THIS ROCKING MOTION, SO GENTLE, SO SOFT. BIRDS Mottle, whose left breast was a white sphere devoid of all pigmentation, in splendid, eye-widening contrast to her dark skin everywhere else, and hence her name's origin, a detail regretfully not as secret among the crew as she'd have wanted – but gods, trapped aboard with all these gruff sailors and the few women among 'em uglier than a priest's puckered arse, and well, what else t'do and besides, she was earning coin, wasn't she? Coin, aye, most useful, since who knew if they'd ever get away with what they were trying t'get away with. Birds Mottle, then, was reluctant to prise open her eyes.

Especially with all the screaming up near the foredeck. And was that a splat of blood or just a bucket of salt water, rivulets running down the steps now, maybe, and well there'd be no use to getting wet now, would there?

And so she opened her eyes. Sat up, found herself facing astern, the cabin hatch slightly off to her right.

From which something wet, slick and murky was creeping into view, heaving over the steps. A chaotic scattering of small, black, beady eyes across a misshapen, mottled, lumpy surface. Slick, wet, yes, wetly slick, scrabbling and skittering noises as of minute claws on the wooden steps, faint slithering sounds, the pulse of organs now, throbbing beneath transparent, leaking skin. Half a face, below a purplish bulge that might be a liver, a glassy eye fixing on Birds Mottle momentarily before the next heave pitched the entire face down and out of sight.

Random locks of greasy hair, black and straight, blond and curly, brown and kinked, each emerging from a seamed patch of native scalp. And was that a lone brow, arching now above no eye, arching indeed above what might be a gall bladder, as if gall bladders were capable of ironic, inquisitive regard, when everyone knew gall bladders could only scowl—

Birds Mottle then realized that she wasn't simply conjuring this slurping, twittering monstrosity out of her modestly equipped imagination. Oh no, this was real.

And it was flowing on to the deck, as if its bulk rode centipede legs, and eyes black and glittering that now, she was certain, glittered directly at her, rife with rodentian avarice. And was that a snaggle of toothy jaws, snapping and slavering above pink noses bent every which way though each lifted up to test the air cute as buttons while the jaws clacked and clicked ominous and minuscule?

Whimpering, she crabbed back across the deck.

A brawny human forearm flopped out from the apparition, from an inconvenient location, and on its wrist gleamed a vivid tattoo of gambolling lambs. A second arm pried loose from folds of organs, revealing a snarling black wolf tattoo. Nails popped off from fingers clawing along the deck as the thing dragged itself forward, intent as a giant slug bolting towards a lump of fresh dung.

Then all at once, its bulk was clear of the steps, and the enormous nightmare scuttled forward, shriekingly quick – as Birds Mottle proved with her open mouth and vocal chords seeking to shatter glass – and, twisting, round to gain her feet, she pitched sideways as her left hand and left leg both plunged into the hold hatch.

She vanished into darkness, bouncing once, twice along the length of the steep steps, and thumping heavily on to the gangway. A swirl of stars spun across her vision, corkscrewing into a burgeoning black maw, that then swallowed her up.

Beautiful, this rocking motion . . .

CAPTAIN SATER DRAGGED AN UNCONSCIOUS MIPPLE TOWARDS the foremast and left her propped there. Sater's longsword was in her gloved right hand. Spatters of blood streaked across the torn remnants of her blouse. Would that she had gone to her own cabin and strapped on her armour and maybe run a brush through her hair – which was what she normally did after sex, something about potential tangles and knots that could yank her head askew – but too late now and regrets were a waste of time.

Especially when that damned lich kept rising out of the solid deck to fold far too many withered limbs about sailors, dragging them back down amidst terrible screams – through splintering wood until all that remained was a hole no sane person could have thought a grown body could be pulled through. But they had been, hadn't they? Right down, the savage edges of wood gouging and tearing away chunks of muscle and shreds of skin and clothes.

And not once, pushing through the panicked mob, had she been able to reach them in time. In the gloom she had seen enough of this lich to know that her sword was likely useless against it. Half again as tall as a man, a massive, elongated melding of corpses wrapped in parchment skin. A dozen or more arms. Jutting, snout-like mouths emerging from shoulder, hip, back of neck, cheekbone. Red-rimmed, unblinking eyes gleaming dull from countless places. Each leg a conglomeration of many legs, the muscles all knotted like twisted braids, a ribcage thrusting forward box-like, with a solid rippled wall of ribs – and cutting through that would be impossible, she well knew. Even a thrust would be turned. And the head – was that Ably Druther's head?

But oh, how Sater wanted to start hacking off those damned arms.

Wister was crawling past in front of her, weeping worse than a babe in soiled diapers, dragging his belaying pin behind him like a giant rattle.

How many were left?

Sater looked about. Here on the foredeck, she saw, huddled a dozen or so. Six gaping holes exuded horror around them in a neat, even circle. The foremast itself had snapped its step somewhere below and now leaned to one side, rocking with each tug of wind against the few luffing, wing-flapping foresails somewhere above. If a gust hit them . . . damn, why did Ably have to get himself killed? That mast might just lift right up and out, or tear most of the foredeck with it as it toppled. Either way would be trouble, she suspected, and as captain she should be thinking about such matters – oh gods! Was she mad? A damned lich was eating her crew!

'Listen! Wister, get on your damned feet!' She pulled a ring of keys from her belt. 'Weapons locker, floor of my cabin! Take Heck Urse – Heck! Never mind bandaging up Gust, he'll live – go with Wister. Break out the cutlasses—'

'Pardon, Captain, we don't have any cutlasses.'

Sater scowled at Wister. 'We don't? Fine, break out the truncheons, pins and the spears for propelling boarders—'

'We ain't got those neither.'

'So what in Hood's name is in my weapons locker?'

'You ain't looked?'

Sater took a half step closer to Wister, the sword in her hand trembling. 'If I knew, you brainless mushroom, I wouldn't be asking you now, would I?'

'Fine. Old Captain Urbot, he kept his private stock of rum down there.'

Sater clawed at her face for a moment. 'All right,' she sighed, defeated, 'break out the rum.'

'Now you're talking!' Wister shouted, suddenly animated. 'C'mon, Heck, you damned deserter! No time to waste!'

The two leaping down on to the main deck, boots thumping, skidding, then returning just as fast. Wister's face was white as a churning chop. Heck's mouth worked but no sound came forth. Snarling, Sater pushed past them to the edge of the forecastle and looked down.

Something like an abattoir's rubbish heap was crawling across the mid-deck, just skirting the edge of the hatch. It had tiny eyes, dozens of them. And hundreds of short slithery tails snarling out behind it. Arms, partial faces, wayward locks of hair, scores and scores of tiny snapping jaws. It was, in truth, the stupidest monster she had ever seen.

With another snarl she leapt down on to the main deck, strode up to the thing and with one savage kick drove it over the edge of the hold hatch. A chorus of piteous squeals as the absurd mound of flesh plunged into the inky darkness. A splatting impact below and more squealing, and maybe a faint shriek – she couldn't be sure and who cared? Spinning round, Sater glared up at Wister and Heck Urse. 'Well, what are you two waiting for?'

I N THE HOLD, NEAR THE HEAD, THE LICH WAS ARGUING WITH
itself. Souls, once bound to the iron nails that had been driven
into their corpses, now revelled in the miasmic concatenation
of flesh and bone that was the lich. The world was meat and
blood and to be in the world demanded fashioning a likeness of
the same. All too rare were those occasions when the ether was so
saturated with sorcery that such conjuration was possible. Such
luck!

To be meat and blood, one must devour meat and blood.
Worldly truths, oh yes.

Fragments of identity persisted, however, each insisting on
its right to an opinion, each asserting its claim to domination
over all the others. And so voices tittered from the lich's various
mouths where it stood amidst dismembered, half-eaten sailors,
most of whom were dead. Voices, aye, yet one remained silent,
ever silent, even as the argument continued to fill the shadows
with a menagerie of once-selves.

'Merchant trader! Why, the hold's big enough, and if we eat all
the sailors, why, the grand conjoining of spirit and flesh should
prove more than sufficient to crew this modest ship!'

'An undead entrepreneur can only be some malevolent god's
idea of a joke,' said another soul in tones of gravel underfoot, and
the strider of words ground remorselessly on, 'Is this what we've
come to, then, after countless generations of dubious progress?
Your presence, Master Baltro, is an affront—'

'And yours isn't?' rasped a vaguely feminine voice, and rasp was a truth indeed, if one were to take a sweet womanly utterance and run a carpenter's tool over it, should such things be possible and why not? 'Sekarand did you in long ago and yet here you are again, chained to us goodly folk like a morally dissolute abscess—'

'Better than a wart!' shrieked the wizard who had been murdered by Sekarand in Lamentable Moll long ago. 'I smell your reek, Hag Threedbore! Victim of disgruntled salamanders – no other possible explanation for your ghastly persistence—'

'And what of you, Viviset? Sekarand fed you into a tomb so warded that not even memory of you escaped! Why—'

'Please, please!' cried Master Baltro. 'I must ask of you all – who else smells his own flesh somewhere nearby?'

A chorus of muted assents tripped from the lich's score mouths.

'I knew it!' shouted Master Baltro. 'We must find—'

'As noble born,' spoke someone else, 'I must claim priority over the rest of you. We must find my self first—'

'Who in Hood's dusty name are you?'

'Why, I am Lordson Hoom, of Lamentable Moll! Related to the King himself! And I too sense the proximity of some crucial part of me – on this very ship!'

'Crucial? Well, that eliminates your brain, at least. I'd wager a pig-like snout.'

'Who speaks?' demanded Lordson Hoom. 'You shall be flayed—'

'Too late, fop, I already was and before the rest of you even ask, no, I'm not from Lamentable Moll. I don't know any of you, in fact. I'm not sure I even know myself.'

'The nails—' began the once-wizard, Viviset, but the stranger's voice cut in.

'I'm not from any damned nails, but I swear I sensed the rest of you arrive. Including the one who refuses to speak and that refusal is probably a good thing. No, I think I was aboard long before any of you. Though exactly how long, I can't really say.

One thing I can say: I preferred the peace and quiet before all you arrived.'

'Why you inconsiderate snob—'

'Never mind him, Threedbore,' Viviset said. 'Look at the opportunity we now have! We're dead but we're back and we're all damned angry—'

'But why?' Master Baltro asked in his weedy voice.

'Why are we angry? You fool. How dare other people be still alive when we aren't? It's unfair! A grotesque imbalance! We need to kill everyone on board. Everyone. Devour them all!'

Souls yelled out in suddenly savage assent to such notions. Lips writhed with various degrees of muscular success in conveying their bloodlust, their hatred for all things living. All about the lich's misshapen, horrid body, mouths sneered, snarled, licked hungrily and blew kisses of death like lovers' promises.

At this moment something huge thundered down from the hatch, the impact reverberating the length of the keel. More voices cried out, these ones thinner, plaintive, pained. Then, in the relative silence that followed, came the snipping and clicking of jaws.

Viviset hissed in horror. *'It's that . . . thing! The thing hunting us!'*

'I smell spleen!' squealed Lordson Hoom. *'My* spleen!'

At last, the silent one, whose silence had been, in truth, the fugue of confusion, the incomprehension of all these strange languages, finally ventured its opinion on matters. The Jhorligg's bestial roar sent selves tumbling, flung about in the cold flesh and cooling blood threads of the lich's manifold body. Stunning all into mute terror.

Mostly incoherent thoughts from the Jhorligg thrashed with the fury of a storm. *Eat! Rend! Flee! Breed! Eatrendfleebreed!* And up rose the eleven arms of the lich, torn, bloody fingers bending into rending positions, tendons taut as cocked crossbow cords. Weapons readied, the creature spinning round to face the monstrosity now crawling ever closer up the length of the wooden walkway.

That monstrosity was dragging something. Something that kicked booted heels against the hull. Kicked and scraped in frenzied panic.

'My spleen!' cried Lordson Hoom again. *'It wants to eat me!'*

'*L*IFE IS LIKE A CLAM,' BIRD MOTTLE'S FATHER ONCE TOLD HER. '*Years filtering shit then some bastard cracks you open and scrapes you into its damned mouth. End of story, precious pearl, end of story.*'

They'd lived by a lake. Her father had fought a lifelong war with a family of raccoons over the clam beds he'd staked out, run fences and nets round, and done just about everything else he could think of to keep the masked thieves from his livelihood. In terms of intelligence and raw cunning, the raccoons had old Da beat, and they drove him both mad and into his grave.

Birds Mottle, who'd had a much sweeter name back then, found herself – as she stared down at the lifeless face of her father, the expression all twisted by that last scream of outrage – contemplating a future comprised of the war that had killed Da. Her sole inheritance, this feud she could not hope to win. What kind of life was that?

Why, it was filtering shit, wasn't it?

Fifteen years old at the time, she'd collected a small pack full of things from the shack that stood on rickety stilts on the mud-flats – home – and set out for Clamshell Track, walking one last time that desultory route into Toll's City where they'd once hawked their harvest. Not much of a city, Toll's. The inner wall marked the modest extent of the town of twenty years past, and as for all the new buildings that rose outside the fortifications, well, not one stood more than two storeys tall.

160

Take a stick and jam it deep into the mud, just up where the waves reach on an easy day. Come back a week or two later and there's a mound of silts gathered round the stick on one side, and a faint shallow pit on the opposite side. Unless a storm arrives to drag the stick away, the mound grows, the hole slowly fills in.

That was Toll's City. A stone keep in the middle for the stick, the slow even drift of people from the countryside, silting up round the keep the way people did. A decade or so of miserable warfare, forcing the building of defences, and then a time of *'the drudgery of peace'*, as the soldiers said to describe all those bells of wasted training and standing sentinel over borderlands no one gave a damn about.

She didn't mind becoming a soldier. She didn't mind the half-mad fools she'd been squad-mates with. Gust Hubb, Bisk Flatter, Sordid and Wormlick. And, of course, Heck Urse, the one she'd ended up taking to bed, as much from boredom as lust – although, and this was indeed a truth – boredom's best answer, every time, was flat out rutting, grunting, frenzied lust. Why, there was a world of married or otherwise committed women bored out of their skulls, when the obvious solution was right there in front of them. Or the hut down the road.

Too bad they'd lost Bisk, Sordid and Wormlick that night. And now maybe it'd all been an accident, the way the other dory popped a knot belly-deep in the trough, sucking itself and its three wailing soldiers right down to the bottom, where the riptide grabbed all it could on its rush back to deeper water. And maybe it was just the Lady's pull'o'luck that the rest of 'em, Sater and Ably included, were in the bigger boat, the one with all the loot, that made it out to the *Suncurl* where it strained its fore and aft anchors in that churning tidal flow in the cut.

And maybe even Sater had been telling the truth about that haul. Toll's own mintage, silver and gold not yet grimed by a single grubby hand, aye, in bound stacks – well, she'd seen those, hadn't she? Seen and heaved up from the boat, o'er the rail and into Ably's waiting arms, the weight of wealth, so much wealth. But what about that other stuff? The burlap-wrapped, bulky objects, massively heavy, with knobs protruding, stretching the ratty fabric? Big as idols, swear up'n down, not that Toll's City had much in the way of stupid-rich temples, like the ones she'd heard about from Bisk – who'd lived up in Korel and only escaped time on the 'Wall by turning in his kid brother. Huge temples, with thousands of poor people coughing up their last coppers into the big bowls even as they reeled glass-eyed from any of a dozen plagues that seasonally tore through the shanty-towns. Rich enough, oh yes, for bloody idols and inset gems on those collecting bowls, and stealing from those soul-eating oh-so-pious crooks was just fine by her, and would've been, too, if that's what they'd done and if those were what those wrapped-up things were, which they weren't.

Half the city's coinage, aye, the hoarded loot of the Chanters – that nasty mob of tyrants ruling the roost – all to buy the services of that cursed mercenary company, them Crimson Guard, and why'd they needed 'em? The unification of all Stratem, oh yes, with Toll's City as the blustery capital. An end to skirmishes and feuds, to trader wars between damned factors out in the bush, to ambushes of furbacks and caravans of pelts burnt to a crisp just to make someone's neighbour starve, babes and old alike and all in between, too. Mercenaries, yes, to deliver the drudgery of peace.

Imagine, then, arriving at the coast where it was said the damned Crimson Guard had landed by the hundreds, only to find the fools gone. Shipped back out, on their way somewhere else, and in a hurry, too.

Well, turn round and take it all back home?

Sater had a better idea, aye.

Maybe better. Maybe Birds Mottle wasn't so sure anymore, now that she was embedded, head, shoulders and at least one tit, within a nightmare blob of squishing, squelching, wheezing, twittering, gasping, blinking and mouthing and throbbing . . . *thing*.

Embedded, aye. And more. Merged. Melded. Each breath a slimy inhalation of bright, cool liquid – air? No, wasn't that. Spit?

Could be, but spit brimming with whatever was in air that kept people alive. Blood? No, too thin. Too cool.

Eyes open, seeing red, mostly, and some pulsing arteries or veins. Not even blinking any more, since more cool liquid, yellowy perhaps, but thin as the lid on a snake's eyeball, kept everything from drying out.

Embedded, the monstrosity dragging itself forward and dragging her in its wake. She struggled to get to her feet, so she could stand – but that wasn't possible, she suspected – she'd never be able to lift this damned thing, not even in her arms much less tottering above uncertain footing.

Oh, what a lousy way to die. What a lousy way to stay alive, in fact. Dead would be good, yes, good indeed.

LIKELY UNNOTICED BY ANYONE, BAUCHELAIN HAD EMERGED on to the mid-deck, found his sword jammed by one edge into the rail off to his left – another hand's length and the precious weapon would have gone over the side. Blood gleamed on the reddish-black iron. Tugging it free, he paused, glanced astern.

Something . . .

Curious, Bauchelain ascended the aft steps to the wheel deck. No one had tied off, leaving the rudder to flap and swing, turning the huge wheel every which way. Frowning, indeed disappointed by such sloppy seamanship, he continued on to stand at the stern rail. Looked out over the gloomy Red Road of Laughter's End.

Crimson swirl, crimson phosphorescence, the wake jagged and random. He saw a faint carved trough, then noted the fishing line looped and knotted at the rail. They were trailing bait, possibly an unwise notion given the circumstances. Likely Korbal Broach's doing. He stroked his beard, musing.

Commotion from the bow. Turning, Bauchelain squinted. The lich had struck again, the Jhorligg's mindless hunger staining every soul with its desperate need. Misapprehension was ever a curse among the undead, alas. Although, given the emboldened strain of raw power curling through the currents on these seas, even misapprehension could acquire a certain . . . corporeal truth.

The lich devoured. And so grew in mass, in strength. A most

curious evolution, quite possibly unique. Without doubt worthy of further study.

A final shriek wavered up from the latest victim.

Thrumming, as of a bass lyre's string being plucked, drew him round once more. The fishing line was sawing back and forth, proof that something had been caught on the hook. A shark? Perhaps.

The line suddenly went slack.

Snapped? Most likely.

He saw dorsal fins in their wake, cutting the red-black water, rushing fast, then out, sweeping round the ship. Scores and scores. One of the sharks broke the surface barely a knife's throw from the rudder – a creature two-thirds the length of the *Suncurl*. It twisted to avoid colliding with the stern, then slid past, buffeting the hull, its shiny buckler-sized eye flashing. Then plunged from sight.

The sharks, Bauchelain realized, were fleeing.

Well, these waters were indeed thick with dhenrabi – and there was one of the gargantuan segmented behemoths, breaching a huge, rolling swell a thousand strokes to the east. Astonishingly fast, he observed. Outracing even the sharks . . .

Bauchelain finger-combed his beard some more.

GAUZE SWADDLED GUST HUBB'S FACE JUST BELOW HIS EYES and wrapping round his head in a thick band, the sun-bleached white material marred by three dark red blooms, one centre, the other two flanking at more or less the same elevation.

Noises assailed him. Chittering, snapping of jaws from one side, swirling water from the other. This was manageable, or so he had just concluded when, from the watery side, there came a devastating crunch and then vast, unbearable pain. The sudden assault was of such force that he bit down on his tongue and now there was even more blood, spurting from his mouth.

He had been kneeling on the foredeck, staring accusingly at everyone else, all of them mocking him with their perfect faces, their rosy noses and squid-hued ears all perfect in their delicate folds and cute lobes. But now he toppled to one side, curling up as agony tore through him from an ear he didn't even own anymore.

And now nipping bites affronted his other missing ear and this, dammit, was very nearly the worst night of his life.

Heck Urse crawled over, brandishing a knife and Gust recoiled upon seeing it.

'Idiot, I ain't gonna cut you or nothing! This is protection, for when that lich pops up again – gods, you'd think its belly was full by now. Look at Mipple, she's only now come round – missed all the fun, didn't she? I hate it when people do that. Anyway, I come to give ya this—' and he showed his other hand, this one gripping a clay jug. 'Rum!'

CAPTAIN SATER DOWNED ANOTHER MOUTHFUL, THEN FLUNG the empty flask to one side. Where had it all started to go wrong, she wondered. Sure, stealing a half-dozen Sech'kellyn statues was probably a bad idea, the way tales of terrible curses swirled around the damned things. They'd been found buried in a neat little row beneath the foundation rubble of Avoidance Alley just behind Toll's Keep, ghastly squatting figures of some foreign, chalk-white marble now stained and mottled by a century or two of kitchen refuse and royal sewage. The expressionless, gaunt faces were all the more chilling for their black iron eyes and black iron canines – seemingly immune to the ravages of rust – and their strange limbs with too many knobby joints, the twice bent knees framing the forward-thrusting heads, the raptor-like, elongated fingers and, most peculiarly, iron collars enclosing their thin necks, as if the six creatures had been pets of some sort.

The court mage – calling them Sech'kellyn, whatever that meant – had claimed them at once, and Sater herself had been among the hapless fools lugging the things up to the sorceror's beehive apothecary perched atop the city's lone hill. A week later she'd helped carry them back to the keep, down into some long unused storage room barred by a newly installed iron door into which the mage gouged so many warding glyphs and sigils the door looked like a flattened crane nest by the time he was done.

The poor sorceror went mad shortly thereafter, and if there

was some kind of connection then no one official wanted to talk about it. Sater hadn't been alone in paying coin for a ritual cleansing at Soliel's Temple behind Cleanwater Well – every other soldier who'd set hands on those statues had done the same, with the exception of Corporal Steb, who'd been picking his nose with a dagger point and, walking up to a door that suddenly opened, drove the point into his brain – amazing the dagger ever found it, truth be told. But then, things had mostly settled and it looked as if they'd escaped whatever curse there'd been. When the mage drowned himself in a bowl of soapy water, well, he'd been mad by then, hadn't he, so it was no real surprise.

Some bright wick had then decided to offer them as gifts to the Crimson Guard – who were, it was said, deep into the arcane stuff anyway. But maybe, Sater now wondered, they'd been less a gift than a not-so-noble desire to get rid of the ugly things.

So then she went and stole them. Why? What insane impulse had taken her then, like a bony hand round her throat? Over the side they shoulda gone, aye, right over the side.

Was it the curse that had conjured to life the miserable lich?

She needed to get rid of them. Now, before it was too late—

An eruption of screams from below – so awful that even her rum-heated blood went icy cold – and the thunder of some collision, as of two massive forms slamming into one another, and the entire ship shivered. More screams, the thumping of blows delivered with savage strength and ferocity.

With hammering heart, Sater glared around, saw a trio of sailors crowded up at the prow. 'Briv! And you too, Briv! And you, Briv! You three, here, take my strongroom key—'

'*Down below?*' one of them shrieked.

'At the stern and it's all quiet there. There's six wrapped statues – I want 'em up here, understand? Up and o'er the rail! Quick!'

All at once a figure was standing at her side. Tall, hulking, a flabby, round, child-like face peering down at her. The thick lips licked beneath bright, beady eyes. 'Statues?'

BRIV, COOK'S HELPER, GLANCED OVER AT BRIV, CARPENTER'S helper, then back at a snuffling Briv, Rope Braider, whose orange mane of hair was strangely tousled, almost askew. He saw terror writ plain on their faces, as much as he himself must be showing on his own. Descending the steps in front of them was the scarier of the two passengers (three if counting the manservant but nobody ever counted the manservant), the over-sized one with the round face and thick lips and tiny voice.

Seemingly completely unafraid, which meant he was insane.

Their escort to the strongroom, rustling in full-length chain beneath a thick woollen black cloak. Pudgy, pale hands folded together like he was a damned mendicant or something.

We're all going to die. Except maybe him. That's how it always is. People in charge always survive, when everyone else gets slaughtered. No, he'll live, and so will Cook, because no one likes to cook and that's just the thing. Cook's a poet.

No, really, a poet. He sure as Hood ain't a cook.

Now if only he was any good at poet stuff. Can't sing, can't play an instrument, can't make a rhyme because rhyming, well, laddie, it's beneath him.

> 'I dreamed this thing
> This thing of dreams
> An army marching close
> Each soldier cut off

At the knees
Which was strange and all
Since they were
Foot-soldiers.'

Aye, Cook's latest, his morning paean to the slop he shovelled into the bowls. That pompous face and that rolling cadence, as if the tumbling refuse of words coughed out from his throat was some kind of profound thing – why, I've read poetry, oh yes, and heard plenty too. Said, sung, whined, gargled, mewled, sniffed, shouted, whispered, spat. Aye, what seaman hasn't?

But what do we know? We're no brush-stroked arched brow over cold, avid eye, oh no. We're just the listeners, wading through some ponce's psychological trauma as the idiot stares into a mirror all love/hate all masturbatory up'n'down and it's us who when the time comes – comes, hah – who are meant to gasp and twist pelvic in linguistic ecstasy.

Yeah, well, Cook can stroke his own damned ladle, know what I mean?

Briv, Carpenter's helper, gave him a nudge. 'Get on wi'ya.'

'Leave me be,' snarled Briv, Cook's helper. 'I'm going, all right?'

And down they went, the steep steps, down into the hold, where horror did abide – up near the head, that is. And all three seamen (or two seamen and one seawoman who was, in fact, a seaman), desperately needed to go to the bathroom.

Briv, CARPENTER'S HELPER, STAYED ONE STEP BEHIND BRIV, Cook's helper, and one step ahead of Briv, Rope Braider who, if she braided ropes as bad as she did her hair, would probably better serve the ship as Cook. Since Cook was a poet.

But then, without a rope braider, things would get unravelled and that wouldn't do. And listen to those demons scrapping near the bow – if he bent right down to look between his own ankles, through the gap in the steps, he might see something of that snarling, hissing, snapping, thumping battle. But what good would that do him, hey? None a whit. They was just up there bashing the precious hull, bruising the wood, punching out the caulk and gouging nasty gouges and if reefs and shoals and rocks and deadheads weren't enough trouble, here they had unmindful demons doing all kinds of damage.

Now, if Carpenter had knowed his business, well, it'd be all right, wouldn't it? But the man was a fool. Killing him had been a gift to the world. Funny, though, how that one death-cry seemed to unleash all the rest of what showed up and now people were dead everywhere and there, see, that was Ably Druther, his body at least, sitting there barely a nail's throw behind the steps. Sitting like he was just waiting for his head to come home. Looked crazy upside down like this, and whatever fought in the gloom further up, well, that was blessedly hard to make out—

'Damn you, Briv,' hissed Briv, Rope Braider, 'you tryin' t'catch your own shit in your mouth or something?'

'You don't sound ladylike,' Briv replied, straightening up then hastening two steps to catch up to Briv, Cook's helper. 'We shoulda brought a lantern.'

The giant eunuch was down on the walkway now and not waiting courteously for the sailors to join him, just heading on sternward to the strongroom. Briv, Cook's helper, should never have given the hairless freak the key. Why, Briv, Carpenter's helper, could have stood up to him easily enough—

'Ow! You're treading on my heel, woman!'

'There's a headless guy sitting behind me, so hurry on, Briv!'

'He's not paying you any mind.'

'There's eyes on my backside, I'd swear it.'

'Not him, if you turned his head it went and fell off.'

'Look, a woman knows these things. When someone's giving 'em the up down left right. Worse on a ship, too, all these letches.'

'Lich, not letch.'

'How do you know? Anyway, since I'm the only decent female aboard, it's all on me, you know.'

'Who's all on you?'

'Wouldn't you like to know.'

'Not really. Just curious.' And, maybe, aghast, but it paid a man to be polite to a woman. Even one whose breasts seemed to float up and down like cork and twine buoys on a swell.

The eunuch had halted before the strongroom door.

Briv, Briv and Briv crowded up behind him.

'Is this a good idea?' Cook's helper asked as the eunuch slid the key into the lock.

'Ooh,' sighed Rope Braider.

Key turned. Tumblers clicked.

'Is this a good idea?' asked Cook's helper once again.

S ECH'KELLYN WERE BAD ENOUGH. BUT SECH'KELLYN WEARING ensorcelled collars, well, that boded ill indeed. Homunculi, of sorts, Sech'kellyn were Jaghut creations, modelled – it was said by the scant few with sufficient authority to voice an opinion – on some ancient race of demons called the Forkassail. White as bone, too many knees, ankles, elbows, even shoulders. Being perfectionists of the worst sort, the Jaghut succeeded in inventing a species that bred true. And, even more typical of Jaghut, they went and made themselves mostly extinct, leaving their abominable conjurations free to do whatever they pleased, which was usually kill everyone in sight. At least until someone powerful showed up to hammer them back down and chain their life-forces and then maybe bury them somewhere nobody would ever disturb, like, say, under a poorly made alley in a fast-growing city.

A powerful enough sorceror could subsequently reawaken the geas on such creatures, could indeed bind them to his or her will, for nefarious and untoward purposes, of course.

Perhaps this was what had been done to the six Sech'kellyn in the strongroom.

But in truth, it was nothing like that at all.

It was much worse.

Oh yes.

WIZARDS DELEGATE. ONE COULD ALWAYS TELL THE WIZARDS who did by the way they sat around in their towers day and night concocting evil schemes of world domination. Somebody else was scrubbing out the bedpan. Wizards who didn't delegate never had the time to think up a black age of tyranny, much less execute what was necessary to achieve it. Dishes piled up and so did laundry. Dust balls gathered to conspire usurpation. Squirrels made the roof leak and occasionally fell down somewhere in the walls where they couldn't get back out and so died and then mummified displaying grotesque expressions after wearing their teeth out gnawing brick.

Mizzankar Druble of Jhant – which had been a city on Stratem that fell into dust centuries past and the presence of which was not even guessed at by the folk of Jatem's Landing, a new settlement not three thousand paces down along the very same shore – Mizzankar Druble of Jhant, then – who had been, it was agreed by all now long dead, a most terrible sorceror, a conjuror, an enchanter, a thaumaturge, and ugly besides – Mizzankar Druble of Jhant, aye – who'd raised a spire of gnarled, bubbly black, glassy stone all in a single night in the midst of a raging storm which was why it had no windows and the door, well, it was knee-high and about wide enough for a lone foot as if that made any sense, since Mizzankar was both tall and fat so everyone who were now dead decided he must have raised that tower from the inside out, since the poor fool ended up stuck in there and Hood knew what terrible plans he was making which more than justified piling up all the brush and logs and such and roasting the evil wizard like the nut in a hazel – Mizzankar Druble, of Jhant, yes, he had been a wizard who had delegated.

Like hounds needing a master, the Sech'kellyn were demanding servants. And as such, the task was indeed full time and not much fun either. Mizzankar Druble – who in truth had been a minor wizard with the unfortunate penchant of attempting rituals far too powerful to control, one of them resulting – in a misjudged battle with an undead squirrel – in the explosive, terrifying eruption of molten rock that rose all round him where he stood in his pathetic protective circle – thus creating a towering prison he never did escape – but Mizzankar Druble, wise enough to delegate, and happily possessing six demonic servants hatefully created by some miserable Jaghut, understood – in a spasmodic moment of clarity – the need for a powerful, preferably enormous, demon that could assume the burden of commanding the Sech'kellyn.

In the most ambitious and elaborate conjuration of his life, Mizzankar summoned such a creature, and naturally got a lot more than he bargained for. An ancient, almost forgotten god, in fact. The battle of wills had been pathetically short. Mizzankar Druble, of Jhant, had, in his last few days of life before the villagers roasted him alive, been set to the task of scrubbing bed pans, rinsing dishes, wringing laundry and chasing dust balls on his hands and knees.

Gods, even more so than wizards, understood the notion of delegation.

Now the tale of the god's subsequent adventures, and all relating to the Sech'kellyn and the tumbling disasters that led to their theft and burial in what would one day be Toll's City, is a narrative belonging to someone else, at some other time.

The vital detail was this: the god was coming for his children.

BLEARY-EYED, HALF-CRAZED WITH THROBBING PAIN IN numerous parts of his head, Emancipor Reese, 'Mancy the Luckless, clawed his way on to his knees, then paused while everything reeled for a few dozen heartbeats. His face pressed against the damp wicker, his gaze shifted so that his left eye took in Bena Younger – crouched once more opposite him, knife raised in case he should lunge murderously her way – but of course that wasn't likely. He might lunge indeed, but if he did it would be to heave out whatever was left of Cook's dubious supper, and the thought of that – a most satisfying image dancing in his mind's eye of the vicious child covered in fetid slop – while gratifying on one level, thrummed a warning echo of blistering pain through his skull.

No, too much action demanded by such explosive, visceral expression. He closed his eyes, then slowly edged up a little further, until his head cleared the basket's tattered edge. Opened his eyes again, blinking smartly. Emancipor Reese found himself looking astern.

Still night? Gods, would it never end?

Black looming overcast blotting out everything above the murky rolling seas. Dhenrabi breaching the surface on all sides, racing faster than any ship. Damn, he'd never seen the behemoths move so fast.

Somewhere below a fight was going on, sounding entirely

unhuman, and reverberations thundered through the ship, rocking the mast with each blow against the hull.

Another massive bulge in the water, this one directly behind the *Suncurl*, swelling, rising, looming ever closer. And Emancipor now saw Master Bauchelain, standing wide-legged a couple strides back from the aft rail, sword held in both hands, eyes seemingly fixed on that surging crest.

'Oh,' said Emancipor Reese.

As two enormous, scaled arms thrust up from the foaming bulge, crashing down in a splintering, crushing grip on the rail – wood snapping like twigs – the long, curved talons plunging into the aft deck. Then, in a massive heave of cascading water, the elongated reptilian head reared into view between those arms. Maw open, articulated fangs dropping down as water slashed out to either side.

The entire ship stumbled, hitched, seemed to stagger into a deathly collapse astern – the prow lifting high – as the apparition pulled itself aboard.

And all of it – the entire scene with creature and Bauchelain, who now leapt forward, sword flashing – raced fast towards Emancipor as the crow's nest and the mast to which it was attached, pitched down. Something slammed into Emancipor's back, driving all the air from his lungs, and then a scrawny body, wailing, was rolling over him, out into the air – ratty hair and flailing limbs – and he threw himself forward, reaching—

THE SUDDEN LIFT OF THE PROW FLUNG LICH AND MISSHAPEN child down hard, collapsing the planks of the o'er keel gangway. At this moment, unfortunately for the child of Korbal Broach's unnatural procreation, the lich was on top. Crushing impact, percussive snapping of various bones, including a spine, and as ribcage buckled, everything unattached within that monstrous body was violently expelled. Spurting, spraying fluids in all directions, and, spat out like a constipated man's triumph, the upper half of a body that had once been deeply embedded within a murky, diluvian world. Coughing, hacking, flinging out gobbets of weird phlegm, Birds Mottle reeled away, falling down between hull and splintered gangway.

While the lich raised itself up from the leaking carcass of its foe, fists lifting in exaltation, head rocking back as it prepared to loose a howl of entirely gratuitous glee.

But even the dullest scholar knew that forces in nature were inextricably bound to certain laws. That which plunges downwards, in turn launches upwards. At least, that which floated on the seas did, just that. Upwards, then, the floor, shooting the lich straight up – another such law, one permitting the invention of things as, say, catapults—

And the gnarled, hard-boned, vaguely Ably Drutherly head – for the lich was all too corporeal at the moment – smashed like a battering ram, up through the foredeck's planks. And jammed there.

Momentarily blinded by the concussion, the lich failed in comprehending the sudden shouts that surrounded it.

'Kick it!'

'Kick it! Kick it!'

All at once, hard-toed boots slammed into the lich's head, from all sides, snapping cheek bones, brow ridges, maxilla, mandible, temporal, frontal. Kick kick kick slam slam slam – and then a boot crashed into the lich's gaping, fanged mouth.

And so it bit down.

A S THE HORRIFYING CREATURE BIT OFF HALF OF HIS RIGHT foot, Gust Hubb howled, staggered back, spinning as blood sprayed, and fell to the deck. Toes – now missing – were being ground to meal in the lich's jaws, crusty nails breaking in all the wrong ways, even as more boots hammered at the crumpled, deformed head. Chewing, aye, just like one ear was being chewed, the other gnawed to nearly nothing now and hearing only slow leaking fluids, and as for his nose, well, he was smelling mud. Cold, briny, slimy mud.

Any more of this and he was going to lose his mind.

Someone fell to their knees beside him, and he heard Mipple cry out – 'Stick his foot in a bucket!' And then she laughed like the ugly mad woman she was.

S NARLING (AND CHEWING), THE LICH RETREATED FROM THE pummelling, back down through the hole, and as it blinked one of its still functioning eyes, it caught the brief blur that was Birds Mottle – who had, upon retrieving Ably Druther's shortsword – rushed to close, the broad, savage blade plunging deep into the lich's chest.

Shrieking, the creature batted the woman away with a half-dozen arms, sending her flying, skidding and finally tumbling.

Tugging out and flinging aside the offending weapon, the lich advanced on the obnoxious mortal. Paused a moment when something big that had been in its mouth suddenly lodged in its throat. Paused, then, to choke briefly before dislodging the pulpy mass of boot leather, meat, bone, nail and, sad to say, hair. Greater indignity followed, when it shook its head, only to have its lower jaw fall off to thump accusingly pugnacious at its feet.

The roar that erupted from its gaping overbite was more a wheezing gargle, no less frightening as far as Birds Mottle was concerned, for, shrieking, she crabbed back along the gangway, into the grainy patch beneath the hold, then past that, heading for the stern – where, from above and indeed, from the strongroom behind her, there came sounds of ferocious fighting.

Long-fingered, clawed hands with bits of meat hanging from them lifted threateningly, and the lich stamped ever closer.

EMANCIPOR REESE'S FRANTIC REACH CAUGHT BENA YOUNGER'S skinny ankle, halting her headlong flight towards the giant fiend scrabbling aboard at the stern. The manservant grunted as the girl's weight nearly ripped his arm from its socket, then, as she swung straight down, he heard the thump of her forehead against the mast, the crack of her arms against the top yard—

At that moment, the ship's prow surged back down, whipping the mast and crow's nest hard forward. Something hammered into Emancipor's back and withered, bony arms buffeted about his head. Toppling backward – dragging Bena Younger back up in the process – Emancipor cursed and flung an elbow at the clattering corpse assaulting him. Elbow into shrunken chest, sending the thing flying – and over the edge—

GUST HUBB ROLLED ON TO HIS BACK, IN TIME TO SEE A GHASTLY hag plunge down from the night sky, straight at him. Screaming, he threw up his hands just as the thing crashed down on to him.

Knobby, desiccated finger stabbed his left eye and Gust heard a *plop!* as of a crushed grape. Shrieking, he flailed at his attacker. An inward drawn breath netted him a mouthful of brittle grimy hair.

'Kill it!' someone shouted, voice breaking in hysteria.

'Kill it! Kill it!'

And now boots slammed into Gust, heels cracking down indiscriminately, breaking bones dead and living it was no matter, no matter at all.

'Kill it!'

'It's already dead!'

'Kill it some more!'

Sudden bloom of light as a boot cracked into the side of Gust's misused skull, then darkness.

IN THE STRONGROOM, OH, IN THE STRONGROOM. AND BACK, NOW, A timeward score of rapid steps—

Striding in, Korbal Broach paused to look round, took another stride and saw torn fragments of burlap littering the floor. Behind him, Briv, Briv and Briv edged in, crouched and whispering and at least one of them whimpering.

The Sech'kellyn attacked from all sides. One moment, gloom and calm, the next, explosive mayhem. Stony fists lashed out, sending Brivs flying in all directions. More fists cracked into Korbal Broach, forcing surprised grunts from the huge eunuch. He started punching back. Deathly white bodies reeled, crunched against the curving walls.

Briv, Cook's helper, glanced over to see all six of the demons close in on the eunuch. *Just as it should be, him in charge and all that.* Then, spying the motionless, crumpled form of another Briv, he crawled over, grasped the sailor by the ankles, and began dragging Briv – Briv, Rope Braider – away from the colossal battle in the centre of the room.

Briv, Carpenter's helper, was suddenly at Briv's side, taking one of Briv's ankles.

'Hey,' Briv, Carpenter's helper, hissed, 'Briv's hair got torn off! Hey, this ain't Briv – it's Gorbo!'

'Of course it is!' snapped Briv, Cook's helper. 'Everybody knows that!'

'I didn't!'

185

Cook's helper paused. 'That's impossible – you slept with him!'

'Only once! And it was dark – and some women like it—'

'Enough of that, help me get him outa here!'

'What about the wig?'

'What about it?'

'Uh, nothing, I guess.'

Hard to tell who was winning – oh, no, easy to tell. Korbal Broach was being beaten to a pulp. Amazing he was still standing, but standing was a good thing, for as long as he stood there the demons weren't bothering with them, and as soon as they got out past the threshold, well, they'd be saved!

A s soon as the god-thing's head cleared the rail, Bauchelain stepped forward and swung his sword. Edge smashing into the creature's snout. At the blow, something spat out from the mouth.

Line, hook and ear.

A giant taloned hand slashed in a lateral sweep that Bauchelain not quite succeeded in evading, and the curved claws raked slashes through his chain hauberk. Black links pattered like hail across the aft deck.

He chopped down at the limb as it passed, felt the iron bite deep into the wrist, slicing clean through at least one of the bones.

The god wailed.

Bauchelain caught but a glimpse of the other arm, slanting down directly from above, and so he brought up his sword in a blocking parry that was, alas, unsuited to the downwards force of the fist's blow, akin to a blacksmith's anvil dropped from a tenement roof.

Blow struck.

Wood crunched, the fist pounding on to the deck, and Bauchelain was no longer on the aft deck.

He landed, amidst showering splinters of wood, in the strongroom.

A Sech'kellyn lunged at him. Instinctively he stop-thrust and watched the demon impale itself on the sword. It cried out, chest shattering like a chunk of marble beneath a mason's spike.

That cry was heard from above. Bellowing, the god began tearing away the aft deck.

The five remaining Sech'kellyn all looked up. Child-like squeals erupted, and all at once the Sech'kellyn was scrabbling up towards the ever-expanding hole. A huge hand reached down and the homunculi climbed it as if scampering up a tree.

A cacophony of screams from just outside the strongroom door. Rising, a bloodied mass of wounds, Korbal Broach shook himself, glanced once at Bauchelain, then walked out of the strongroom.

B IRDS MOTTLE STARED UP AT THE LOOMING LICH. SHE WAS STILL trying to scream but her voice was gone, completely gone, and now she was – absurdly – making sounds virtually identical to the lich.

Briv, Briv and Gorbo tumbled into her, the relief on their faces transforming in an instant to mindless terror upon seeing the lich, still looming as dastardly monsters were wont to do.

At that precious moment, with death mimed by every spasmodic clutch of those all-too-many clawed, skeletal hands, with eyes of lifeless black inviting the blackness of lifelessness, with the princely overbite and nasal, wheezing haw-hawing of what was probably intended to be gleeful triumph – at that moment, aye, the lich looked up from its intended victims.

As Korbal Broach strode up to it, stepping right over Bird Mottle's despair-numbed legs, and, smiling, closed his thick-fingered hands to either side of the lich's misshapen head.

A sudden twist to one side, a sharp snap.

Then another sudden twist, to the other side, and grinding sounds.

A twist the other way again, then back again, faster and faster.

With a dry sob the lich's body dropped away beneath the head, clattering on to the gangway in a jumble of limbs, brows, mouths and stuff.

Korbal Broach held the head before him. Still smiling, he turned about.

And looked over to Bauchelain, who appeared in the threshold and was now brushing splinters of wood from his shoulders.

'Look!' piped Korbal Broach.

Bauchelain paused. 'I see.'

Tucking the mangled head under an arm, Korbal Broach walked to the steps, and up he went.

EMANCIPOR REESE LOOKED DOWN ON THE WRECKAGE THAT was the *Suncurl*. Oh, the damned thing still floated, and that was something. The giant reptile thing and its pallid pups were gone, back over the ruined stern, back down into the wretched waters of Laughter's End.

Captain Sater was drunk, leg-sprawled with her back against the prow step, with Cook beside her intoning some discordant declamatory drivel the genius of which was so loftily profound that only he had the wit to comprehend it. Or at least pretend to, which in this world and all others was pretty much the same thing, amen.

He saw Korbal Broach emerge from the hold hatch, something tucked under an arm and guess what that might be – no need, oh no, but guess anyway – and followed a moment later by four sailors all watery with relief and then Bauchelain, who was not quite as solid on his legs as was usual.

To the east, the sky was paling, moments from painting the seas blood-red but too late for that, hey?

A raspy voice cackled behind him, then said, 'Mother did what needed doing. We're safe, lass, safe as can be now!'

Emancipor Reese glanced back over a shoulder, then sighed.

Fools.

Groaning, with a last look back at Bena Younger, Emancipor Reese clambered out of the crow's nest and began the climb down.

KORBAL BROACH REAPPEARED BRIEFLY ON DECK ONLY TO descend into the hold once more. He emerged a hundred heartbeats later grunting under the weight of a massive, misshapen bladder-like thing replete with limp rat tails and tiny clawed feet all curled in tragic demise. And hundreds of dusty, wrinkled, tiny black eyes none of which took note of the small crowd of staring sailors while Korbal carried it to the foredeck.

Once there he unhitched a grappling hook, checked its knot at both ends, then, crouching down, he impaled the mass of meat on the hook, straightened with a grunt and heaved the mess over the side. A loud splash, then the line paid out for a time.

Standing nearby, quite apart from the crew and their captain who'd watched with mouth hanging open and now a thread of drool dangling, Emancipor Reese frowned at his master at his side. 'Uh, fishing with that . . .'

Bauchelain gave a single nod, then clapped his manservant on the shoulder – making Emancipor wince as a bruise flared beneath that friendly blow – and said, 'Think even a dhenrabi, crazed as it might be in this season of mating, would pass up such a sweet morsel, Mister Reese?'

Emancipor shook his head.

Bauchelain smiled down at him. 'We shall be towed for a time, yes, to hasten our journey. The sooner we are freed of the lees of Laughter's End, the better, I should think. Do you not agree, Mister Reese?'

'Aye, Master. Only, how do we know where that dhenrabi might take us?'

'Oh, we know that, most certainly. Why, the dhenrabi breeding beds, of course.'

'Oh.'

'Stay close to the prow, Mister Reese, with knife at the ready.'

'Knife?'

'Of course.' Another savage clap on the same shoulder. 'To cut the rope at the opportune moment.'

Emancipor squinted forward, saw the line's sharp downwards angle. 'How about now, Master?'

'You are being silly, Mister Reese. Now, I think I shall take my breakfast below, assuming Cook is willing.'

'Willing? Oh, aye, Master, he is that I'm sure.'

'Excellent.'

GUST HUBB OPENED HIS REMAINING EYE AND FOUND HIMSELF staring up at Heck Urse's face.

That now smiled. 'Ah, awake now, are ya? Good. Here, let me help you sit up a bit. You lost more than a bucket full of blood, you need your food and Cook's gone and made up some gruel just for you, friend. No ears, no nose, half a foot and broke bones, you're a mess.'

'Bucket?'

'Oh, aye, Gust, more than a bucket full – I saw the bucket, I did.'

Heck Urse then spooned some slop into Gust Hubb's mouth.

He choked, fought back a gag reflex, swallowed, then swallowed some more, finally coming up for a gasp of air.

Heck Urse nodded. 'Better?'

'Aye. Cook's a poet, Heck, a real poet.'

'That he is, friend. That he is.'

DISPERSED, NAY FLUNG AWAY LIKE SO MUCH DROSS, SOULS found themselves once more trapped within iron nails embedded in wood.

'I told you a mercantile venture would've been better,' Master Baltro said.

'I'm not ready for oblivion, oh no,' hissed Viviset. 'Once I escape—'

'You won't escape,' cut in the one voice (apart from the Jhorligg's and they'd heard just about enough from it, thank you very much) that didn't belong to any nail. 'Dead currents are cutting into the Red Road now. Our chance is lost, forever lost.'

'Who in Hood's name are you, anyway?' demanded Hag Threedbore.

'I wish I knew.'

'Well, go away,' said Threedbore, 'we don't like your kind around here.'

'A mercantile venture—'

'Something's nibbling my spleen!' cried Lordson Hoom.

THROUGH THE SCARRED CRYSTAL LENS, THE *SUNCURL* wallowed fitful and forlorn, and the huge man standing at the prow of *Unreasoning Vengeance* slowly lowered the eyepiece. He turned about and studied his eleven brothers and two sisters, not one short or even of average height, not one not bound in massive muscle – women included – and he smiled.

'Blessed kin, we have them.'

All fourteen now set to preparing their weapons. Two-handed axes, two-handed swords (one of them a three-hander thanks to an overly ambitious but not too intelligent weapon smith back in Toll's City), falchions, mattocks, mauls, maces, flails, halberds and one very nasty looking stick. Armour glinted as it was wont to do in morning sunlight; helms were donned, indeed, jammed down hard over thick-boned skulls. Silver-sheathed tusks gleamed on a few of the men who betrayed more than the normal hints of Jhag blood.

Around them swarmed the crew, all undead since that saved feeding and watering them and they never slept besides, while down below in the hold enormous, starving beasts growled and roared in frenzied hunger, pounding against their cages.

Tiny Chanter, the eldest in the family and so its leader, unslung his own weapon, a two-ended thing with one end a crescent-bladed axe and spike and the other a studded mace that had the word SATRE painted on it in red, because Tiny couldn't spell, and then scanned his kin once more.

'We have them,' he repeated.
And he smiled again.
All the Chanters smiled.
One undead sailor, noting this, screamed.

THE HEALTHY DEAD

Warning to lifestyle fascists everywhere.
Don't read this or you'll go blind.

*'Those who die healthily are stuffed and displayed
in glass-cased shrines as examples of good living'*

IMID FACTALLO, FOREMAN OF THE WORK CREW RE-LAYING THE cobbles round back of the Wall, was struck unconscious by a collapsing wagon, and so became a saint. His fellow workers, their faces smeared in dust, stared down upon him in wonder as he blinked open his eyes. The sky behind those mundane visages looked indeed the resplendent residence of the Lady of Beneficence, the Goddess of Wellness, into whose finely-boned arms Imid Factallo felt himself on the verge of falling. If, of course, one could indeed fall upwards, plunging clear of the heavy, laden earth, and dive with keening joy into the vast blueness overhead.

But the glorious ascent never arrived. Instead, runners had set out to the Grand Temple and were now returning, this time leading worthies, their pink shirts and pantaloons bound at the joints, arms and legs filled out with padding to infer to any and all onlookers the musculature of vigorous health, their drawn faces painted in flushed tones. And joining them, three Well Knights, white-cloaked and clanking in the highly polished, silver-etched armour of their exalted rank – and Imid saw, foremost among these three, none other than Invett Loath, Purest of the Paladins, who needed no rouge to colour his square-jawed, large-nosed face, which was very nearly purple, so thoroughly blooded the veins and arteries beneath the only-so-slightly spotty skin. Imid knew as well as any other citizen that one might, upon seeing Knight Invett Loath for the first time, assume the very worst – that the Paladin was far too fond of ale, wine and the other forbidden vices of slovenly living – but this was not the case. Invett Loath could not be pre-eminent among the Knights were he such a fallen soul. In fact, nothing untoward had passed his lips his entire life. At least inward.

'You, sir,' he now rumbled, glaring down from beneath the rim of his blindingly sunlit helm, 'are the unworthy leach of the salt marshes they call Imid Factallo? Has your skull cracked entirely open, then? Are you now mute as well as dumb? The Goddess abides both the physically and the mentally inept, you will be pleased to know, sir. Thus leaving you twice, if not thrice blessed. It is a distinction to ponder, is it not? Yet I see your eyes dart, suggesting that sight has not left you. Twice, then, as I first surmised. Well, Imid Factallo, once foreman of the Wall's Third Reach road-tossers, you will now be honoured to know that, by your fated accident which has spilled your blood so messily on to your face and the stones beneath you, I now pronounce you a Saint of the Lady.'

Imid Factallo stared up at the Knight, then, squeezing shut his eyes, he groaned and wished, with all his heart, that the damned wagon had killed him.

'THE TRADER CALLED THE CITY QUAINT,' EMANCIPOR REESE said, squinting at the distant high walls with their strange banners dangling limp two-thirds of the way up. The battered wagon beneath the two men pitched wildly on the rocky path.

'Well,' Bauchelain sighed beside him, 'there is little I see to support that observation.'

'No, Master, it is actually called *Quaint*, the last and most remote of the city-states on this peninsula. And, given that we've seen naught of even so much as a hamlet in the past six days, I would agree with the trader that it is indeed remote.'

'Perhaps,' the sorceror conceded, pulling at his pointed beard. 'Nonetheless, the only quality I can discern from this distance that might be construed as quaint is that tidy row of corpses spiked to the inland wall.'

Emancipor narrowed his gaze even further. Not banners, then, dangling so limp. 'And you call that quaint, Master?'

'Yes, I do, Mister Reese. Korbal Broach will be pleased, don't you think?'

The manservant leaned back on the wagon's buckboard, easing the knots in his lower back. 'I would hazard, Master,' he offered, 'that the city's authorities would not look kindly upon the theft of their . . . uh, decorations.'

'I imagine you are correct,' Bauchelain murmured, his high brow wrinkling in thought. 'More alarming, perhaps, is the notion that our recent escapades in the previous city might have preceded our mortal selves.'

Emancipor Reese shivered and clutched tighter the traces in his gnarled hands. 'I sincerely hope otherwise, Master.'

'Perhaps, this time, we ought not to risk it. What do you say, Mister Reese? Circumvent the city. Find ourselves an outlying village and purchase a worthy sea craft, and so make our way across the bay?'

'Excellent idea, Master.'

The road had been empty of passersby during the course of their conversation, and the dust trailing the wake of the trader who had been heading the other way was already settling on the tree-tops visible beyond the road's crumbly edge. As if to challenge Bauchelain's decision, however, there came the sound of boots scrabbling up the track towards them, and a moment later two figures climbed into view. A man and a woman, carrying between them a small but clearly heavy chest.

I N THIS WORLD OF VIRTUES, THE THIRD AND MOST REVILED DEMON, Vice, knew loneliness, despair and misery. Which wasn't right, all things considered. Of the three emotional states previously mentioned, Ineb Cough was well-acquainted with the latter two. Despair and misery, but they were what he delivered unto others. To suffer beneath identical torment as those who succumbed to his lures was unconscionable. Well, perhaps that was the wrong word to use, but the sentiment fit.

Which was more than could be said of the foppish dancer's clothes he was presently wearing, clothes that clearly had belonged to a much taller, wider-shouldered individual. It was a sad truth, he reflected as he poked through the rubbish in the alley behind The Palace of Earthy Delights looking for . . . something, anything. A sad truth, that the arts of the flesh could not but surrender to decrepitude, eventually. That talent and prowess gave way to aching muscles and brittle bones. The world had no place for aged artists, and that brutal fact could not have been made more evident than with the demon's discovery of the dead dancer. His wrinkled face staring sightless up at the sky, the expression revealing faint surprise, perhaps even outrage, to announce the final realization that, bent and old as he'd become, he could no longer perform that particular move. That, indeed, the loud crack that had no doubt accompanied that final spin and twirl was unquestionably a bad thing.

The demon doubted that there had been an audience. Another

sordid fact of aged artists – no one watched, no one cared. Spin, twirl, snap, sprawling on to the grubby cobblestones, there to lie undisturbed by any but the tiny eaters of the flesh that dwelt within a living body and would only now come out to feed.

Vice had always been the retreat of artists. When naught else remained, there was always drink. Dubious carnal appetites. An excess of indulgences served on overflowing plates. The host of delectable death-wishes to sample among the myriad substances that were offered. Or, had been offered. Back in the good old days.

But now, in Quaint, virtues ruled, righteous and supreme. And people danced in the streets. Well, some people did, or tried to, only to die trying. Likely a final flourish. There were plenty of those these days. To live clean, to live with unobstructed vigour. To die slow. To die sudden. But always to die, alas. The demon, who might well have wished to die, could not. He persisted, in the manner of hidden desires, and so was witness to the unchanging realities of these sad mortals. Ducking and dodging the inevitable awakening of those tiny eaters of flesh. In the end . . . was the end, and only the end. Poor sods.

How many pleasures, Ineb wondered morosely, were truly pristine? How many lives swanned past the multitude of ambushes the physical world set in their path? This was another kind of dance, with frantically flapping wings on the heels, and it was a style singularly unattractive. Strident, precious, defensive in gesture, spasmodic in extremity. The demon found it depressing to witness. After all, what *didn't* kill?

Amidst the rubbish behind the Palace of Earthy Delights, his rummaging hands touched and closed on an object. A large bottle of fired clay, the base chipped and the neck broken off, but otherwise . . . perfect. The demon drew it into view. Yes, it had once held liquor.

Ineb could not help the broadening smile that split his pocked, grubby face, as he lifted the bottle to his nose and breathed deep its stale aroma. Years old, likely, back when the Palace had been an altogether different kind of establishment, when within its confines something other than green leaves had been on offer.

His flabby lips reached out to caress the cold glaze, to nibble at the smooth pattern of the maker's seal. Red-tipped tongue flitted out along the neck's sharp edge. He sniffed, snorted, stroked with his fingers, and crouched down in the rubbish. Just as there were tiny eaters of flesh, so too were there tiny, unseen creatures that clung to the memories of flavour, of smell. It would take him half the night before the bottle yielded the last morsel.

'HAVE YOU EVER WONDERED, WHAT HAPPENED TO LUST?'
Nauseo Sloven's miniscule eyes thinned amidst the flaccid folds of fat, but the only reply he made was a loud, bilious exudence of gas from somewhere below. He reached out one oily, smeared hand and plucked up a fat grub from the heap of rotting vegetables, and carefully set it down on his protruding tongue, which then snapped inward. A brief crunch, then a smack of lips.

'You'd think,' Senker Later continued, stifling a yawn, 'that of us all, she'd be the most . . . persistent.'

'Maybe,' Nauseo wheezed, 'that is why we never see her.' He waved a hand about. 'This alley evinces our poor lot these days, abandoned as it is to underfed rats, squealing maggots, and diffident memories of past glory. Not to mention our pathetic brother, Ineb Cough.'

'Your memories, not mine,' Senker Later said, wrinkling her small, button nose. 'Your glories existed in excess, all of which was far too frantic for my tastes. No, this alley and its modest pace suits me just fine.' She stretched her less than clean bared legs out and settled deeper amidst the rubbish. 'I see no reason to leave, and even less to complain.'

'I applaud your consistency,' Nauseo said, 'and your aplomb, even as you lie here night after night witnessing my diminishment. Look at me. I am nothing but folds of skin. Even the smell about my person has gone from foul to musty to earthy, as if I was no more than a rotting tree stump in some sunlit glade. And, might I point out with apologies for my seeming indelicacy, you are far less than you once were, my dear. Who has succumbed to your charms of late?'

'No one. But I admit I can't be bothered to worry much about it.'

'And so you will while away into extinction, Senker Later.'

She sighed. 'I suppose you're right. Something should be done.'

'Such as?'

'Oh, I'll think about it later. Look, there's a nice fat grub, crawling out – there!'

'I see it. Too far away, alas.'

Senker Later smiled at him sweetly. 'That was nice, thank you.'

THE CHEST WAS FILLED WITH COINS. SUNSET GOLD AND PISS-bleached silver, a glitter of poison to Emancipor Reese's jaded eyes. Nothing good ever came of riches, nothing, nothing at all.

'We're Saints of Glorious Labour,' the one named Imid Factallo said.

'This seems a worthy title,' Bauchelain observed as he stood before the two Quaint citizens with hands clasped behind his back.

Nearby, Emancipor had started a small cook fire and was now preparing mulled wine against the growing chill. Modest, mundane tasks had a way of accompanying egregious, enormous evils. It had always been so, he believed. Especially in the company of his masters. And he sensed that something truly ignoble was in the offing.

'A worthy title, you say,' Imid replied, looking like he had just swallowed a mouthful of ashes. 'So you'd think!'

'So I do,' Bauchelain replied, brows lifting, 'and have just stated it.'

'Well, it's a misery, I tell you,' Imid said, a twitch rippling along his left cheek. 'I'm out of work. Now I spend all day praying with a thousand other saints. Saints! The only thing we all have in common is clumsy stupidity or rotten luck, or both.'

'You are too harsh on yourself, sir,' Bauchelain said. 'To have earned such a noble title—'

'One must nearly die whilst working,' the woman cut in, her voice harsh. 'Mistakes, accidents, blind chance – these are what makes saints in Quaint!'

Bauchelain had frowned at the interruption, and now the frown deepened. He drew his long, silk-lined cloak tighter about himself. 'If I am to understand you, the proclamation of sainthood depends upon injuries sustained in public service?'

'You have it precisely,' Imid Factallo said. 'Let me explain about Quaint. It all began with the sudden death of the previous king, Necrotus the Nihile. Your usual kind of ruler. Petty, vicious and corrupt. We liked him just fine. But then he died and his little known brother assumed the throne. And that's when everything started to unravel.'

The woman beside Imid said, 'King Macrotus, the Overwhelmingly Considerate, and there's no love in that title.'

'And your name is?'

'Saint Elas Sil, sir. I had a fellow worker trip into me with a knitting needle. Stabbed me in the neck, the idiot. I bled all over the wool, and it turns out that's a debt even being a saint doesn't forgive. Only, how can I make restitution? I'm not permitted to work!'

'A newly invoked law by your new king, then.'

Emancipor stirred the mulling wine. The smell was making him light-headed in a pleasant, dreamy manner. He leaned back on his haunches and began stoking his clay pipe with rustleaf and durhang. His actions had snared the attentions of the two saints, and Emancipor saw Elas lick her lips.

'It is the Will of Wellness,' Imid Factallo said, nodding up at Bauchelain. 'Macrotus has elevated the cult of the Lady of Beneficence. It now stands as the city's official – and only legal – religion.'

Emancipor narrowed his gaze as he met the woman's eyes. She would have been attractive, he mused, had she been born someone else. As it was, Elas Sil, the saint with the puckered neck, might or might not have been the victim of an accident. The servant set burning ember to his pipe. He recalled, vaguely, that some old hag in his home city of Lamentable Moll had lived by similar notions of wellness. Perhaps the trend was spreading, like some kind of horrific plague.

Imid Factallo continued, 'The new Prohibitions are filling volumes. The list of That Which Kills grows daily and the healers are frantically searching for yet more.'

'And all that kills,' Elas Sil said, 'is forbidden. The king wants his people to be healthy, and since most people won't do what's necessary for themselves, Macrotus will do it on their behalf.'

'If you want the Lady's Blessings in the afterlife,' Imid said, 'then die healthily.'

'Die *un*healthily,' Elas said, 'and there's no burial. Your corpse is hung upside-down on the outer wall.'

'Well,' Bauchelain said, 'how is it that we may help you? Clearly, you cannot be unmade saints. Nor, as you see, are we simple travellers in possession of an army.'

Though there's one chasing us. But Emancipor kept that addendum to himself.

Imid Factallo and Elas Sil exchanged looks, then the former ducked his head and leaned slightly forward. 'It's not the traders' season, but word travels anyway. Fishing boats and such.' He tapped his misshapen nose. 'I got a friend with a good sight on this road, starting at the top of Hurba's Hill, so word came in plenty of time.'

'You're the ones,' Elas Sil said in a low voice, her eyes still fixed on Emancipor as he stirred the wine. A flicker towards Bauchelain. 'Two, but three in all. Half of the last city you visited is nothing but ashes—'

'A misunderstanding, I assure you,' Bauchelain murmured.

Imid Factallo snorted. 'That ain't what we heard—'

Bauchelain cleared his throat, his warning frown silencing the saint. 'One must presume, therefore, that even as you anticipated our salubrious arrival, so too has your king. Accordingly, it is unlikely he would welcome our presence.'

'Macrotus cares little for tales from neighbouring cities – they're all cess-pits of depravity, after all.'

'And his advisors and military commanders are equally ignorant? What of his court mages?'

'They're all gone, the mages. Banished. As for the rest,' Imid shrugged, 'such interest would be direly viewed by Macrotus, hinting as it would of unpleasant appetites, or at least dangerous curiosity.'

'The wine is ready,' Emancipor announced.

The heads of the two saints snapped round with avid, hungry stares.

Elas Sil whispered, 'We are forbidden all such . . . vices.'

The manservant's brows rose. 'Absolute abstinence?'

'Weren't you listening?' Imid growled. 'All illegal in Quaint. No alcohol, no rustleaf, no durhang, no dream-powders. Not for saints, not for anyone.'

Elas Sil added, 'No meat, only vegetables and fruit and three-finned fish. Butchery is cruel and red meat is unhealthy besides.'

'No whoring, no gambling,' Imid said. 'All such pleasures are suspect.'

Emancipor grunted in reply to all of that. He tapped his pipe against his heel and spat a throatful of phlegm on to the fire.

'Curious,' Bauchelain said. 'What is it you wish us to do for you?'

'Usurp the king,' Imid Factallo said.

'Usurp, as in depose.'

'Right.'

'Depose, as in remove.'

'Yes.'

'Remove, as in kill.'

The saints looked at one another again. But neither replied.

Bauchelain turned to study the distant city. 'I am inclined,' he said, 'to preface my acceptance of your offer with a warning – a last opportunity, if you will, to say not another word, to simply collect your coins and return home – and I and my entourage will blithely move on to some other city. This warning, then. In this world, there are worse things than a considerate king.'

'That's what you think,' said Elas Sil.

Bauchelain offered her a benign smile.

'That's it?' Imid Factallo demanded. 'No more questions?'

'Oh, many more questions, my good sir,' Bauchelain replied. 'Alas, you are not the ones to whom I would ask them. You may go.'

WELL KNIGHT INVETT LOATH STOOD ABOVE THE BASKET WITH the wailing baby and glared at the half-dozen women talking near the well. 'Whose child is this?'

One woman separated herself from the group and hurried over. 'It's colic, Oh Gloriously Pure One. Nothing to be done for it, alas.'

The Well Knight's face reddened. 'Absurd,' he snapped. 'There must be some sort of treatment to silence this whelp. Have you not heard the most recent Prohibition? Loud babies are to be confiscated for disturbing the well-being of citizens. They are to be delivered to the Temple of the Lady, where they will be taught the Ways of Beneficence, said ways including vows of silence.'

The hapless mother had gone pale at Invett's words. The other women at the well were quickly collecting their children and hastening away. 'But,' she stammered, 'the medicines we used to use are now illegal—'

'Medicines made illegal? Are you mad?'

'They contained forbidden substances. Alcohol. Durhang—'

'You mothers were in the habit of befouling the blood and spirit of your children?' The notion made Invett apoplectic. 'Is it any wonder such gross abuse was forbidden? And you dare call yourself a loving mother?'

She picked up the basket. 'I didn't know! I'll take her home—'

'Too late for that.' He gestured and the three worthies standing behind him rushed forward. They struggled with the woman for control of the basket, until one of the worthies poked the mother in the eye. She yelped and staggered back, releasing her grip on the basket, and the worthies hurried off with it down the street. The woman wailed beseechingly.

'Silence!' Invett bellowed. 'Public displays of emotion are forbidden! You risk arrest!'

She fell to her knees and began pleading in a most unseemly manner.

'Clean yourself up, woman,' Invett said, lip curling, 'and be glad for my mercy.'

He marched off, in the wake of his worthies with their shrieking charge.

Before long they arrived at the Grand Temple of the Lady. The formal front entrance with its raised platform and the blockish altar sitting atop it – from which the Lady's voice periodically emerged to deliver her pronouncements – had been deemed too public for the delivery of wailing babes. Accordingly, Invett and his worthies approached a side postern where one worthy knocked in elaborate rhythm. A moment's wait, then the door creaked open.

'Give me that,' Invett said, taking the basket with its blubbering, red-faced infant. He stepped into the corridor beyond and closed the door behind him.

The priestess facing him, veiled and robed but not so disguised as to hide her near obesity, was staring down at the babe with hungry eyes. 'Most excellent,' she whispered. 'The third today. The Lady is delighted with this new Prohibition.'

'I'm surprised,' Invett growled. 'Soon you will have a thousand screaming babes in here, and how will the Lady know peace?'

The priestess reached out and pinched the soft part of the baby's nearest arm. 'Plump,' she murmured. 'Good, yes. The Temple's peace will not suffer for long.'

Invett Loath frowned, wondering what it was in her words that made him slightly uneasy, then with a grunt he dismissed it. Not for the Well Knight to question other servants to the Lady. He handed her the basket.

The baby, that had been screaming all this time, all at once fell silent.

Knight and priestess leaned forward, studied its suddenly wide eyes.

'Like a newborn sparrow,' the priestess murmured, 'when a jay is near.'

'I know nothing of birds,' Invett Loath said. 'I am leaving now.'

'Yes, you are.'

A CROW PERCHED ON THE BUCKBOARD OF THE WAGON, feathers ruffling in the breeze that had sprung up as the sun's light faded. Emancipor noted its arrival with a scowl. 'Is he hungry, do you think?'

Bauchelain, who was seated on a folding camp stool opposite his manservant, gave a single shake of his head. 'He has fed.'

'Why are you looking at me like that, Master?'

'I have been thinking, Mister Reese.'

Oh no. 'About deposing this kindly king?'

'Kindly? Do you not realize, Mister Reese, how perfectly diabolical is this king's genius? Every tyranny imaginable is possible when prefaced by the notion that it is for the well-being of the populace. Patronizing? Of course, but when delivered with wide-eyed innocence and earnestness, what is a citizen to do? Complain about the benefits? Hardly, not when guilt is the benign torturer's first weapon of choice. No,' Bauchelain rose to his feet and turned to face the dark city. He used both hands to sweep his hair back, his eyes glittering in the gloom. 'We are witness to genius, plain and simple. And now, we are about to match wits with this clever king. I admit, the blood rushes about my being at the challenge.'

'I am happy for you, Master.'

'Ah, Mister Reese, I gather you still do not understand the threat this king poses to such creatures as you and I.'

'Well, frankly, no, I don't, Master. As you say.'

'I must perforce make the linkage plain, of sufficient simplicity to permit your uneducated mind to grasp all manner of significance. Desire for goodness, Mister Reese, leads to earnestness. Earnestness in turn leads to sanctimonious selfrighteousness, which breeds intolerance, upon which harsh judgement quickly follows, yielding dire punishment, inflicting general terror and paranoia, eventually culminating in revolt, leading to chaos, then dissolution, and thus, the end of civilization.' He slowly turned, looked down upon Emancipor. 'And we are creatures dependent upon civilization. It is the only environment in which we can thrive.'

Emancipor frowned. 'The desire for goodness leads to the end of civilization?'

'Precisely, Mister Reese.'

'But if the principal aim is to achieve good living and health among the populace, what is the harm in that?'

Bauchelain sighed. 'Very well, I shall try again. Good living and health, as you say, yielding well-being. But well-being is a contextual notion, a relative notion. Perceived benefits are measured by way of contrast. In any case, the result is smugness, and from that an overwhelming desire to deliver conformity among those perceived as less pure, less fortunate – the unenlightened, if you will. But conformity leads to ennui, and then indifference. From indifference, Mister Reese, dissolution follows as a natural course, and with it, once again, the end of civilization.'

'All right all right, Master, we are faced with the noble task of confounding the end of civilization.'

'Well said, Mister Reese. I admit I find the ethical aspects of our mission surprisingly . . . refreshing.'

'Have you a plan, then?'

'Indeed. And yes, you will be required to play an essential role.'

'Me?'

'You must enter the city, Mister Reese. Unobtrusively, of course. Once there, you must complete the following missions . . .'

THE SIGHTLESS EYES HAD BEEN STARING A LONG TIME WITHout seeing anything. Not surprising, since ravens had long since eaten everything there was to eat within those hoary sockets. No lids left with which to blink, nor any fluids to bring tears to those withered rims. Even so, Necrotus the Nihile, once king of Quaint, was not entirely surprised to find a grainy, misshapen scene slowly form, spreading to fill the vista his soul faced, a vista that had heretofore been naught but darkness – the welcome that was the Abyss.

Being dragged back and made to inhabit this bird-picked desiccated corpse hanging on the city's north wall, the flesh he had once called his own in better days, was, while not surprising, nonetheless disappointing. Worse yet, he found he could talk. 'Who has done this to me?'

A voice answered from somewhere below, not far, perhaps level with his chest. 'To that, I have more than one answer, King Necrotus.'

The tether upon which his soul was bound to this body was not so tight as to prevent a slight wandering outward, in order to look down. So that he could see the two crows perched upon the rusty spike projecting out from the wall, upon which his corpse had been impaled. 'Ah,' Necrotus said, 'now I understand.'

One of the crows cocked its head. 'You do? How charming.'

'Yes. You have come to discuss me. My life. My fate, all the lost loves of my mortal years in this world. Only, why must I witness this ironic indulgence?'

'Actually,' the first crow said, 'we would discuss, not you, but your brother.'

'Macrotus? That snivelling worm? Why?'

'For one, he is now king.'

'Oh. Of course. I should have thought of that. No heirs. Well, plenty of bastards, but the laws are strict on that. I was planning on officially adopting one, but then he died. And before I could choose another, so did I.'

'Indeed. That strikes me as careless,' the first crow said. 'In any case, my companion has done some cursory examination of your corpse here, and has detected the remnants of poison.'

Necrotus thought about that. 'That runt did me in! Gods below, I never thought he had it in him!'

'More precisely,' the crow continued, 'he fouled your life-extending alchemies, Necrotus. Which strikes us as odd, given his eagerness for health.'

'I was cheating, though, wasn't I? He hated that. He invented a mechanism, you know. Fills an entire room. He climbs into a harness and it works all his muscles, all his joints, it exercises him, jerks him about. He spends half his day in that thing. I concluded he'd gone insane.'

'Tell us,' the crow said, 'of this Lady of Beneficence.'

'A goddess, a minor one. Severe, miserable, a nose like a pig's, tilted up, you understand. At least it's so on the statues and idols depicting her.'

'A goddess?'

'I assume so. Believed to dwell in a pit in the Grand Temple. Why?'

'She is now the city's official patroness.'

'That bloodthirsty bitch? Gods below! If I wasn't a shrivelled up thing hanging here, I'd – I'd – well, it'd be different!'

'Well, King Necrotus, I would point out, you are not alone here on these walls.'

'I'm not?'

'And so I now ask you, are you of a mind to partake in ousting your brother, the King of Quaint?'

'Beats hanging around. Let's hear your plan, corbies.'

EMANCIPOR STOOD IN FRONT OF THE SMALL BUSH, LISTENING TO the birds chirp to greet the morning whilst he emptied his bladder.

'Look well on that yellow, murky stream, Mister Reese—'

The manservant started at the voice beside him. 'Master! You, uh, surprised me.'

'Thus reducing you to a trickle. I believe, in case you are interested, that only a few minor cantrips would convert the toxins in your flow, such that a single gesture could set that unfortunate shrub to flame. But as I said, look well, Mister Reese. In a few days you will be astonished to witness a stream issuing from you so clear that it is nigh water.'

Emancipor finished with a few final, spasmodic spurts, gave himself a shake, tucked in, then fumbled at retying the front of his trousers. 'I'm afraid I don't understand you, Master—'

'To dwell unobtrusively in the city, Mister Reese, you shall have to abstain from all unhealthy indulgences. You might well return from this mission a new man.'

The manservant stared at Bauchelain. 'Abstain? Completely? But, can't I sneak anything—'

'Absolutely not, Mister Reese. Now, divest yourself of the relevant items on your person. The crowd of traders on the low road is reaching ideal density.'

'I'm not sure I want to do this.'

'Ah, but you are in my employ, are you not? Our contract stipulates—'

'All right! Of course, Master,' he added. In a calmer tone, 'Can I not break my fast, as it were, before heading down there?'

'Oh, very well. Let it not be said I am a cruel master.'

They returned to the encampment, where Reese quickly filled his pipe with rustleaf and durhang, and broke the wax-sealed stopper on a bottle of wine.

'When you are done,' Bauchelain said, standing nearby and watching, 'there is some wild anise growing here beside the trail. Chew the feathery leaves. This should assist in hiding the various smells emanating from your person. Would that we could find some wild garlic, onions, skunk-bulbs . . . Not too much of that wine, Mister Reese, it will not do to have you weaving and staggering at Quaint's gates. You are producing enough smoke to launch a fire-fighting crew from the city – I think that will be enough, Mister Reese. The anise—'

'It's fennel, Master,' Emancipor said.

'It is? Well, whatever.'

Head buzzing, the manservant marched over to the weeds and began pulling the thin spidery leaves from the stalks. 'I feel like a damned caterpillar.'

'The white and black banded ones?' Bauchelain asked. 'I am pleased to inform you that those transform into the most beautiful butterflies.'

Emancipor stared over at his master.

Who stared back.

A moment of silence, then Bauchelain cleared his throat. 'Yes, well, off you go, then.'

I MID FACTALLO WANDERED DOWN RUNNER'S AVENUE, STRANGE twitches spasming across half his face. They had started up a few days ago, some consequence of the wound he had received in his head, which he'd thought fully healed. But now . . . in addition to the twitches he was having strange thoughts. Desires. Illicit desires.

He wondered if he and Elas Sil had done the right thing. But it was too late now. That sorceror, Bauchelain, was . . . frightening. In a peculiar, uncanny way. As if a warm thought had never once entered his mortal soul, and all that hid within was dark and cold. And the stories Imid had heard from the city up the coast . . . there was said to be a second sorceror, given to hiding, with the most venal appetites. Thus . . . *evil*.

A concept Imid had rarely thought about, but now it haunted him. There had been little particularly good about old Necrotus the Nihile. The usual assortment of unsavory indulgences common to those with absolute power. A score of repressive laws intended, as Elas Sil explained, to keep the king rich and free to revel in excess at the expense of the common folk. But if you paid your tithes and killed or robbed nobody important, you could live out your life without once crossing the path of trouble. And of course, such systemic corruption flowed down easily enough, the poison of cynicism infected the lowest city guard as much as it did the king. Bribery solved most problems, and where it couldn't, swift and brutal violence did. In other

words, life was simple, straightforward and easily understood.

And, perhaps, *evil*. In the way of apathy, of indifference, of
tacit acceptance of inhumanity. A cruel king made cruel nobles,
who in turn made cruel merchants, and so on down to cruel
stray dogs. And yet, Imid Factallo longed for a return to those
times. For, it turned out, an earnest king, a king obsessed with
goodness, delivered to all below him a certain zeal from which all
manner of cruelty derived. Born of harsh judgementalism – Elas
Sil insisted such a word existed, and if didn't before then it did
now – the sheer frenzy of noble ideals put into practice without
flexibility or compassion was proving as destructive to the human
spirit as anything Necrotus and his ilk may have contrived to
inflict upon the people.

Evil possessed myriad faces, and some of them were open and
genuine.

Whilst others, like Bauchelain's, revealed nothing, nothing at
all.

Imid could not decide which of the two was more frightening.

He arrived at the home of Elas Sil, knocked thrice as custom
dictated, then entered, as the law now permitted since privacy
invited . . . private things. Entered, then, to find her quickly
emerging from the curtained backroom, adjusting her tunic with
a decidedly guilty expression on her face.

Imid stopped two steps in from the doorway, frozen in horror.
'Who's back there?' he demanded. 'He'll get castrated! And you
– you—'

'Oh be quiet, there's no one back there.'

He stared at her. 'You were masturbating! That's illegal!'

'Nobody's ever proved the unhealthiness of it, have they?'

'Not physically, no, but emotionally unhealthy! Is there any
doubt of that, Elas Sil? Your mind is drawn into base desires, and
base desires lead to sordid appetites and sordid appetites leads to
temptation and temptation leads to—'

'The end of civilization. I know. Now, what do you want,
Imid?'

'Well, uh, I was coming here to, uh, confess.'

She advanced on him, smelling of women's parts, and with a growing sneer said, 'Confess, Imid Factallo? And what must you confess to a fellow saint, if not *temptations*? You hypocrite!'

'I confess my hypocrisy! There, satisfied? I'm having . . . impulses. All right?'

'Oh, never mind,' Elas said, turning away and sitting down on a nearby chair. 'It's all so pathetic, isn't it? Did you hear? They're stealing babies, now. If it screams, it's breaking the law. If children play-fight in the street, they're breaking the law.' She looked over. 'Have you done your required exercises today?'

'No.'

'Why is your face twitching?'

'I don't know. Must be a side effect.'

'Of good living?'

'Oh, aren't you funny.'

'Well, should we exercise together?'

Imid's eyes narrowed. 'What do you have in mind?'

'Something seriously illegal. Your visit interrupted me.'

'That's not exercise!'

'Now there's a depressing confession for you to make, Imid Factallo. Of course, I could take it as a challenge.'

'You're disgusting.' He paused. 'Say some more disgusting things.'

EMANCIPOR REESE WAS SWEATING BY THE TIME HE PASSED unaccosted through the city gate. His nerves were jumping wildly and he felt slightly sick. Likely the dust and the stench of ox and mule sweat, he told himself as he jostled among the farmers driving their loaded carts through the narrow passage. With Oponn's blessing, he would have completed his tasks by tomorrow, and so could return to a sane lifestyle – or, as sane as was possible whilst in the employ of two homicidal masters.

He hoped his wife was living well on his earnings back in Lamentable Moll. The brats would be in school, still, although the eldest might well be apprenticed out by now. It had been four years, after all. A lifetime, given what the manservant had lived through since that fateful drunken day when he'd knocked on the door to Bauchelain's room at Sorrowman's Hostel.

She'd have found lovers by now, too, he suspected. Sailors, fishers, maybe even a soldier or two. He didn't begrudge that, much. It could be a lonely life, being a mother with no husband close by.

Twenty paces in from the gate, Emancipor moved off to stand clear of the carts and braying beasts of burden filing past. He looked round, trying to sense what was different about this place, compared to the countless other cities he had visited. It was quieter, for one thing. Off to the right, at the end of a narrow passage, was something like a square, in which citizens stood in rows waving their arms about and jumping in place. He wondered if these people might also be saints, all of them skull-cracked and now entirely insane. There were few urchins to be seen, and none of the hopelessly destitute begging for coins in the gutters. Indeed, the street looked surprisingly clean.

If this was the good life, then it wasn't so bad, he concluded.

Of course, it was not going to last. Not with Bauchelain and Korbal Broach scheming its downfall. He felt a pang of regret.

'What are you doing here?'

Emancipor turned. 'Excuse me?'

The woman standing before him was wearing white enameled armour, a white cape lined in gold silk. Her face belonged to that of a marble statue carved by some artist obsessed with perfection, down to the pallid dust on her cheeks and to either side of her even, pert nose. The red paint glistening from her lips made it appear she had just drunk a flagon of blood. Cold, hard blue eyes were fixed on his with haughty contempt. 'You're loitering, citizen.'

'Actually, I was hesitating.'

She blinked, then frowned. 'Is there a difference?'

'Of course,' Emancipor replied. He considered explaining the difference, then decided not to.

'Well,' she finally said, 'we don't like hesitation much, either.'

'Then I will be on my way.'

'Yes, but first, where are you going? By your accent you are some sort of foreigner – don't deny it! And we have concerns about foreigners. They possess unruly ideas. I need to know everything about you, beginning with your reason for coming to Quaint. Now, start talking!'

Her tirade had attracted onlookers, all of whom now turned with unveiled suspicion to Emancipor to await his answer.

Sweat beaded Emancipor's wrinkled brow. It should have been Bauchelain answering these damned questions. Or, even more amusing, Korbal Broach – with those flat, beady eyes, that flabby, placid smile. Inspiration struck the manservant, and he swung a glazy look on the fierce woman. 'Who are you? My head hurts. Where are we?'

Her scowl deepened. 'I was the one asking the questions.'

'What has happened?' Emancipor asked. 'I woke up outside the gate. I think. I was . . . I was working. Yes, I was working, with a crew, clearing a drainage ditch. There was this big rock, they wanted it moved – I was straining. Then – pain! In my head! By the Lady, I don't even know who I am!'

A gasp from the crowd. Then, *'He is a Saint!'*

The woman asked, 'Have you been proclaimed by a Well Knight?'

'Uh, I don't think so. I don't remember. Maybe. What day is this?'

Someone in the crowd answered, 'Saint Ebar's Day, oh chosen one!'

'Seven months!' Emancipor exclaimed. Then cursed himself. That was too long. What was he thinking?

'Seven months?' The Well Knight stepped closer. *'Seven months?'*

'I—I think so,' Emancipor stammered. 'What year is this?' Idiot! He was making it worse!

'The Second Year of the Rule of Macrotus.'

'Macrotus!' the manservant exclaimed. Blathering fool, stop this! Now! Another inspiration. Emancipor rolled his eyes up, groaned, and collapsed on to the cobbles. Shouts from the crowd, figures moving close.

Conversations.

'Is he the one, then?'

'The very first Saint of Glorious Labour? He said seven years, didn't he? I'm sure he did. *Seven!*'

The Well Knight growled then, and said, 'The myth of the First Saint – I mean, we have looked and looked and never found him, or her. Besides, this man's a foreigner. The First Saint cannot be a foreigner.'

'But, Blessed Knight of Wellness,' someone persisted, 'all that he said fits! The First Saint, the harbinger of all that was to come! The Royal Prophecies—'

'I know the Royal Prophecies, citizen!' the woman snapped. 'Careful, lest I conclude you are arguing loudly in a public place!'

A voice from further out, stentorian. 'What is happening here?'

The woman replied with some relief. 'Ah, Invett Loath. If you would be so kind, please assist in the adjudication of this situation.'

The man's voice came closer. 'Situation? Situations are frowned upon, Storkul Purge. Even a low-ranking Well Knight such as you must know this.'

'I endeavour to promulgate conformity at every turn, Oh Purest of the Paladins.'

'And well you should, lest by your actions you prove singular or, Lady forgive us, unique. You do not deem yourself unique, do you, Storkul Purge?'

Her voice was suddenly small. 'Of course not. The purity of my innate mediocrity is absolute, Purest. Of that I can assure you.'

'What is happening here? Who is this unconscious man?'

The persistent citizen was quick to answer, 'The First Saint, Purest Paladin of Wellness! A man without memory, for the last seven years!'

'Then why is he unconscious?'

'He succumbed to the Well Knight's questioning. It was . . . shocking. Blessed be the Lady that you have arrived!'

No retort nor refutation came from the hapless Storkul Purge, and, lying at her very feet, Emancipor felt a surge of sympathy. That quickly went away. Let her roast, he concluded. And opened his eyes – immediately noticed – then fixed them on Storkul Purge. Another groan, another apparent plunge into oblivion.

'She did it again!' the citizen said in a gasp.

'Excuse yourself, Storkul Purge,' Invett Loath commanded, 'and await the Knightly Judgement at the Day Temple of Wellness.'

A muted, 'Yes, Purest Paladin.'

Emancipor heard her boots scuff away.

'Awaken, First Saint,' Invett Loath said.

This was perfect. Emancipor's eyes fluttered open. Bewildered, then resting with apparent recognition on the beat-stained, chiselled features of the armoured Knight standing over him. 'I—I have never seen you before,' the manservant said, 'yet I know the purity of your soul. You must be the Paladin. You must be Invett Loath.'

A gleam of pleasure lit the man's sharp blue eyes. 'You are correct, First Saint. There is a little known prophecy that I would be the one to find you, and deliver you to our king. Are you well enough to stand?'

Emancipor struggled to his feet. Tottered momentarily and was steadied by a gauntleted hand.

'Come, First Saint of Most Glorious Labour—'

The manservant's knees buckled, forcing the Paladin to quickly clutch at him.

'What is it, my friend?' Invett Loath asked in alarm.

Ignoring the massive crowd surrounding them, Emancipor straightened once more, then leaned close to the Paladin. 'A – a vision, Oh Purest. A terrible vision!'

'This is fell indeed! What have you seen?'

Emancipor lifted his head slightly. He would have to think of something, and fast. 'For the ears of you and the King and none other!'

'Not even the Grand Nun of the Lady?'

'Oh, yes. Her too.'

'Then we must be away. Here, take my arm . . .'

WELL KNIGHT STORKUL PURGE LEANED AGAINST THE BACK wall of the Day Temple, staring sightlessly as waves of dread swept through her. She was doomed. Knightly Judgements never favoured the judged. She had participated in them enough times to know that as an unmitigated truth, and she well recalled the secret visceral pleasure when adding her voice to the chorus of condemnation. Crimes against Wellness were without question the most serious offences these days, and that seriousness was only getting more serious. She frowned at that thought, then shook her head, suddenly fearful that she was losing her mind.

Then again, perhaps that was for the best. Insanity like a cocoon wrapped about herself before the moment of adjudication.

Damn that Invett Loath! Every Well Knight knew that the myth of the First Saint was an invention. The foreigner was little more than a quick-witted opportunist, clever enough to make mockery of treasured superstition whilst, at the same time, stroke Loath's ego. If anyone deserved adjudication, it was the Paladin of Purity, stomping about the city in the blinding cloud of his unsullied righteousness, a cloud thick enough to choke the fittest citizen.

Ah, did she have something there? Had not Invett Loath set himself above all others? Was he too not bound to conformity and secure mediocrity? Dare she challenge him?

'He will devour me alive,' she whispered. 'Who am I fooling? He's already sharpening the spike for me on the wall. By the Lady,

I need a drink!' Her mouth shut with a click of teeth at that exclamation. Looking about, she saw, with relief, that no one was close.

Then, a small, raspy voice whispered, 'Did someone mention a drink?'

Storkul Purge's head snapped round. The voice seemed to have come right beside her, but there was no one there. 'Who spoke?' she demanded.

'I've caught a most delicious trail.'

The Well Knight looked down, and saw a small, gaudily dressed shape lying beside her right boot.

The thing sniffed. 'Do you not recognize me, Storkul Purge? Granted, these clothes ill fit me. T'was a dancer, a twirling, spinning celebrant—'

'You fool,' Storkul said, sneering, 'those clothes belonged to a puppet. I can still see the strings.'

In a small voice, the thing said, 'A puppet? Oh! I'm wasting away!'

'You are Vice,' she said. 'You are Ineb Cough. Why aren't you dead yet?'

'Oh, you don't understand! It was all I could manage to crawl to you! The lure of your desire – I heard it!'

'You are mistaken—'

'Ah, a lie! Good! Yes, lies are good. Lies are where I begin!'

'Be quiet! People will hear.'

'Better and better. Yes, we will whisper, you and I. A drink, yes? Spirits, yes? I have caught a trail, leading out through Inland Gate. A trail, I tell you, redolent with all manner of indulgences. Liquor, rustleaf, durhang—'

'Inland Gate? Why, I was just there!'

'Someone has entered the city, my dear . . .'

'Someone? A foreigner? Yes, a foreigner!' She knew it!

'We must backtrack along his trail, you and me, Storkul Purge. We must!'

She was silent, thinking. Visions raced through her mind. Dramatic pronouncements, scenes of triumph at the fall of both the foreigner and Invett Loath. But it would not do to act too quickly. No, the two must become further entwined, each the champion of the other in their grand deceit. Yes, she could see it now. Soon, there would be a new champion of purity in Quaint.

But first . . . 'Very well, Ineb Cough, backtrack we shall.'

'Delicious! Pick me up, then, my dark-hearted woman. Through Inland Gate, on to the open road beyond!'

'Quiet! You're getting too loud!' She reached down and collected the puny creature that was Ineb Cough. 'Say nothing more,' she whispered, 'until I tell you it's safe.'

Approaching the gate, she saw a guard step out, his eyes on her. 'Well Knight, what have you there?'

'A most horrible child,' she replied. 'Infected.'

The man edged back slightly. 'Infected?'

'Children are not innocent, only inexperienced. It is a common enough misapprehension. This one is loud, boisterous, aggressive and cares only for itself.'

'A singular child, then.'

As any mother would tell you, you stupid mule-turd, I just described every child in this world. 'Indeed, so singular we have no choice but to remove him bodily from the city.'

'And what do you mean to do with him?' the guard asked.

'Leave him to the wolves. Launch him in a basket on the outgoing tide. Sell him to pernicious but unsuspecting slavers. I have not yet decided, guard. Now, if you would stand aside, lest the vapours of this wretched imp poison you . . .'

The guard took another step back, then waved her on with a nervous gesture.

Once out on the road, she paused. 'All right, no one's close. Which way?'

'Straight ahead,' Ineb replied, 'forty paces, then left on the drover's track, up the hill. The very top. Gods below, the scent is strong and oh so lovely!'

Her basest desires urged her every step onwards. Very disturb-ing. True, she'd once been, long ago, a most indulgent creature, sweet seductress in service to this very demon tucked under her arm. Like honey in a wasp trap, a furry mouse in a snake-pit, a whore at the temple backdoor. And it had been a good, if toxic, life. She admitted that she missed those days, rather, those nights. Yet, had not that foreigner and Invett Loath conspired her imminent downfall, she knew she would have gone on in her new, unstained life as a Knight of Wellness, pure of thought – all right, most of the time – and in the pious straits of healthy living. Respected and feared, representative and exalted far above the miserable mass of wretches crowding Quaint's streets. Wretches deserving little more than her sneering contempt.

And there was a little known truth. Healthy pursuits should have noticeably extended lives by now, but the sheer stress of the endeavour was killing people like mayflies. Clearly, your average citizen wasn't up to the task of living well. Victims of exercise and too many vegetables. Beneficence was a costly glory, it turned out. The chirurgeons were reporting that the most common complaint these days was blocked bowels. 'And there you have it,' she muttered under her breath as she climbed the drover's track, 'what this city needs is a good dump, hah.'

'For starters,' Ineb Cough replied. 'Yes indeed, a good clearing out of the system. An explosive expulsion of—'

'That's enough from you,' Storkul said in a growl. 'I was talking to myself.'

The demon sniffed in a muffled fashion, 'Didn't sound like it to me.'

'Well, I was.'

'Fine, but that's not what I heard, that's all.'

'You heard wrong.'

The creature spasmed under her arm, gaudy limbs writhing. 'All right! I'm sorry! I'm sorry!'

'That,' said a third voice, 'was well done.'

It originated from the summit, three strides ahead. Storkul Purge halted, stared up at the man. 'What?' she asked. 'What was well done?'

'You are a ventriloquist, yes? A fascinating profession, I have always thought, fraught with arcane sorcery and strange mental peculiarity—'

'She's not a ventriloquist,' Ineb Cough snarled, still thrashing about.

The grey-bearded, elegantly dressed man almost smiled. 'Please, ah, *both* of you – I am a most appreciative audience and you will be pleased at the gratuity I shall pay you for the performance.'

'I am Well Knight Storkul Purge, *not* a caster of voices! Who are you and what are you doing here? Is that a camp on the summit behind you? Answer my questions, damn you, in the name of the Lady of Beneficence!'

'Answer her!' the demon added in a vicious rasp.

The man clapped his long-fingered hands. 'Oh, very good indeed.'

Knight and demon howled their outrage.

'Spectacular!'

Storkul Purge flung the demon down and advanced on the man. Flopping in the dust behind her, Ineb Cough screamed, 'I smell rustleaf!'

The stranger took a step back, thin brows rising. 'Exquisite drama,' he said. 'And highest sorcery, since I do not see the strings—'

'Silence, you wretched cur!' She saw the wagon at the far edge of the summit, and two bone-white oxen lolling stupidly as oxen were wont to do – although as both beasts swung their heads to regard her, the Knight faltered upon seeing their onyx black eyes. Nearby was the remnant of a cook fire, and lying close to the ring of stones were two wine bottles. 'Alcohol! As I suspected!' She rounded on the foreigner. 'Ignorance of the prohibitions is not an acceptable defence! I should have you arrested and—'

'A moment,' the man interrupted, lifting one finger, which he then set to his bearded chin. 'Whilst ignorance of prohibitions may not be an acceptable defence, what of ignorance of what constitutes an acceptable defence?'

'What?'

'And what of your ignorance of the proper charge to be made

against me?' the man inquired, the finger now tapping a steady rhythm. 'Do you have an acceptable defence regarding that?'

'I *know* which are the proper charges!'

'Then why are you being so vague about them?'

'I'm not being vague!'

'Ahh,' he said with a slight smile, and the finger wagged lazily.

'Be quiet both of you!' the demon shrieked as it clawed its way to the summit. 'Storkul Purge, have you forgotten your own desires? Forgotten what has brought us here?'

The Knight spun round and stared down at Ineb Cough, struggled against the impulse to crush him underfoot. Then, mastering herself, she faced the foreigner once more. 'The demon is right. I am not here in the capacity of a Knight of Wellness.'

'A Knight of Wellness? I see,' the foreigner said, slowly nodding. Then his placid gaze slid down to Ineb Cough. 'And a demon in truth, although much diminished. Mind you, well suited to ornamental functions. Had I a mantle piece . . . alas, such are the vicissitudes of travel.'

'A *mantle piece*,' the demon hissed in outrage. 'I was once a giant! The Tyrant of Hedonism! That's what they called me. The Demon of Vice, you damned conjurer, had no equal! They all bowed to me – Corpulence, Sloth, even Lust!'

'You were manifest in Quaint?' the man asked. 'How extraordinary. Whomever was responsible for you displayed exquisite extravagance – I would have liked to meet that woman.'

Storkul Purge cocked her head. 'Woman? How do you know it was a woman?'

The man eyed her for a moment, then he turned away. 'Come, my friends, join me at this modest hearth. Here, in my manservant's pack, we shall find no modest supply of illegal condiments, I am certain.' A gesture towards the heap of ashes, the flicker of magic—

A nearby bush burst into flames.

The man started. 'My humblest apologies. That was unintended, I assure you.' He gestured again, and wood appeared in the hearth, heat curling and sudden snaps announcing ignition. In the meantime the bush still raged, throwing up strangely coloured tongues of fire. Eyeing it askance, Storkul Purge edged closer to the hearth. Behind her, Ineb Cough crawled with minute grunts and gasps – he seemed to be heading for the wine bottles.

'Do not think,' the Knight said, 'I am here with the intention of imbibing in unwholesome habits.'

'Unwholesome, you say,' the man said, his broad forehead wrinkling in a frown as he rummaged through the frayed leather sack. 'Certainly a matter of opinion. I favour wine for the most part, and consider it salubrious and, in moderation, enlivening. As such, nothing unwholesome.'

'It deadens the brain,' she replied harshly. 'Indeed, kills it minutely, in increments. More pernicious than that, it assaults the blood and loosens natural discipline.'

'Natural discipline? Gods below, what a peculiar notion!'

'Nothing peculiar to it,' she said. 'It is the mechanism employed by the instinctive desire for health.'

'As opposed to well-being.'

'Health and well-being are not in opposition.'

'A fierce pronouncement, Miss Purge. Oh, I have been rude. I am Bauchelain. As you see me, no more than a gentle traveller, with no intention – no, none indeed – of settling in your fair city.'

'What is with your oxen, Bauchelain?' she demanded. 'Those eyes . . .'

'A rare breed—'

Ineb Cough snorted as he clambered on to the first wine bottle, head thrust out, tiny tongue poking towards the bottle's neck. 'Ynah. Nhn. Yhn.' His tongue flicked cat-like against the dark, pocked glass.

'Here we are,' Bauchelain said, drawing forth a number of objects. 'Rustleaf. Durhang, in dried leaf form, in soft ball form. White nectar – where in Hood's realm did he come by that, I wonder? Uthurl poppy . . . hmm, an assortment of medicines all sharing the theme of stupor, employed to calm highly beset nerves. I had no idea my phlegmatic manservant suffered such ailments. And here, some wine. And peach liquor, and pear liquor, and here is some whale sperm – Queen of Dreams, what does he do with that, I wonder? No matter, we are each and all mysterious miracles in our own ways, yes? Now, I am certain Mister Reese will not begrudge your partaking of his prodigious supply – imbibe as you desire. I myself shall sample some of this Falari wine . . .'

Storkul Purge stared down at the vast array of prohibited substances. A small whimper escaped her.

BEYOND THE FORMAL ENTRANCE WAS A LONG, WIDE COLONNADE lined on each side with upright corpses set in coffins. The lids were glass, murky and bubbled but not, alas, sufficient to disguise the inhabitants. Positioned between narrow, marble columns, a host of blurry, shrunken eyes seemed to track Emancipor and Invett Loath as they made their way down the vast hallway. A set of double doors waited at the far end.

'The Healthy Dead,' the Paladin of Purity said, one arm still taking most of the manservant's weight. 'As you can see, they are all well. Clean of spirit and hale. Glorious evidence of the rewards that come with living unsullied by the foul indulgences that once cursed our people.'

'Why are they all grimacing?' Emancipor asked.

'The Lady takes most mortals unto her bosom by maladies of the colon.'

'Death by constipation?'

'The zeal of health. Many citizens eat grass to excess.'

'Grass?'

'Have you no memory of such things? No, how could you? Having been made a Saint in the time of Necrotus the Nihile. Indeed, grass, a fine substitute for meat. Our chirurgeons have dissected all manner of corpses – early on, they often slit open stomachs to find solid pieces of meat, resident in undigested fashion for years in the victim. Truly horrific. Now, of course, they find knotted bundles of grass, which as you might imagine

241

is a far less disgusting discovery – after all, cows die of that all the time.'

'And now, cows and citizens both.'

'You'd be surprised, First Saint, at the similarities.'

Emancipor glanced up to see something dark and satisfied in the Paladin's flushed face. After a moment, Invett Loath resumed, 'Peruse this corpse, here . . . that one, for a moment.' They halted before one of the coffins. 'See the even pallor? See how shiny all that newly grown hair is? This, my friend, is a thing of beauty, a monument to supreme healthiness.'

'I couldn't agree more,' Emancipor said, staring in fascination at the fixed pain-wracked expression on the poor lady's face behind the blue-green glass. 'I imagine her relatives are very proud to have her here in the palace.'

'Oh no,' Invett Loath said, 'not in the least. Madness struck them one and all upon her death – I tell no lie when I say that their lust for meat led them to eat most of her left leg – yes, the wrapped one. Thus, the rest of her family will be found on the spikes.'

Emancipor stared at the Paladin, aghast. 'What could drive loved ones to do such a thing?'

'Moral weakness, First Saint. It is a plague, ever ready to spread its infection upon the citizens, and this is the greatest responsibility of the Well Knights, to ensure that such weakness is rooted out and mounted high on the walls. And I can tell you, we are as busy today as we were a year ago, perhaps busier.'

'No wonder there are so few people on the streets.'

'Diligence, First Saint. An unending demand, but we are equal to it.'

They resumed their journey down the cavernous hall. 'But not that . . . woman who first accosted me,' Emancipor said.

'Storkul Purge? I've had my eye on her for some time. She was a prostitute, did you know that? Before the Prohibitions. A fallen woman, a creature of disgusting vices, a seductress of dreadful hedonism, a singular threat to civilization – her conversion was so sudden that I was instantly suspicious. We have done well, you and I, to expose her inequities. She shall suffer adjudication, this very night.'

Emancipor winced, overwhelmed by a flood of guilt. 'Can there be no second chance, Paladin?'

'Ah, you are a saint indeed, to voice such sentiment. The answer is no, there cannot. The very notion of fallibility was invented to absolve mortals of responsibility. We can be perfect, and you can see true perfection walking here at your side.'

'You have achieved perfection?'

'I have. I am. And to dispute that truth is to reveal your own imperfection.'

They arrived at the double doors. Invett Loath reached for the large rings – but the door on the right suddenly opened, the edge cracking against the Paladin's nose with a wet crunching sound. The man reeled back, blood spurting.

Emancipor stumbled, then, his boot settling on a smear of blood, he lost his balance and pitched forwards, through the open door, where he struck a dumbfounded servant, his head sinking into the woman's belly.

Breath exploded from her and, as Emancipor fell face first on to the floor, she collapsed on to him, the large bowl perched on her head wheeling away, a brain-sized mass of wet grass heaving into the air like a thing alive to splat and slide in runny mint sauce across the tiles—

—directly beneath Invett Loath's left boot as he stepped down. The Paladin skidded, landed with a solid thump on his backside.

Groaning, Emancipor pushed the woman off, then rolled on to his side. In the hallway behind him, he could hear Invett Loath's spattering gasps. Beside the manservant, the servant dragged in her first breath after a long moment of eye-bulging, gaping panic. And, somewhere in the chamber beyond, there came to Emancipor's ears a strange mechanical sound, repeating in steady, indifferent rhythm. Blinking tears from his eyes, he climbed to his hands and knees and looked up.

A massive, iron-framed, hinged and wheeled and cabled contraption dominated the chamber, and in its midst, bound by straps and padded shackles, there was a figure. Suspended an arm's length above the floor, limbs gyrating incessantly, as if the man was climbing air, trapped in place, his shaggy-haired head slowly lolling in time with the various fulcrums and pulleys and ratcheting gears.

The mechanism was so large there was no way to get close to the figure hanging in its centre, and with his back to the doors, it was clear that King Macrotus – for who else could it be? – had heard nothing of the commotion at the entrance. He exercised on, unceasing, steadily, a man in perpetual motion.

Invett Loath staggered through the doorway, his face streaked with blood running down the nostrils of his broken nose. He spat, pain-pinched eyes fixing upon the servant who still sat on the floor. 'Whore's beget! Slayer of civilization! I shall adjudicate you here and now!'

To this bellow King Macrotus paid no visible attention, arms rising in turn, legs pumping in counterpoint – the man looked frighteningly thin, yet strangely flaccid, as if his skin had lost all elasticity.

Emancipor clambered upright. 'Paladin of Purity, it was an accident!'

'Accidents are signs of weakness!'

Invett Loath, the manservant could see, was in a hot, blinding rage. ''Ware your words!' Emancipor snapped.

The huge man wheeled on him, red jaw dropping.

Heart pounding, Emancipor stabbed out an accusing finger. 'Do you condemn this city's Saints of Glorious Labour, Paladin? One and all? Victims of accidents, are they not? Dare you adjudicate in defiance of *my* people? Before our beloved king himself?'

Invett Loath stepped back. 'Of course not!' Eyes flicked to Macrotus in his harness, then back to Emancipor. 'But she is little more than a wench—'

'Serving the king himself!' Emancipor said. 'Moreover, she has been injured . . . whilst,' he added with sudden inspiration, 'conducting glorious labour!' The manservant reached down to settle his hand on the trembling woman's head. 'She is now a Saint!'

'Such proclamation,' the Paladin said, 'must be sanctioned by a Well Knight . . .'

'Indeed, by none other than you, Invett Loath. Is King Macrotus to witness hesitation?'

'No! I do hereby sanctify this woman as a Saint of Glorious Labour!'

Emancipor helped the woman to her feet. Close to her ear, he whispered, 'Get out of here, lass. Quick!'

She bowed, collected her bowl, then scurried away.

Emancipor found a handkerchief in a pocket and handed it up to the Paladin, watched as Invett cleaned up his face, wiping the cloth back and forth, then again, back and forth. And again, back and forth beneath the suddenly glittering, suddenly wide eyes. Slowly, shock filled the manservant.

That handkerchief . . . D'bayang poppy spores . . . oh dear . . . 'Paladin, the King seems indisposed at the moment . . .'

'As always,' Invett Loath said in an odd, jumpy voice. 'But yes. Too busy. Exercising. Exercising. Up down up down down up down exercise! We've tallied too long. Lethargy is a sin. Let us get going.' He held the cloth to his nose again. 'Exercise. I need to patrol the streets. All of them, yes, by dusk. I can do that. You don't believe me? I'll show you!'

The Paladin charged out of the chamber.

And Emancipor found himself alone.

With King Macrotus. Who exercised on, and on.

'THESE CLOTHES ARE TOO TIGHT,' INEB COUGH COMPLAINED.

'You have burgeoned some,' Bauchelain observed. 'Here, have more wine, my friend.'

'Yes, very good. I will. But I'm feeling . . . constricted.'

Nearby, Storkul Purge paced, a woman at war with herself. Ineb was disappointed that she still resisted the delicious lure of all these wondrous condiments. Taking another mouthful from the bottle, the demon edged closer to Bauchelain. 'Sorceror,' he whispered, then smiled, 'Oh yes, I know you for what you are. You and that crow circling overhead. Necromancers! Tell me, what are you doing here?'

Bauchelain glanced over at the Well Knight, then fixed his regard on the demon. He stroked his bearded chin. 'Ah, now, that is something of a mystery, isn't it?'

'That manservant you mentioned. He's in the city, isn't he? Purchasing supplies for your journey? Perhaps, but more than that, I suspect.' Ineb smiled again. 'I can smell conspiracies, oh yes.'

'Can you now? I would ask you, where are your fellow demons?'

'In some alley, I expect. Except for Agin Again – she's disappeared.'

'Agin Again?'

'The Demoness of Lust.'

'Disappeared? For how long, Ineb Cough?'

'Around the time of Necrotus's sudden demise.'

'And how soon, upon taking the crown, did Macrotus announce the prohibitions?'

'These clothes are strangling me!'

Bauchelain reached down. 'Allow me to un-do those buttons – oh, they're just for show. I see. Well, shall I cut you free?'

'No. Another drink would be better. Yes. Excellent. The prohibitions? About a week, during which he'd already begun . . . preparing the way. Elevating the Lady of Beneficence to the official religion. If you think on it, that act foreshadowed all that followed. A newly recruited army of piety, sanctioned to police the behaviour of every citizen in Quaint. By the Abyss, we should have seen it coming!' Yanking at his collar, Ineb stole another glance over at Storkul Purge, then leaned even closer to the sorceror. 'You're planning something, yes? What? Tell me!'

'I was considering removing, from your companion, a certain quantity of blood.'

The demon stared at the sorceror, then licked his lips. 'Oh. How . . . how much blood did you have in mind?'

Bauchelain had picked up the bottle of whale sperm and was studying it. 'Well, that depends on its purity.'

'Ah, I see. It must needs be pure. I think, Bauchelain, that her blood is very pure indeed. Given that . . . are we talking a fatal amount?'

The sorceror's brows rose. He raised the bottle and peered at the thick sediments at the base, then gave it a shake. 'Difficult to say, alas. Oh look, they're still alive – how can that be? I am no longer convinced this sperm belonged to a whale. No, not at all. Curious.'

'Were you planning on asking her for it?'

Surprise flitted across the sorceror's ascetic features. 'Ask? I admit I had not thought of that.'

'And this blood,' Ineb said, pulling himself into a tightly bound crouch, 'what do you intend on doing with it?'

'Me? Nothing. My travelling companion, however, shall employ it in a ritual of resurrection.'

The demon scanned the sky, seeking sight of the crow. It wasn't around at the moment. He shifted uneasily. 'Resurrection. Of course, why didn't I think of that? I can answer that question. I couldn't because you won't tell me what you're planning.'

'Nothing dramatic, I assure you. The overthrow of King Macrotus. We shall endeavour to preserve as much of the city's population as possible.'

'You want Quaint's throne?'

'For ourselves? Hardly. What would we do with it? No, consider it a favour.'

'A favour?'

'Very well, we are being paid to achieve the swift extinction of this deadly trend towards healthiness. Although, truth be said, I am not much interested in material wealth. Rather, it is the challenge that intrigues me.' Bauchelain straightened and faced Storkul Purge. After a moment, the sorceror drew out a knife.

IMID FACTALLO'S LIFE HAD NEVER AMOUNTED TO MUCH, THUS far. such was his considered opinion in any case. No wife, no children, and he not a man women would chase, unless he'd stolen something from them. And so he'd known loneliness, as familiar as an old friend, in fact. Although, presumably, to have a friend was to be other than lonely. Thinking on that, he was forced to conclude that loneliness was not anything like an old friend. Indeed, had he a friend, he would have been able to discuss his thoughts, since that's what friends did, and clearly the conversation would have been scintillating.

He sat on the front step of his modest, friendless abode, watching a squirrel twitch confusedly at the base of a tree. It had been busy for weeks storing various things in anticipation of the winter to come. Curiously, it seemed such rodents despised company. Loneliness was their desired state. This is what came, he concluded morosely, of eating nuts and seeds.

The creature's present confusion had no outwardly apparent cause, suggesting to Imid that the source of its troubles came from within, a particular cavort of agitation in its tiny brain. Perhaps it was experiencing an ethical crisis, making it jump about so in chittering rage.

All the fault of that damned manservant, Imid told himself. Mulled wine and rustleaf and durhang, a veritable cornucopia of forbidden substances, and his indifferent aplomb in the consumption of those items had taken Imid's breath away. Cruel as a squirrel, he'd been. Driving the Saint of Glorious Labour to distraction, and worse . . . thoughts of violence.

He became aware of a susurration of noise from down the street, in the direction of the Grand Temple of the Lady. A crowd. Distant screams.

Imid Factallo saw the squirrel freeze in its tracks, head cocked. Then it fled.

The sounds were getting louder.

The saint leaned out slightly, peering down the street.

More screams, shattering pottery, a heavy crash – he saw a mass of motion, filling the space between the buildings. A mob, in full charge now, coming this way.

Alarmed, Imid Factallo rose from the step.

A hundred citizens, maybe more. Faces twisted in terror and panic, Saints of Glorious Labour among them. And worthies. And nuns – what was this?

They swept opposite Imid where he stood, clawing each other, clambering over those who fell. A wailing baby rolled to the bottom step, directly below Imid, and he snatched it clear a moment before a worthy's boot slammed down on that spot. Staggering backward until his shoulders struck the door behind him, Imid stared as the mob surged past.

And, in its wake, the Paladin of Purity, Invett Loath. He'd drawn his sword, the polished steel flashing as he waved the weapon above his head, marching as if leading a parade. Or driving sheep.

'Weaklings!' the Paladin bellowed. 'Run, you assorted pieces of filth! You are all being adjudicated! I have seen your faces! Smelled your foul breaths! Unclean, all of you! None of you shall escape my judgement!'

Noting Imid standing with the now-silent babe in his arms, Invett Loath pointed his sword at them. 'You are witness!'

Imid stared. In his arms, the babe stared. From the rooftop directly overhead, the squirrel stared.

In Invett's other hand was a handkerchief, which the Paladin used to wipe dried blood from his face. The man's eyes glittered, appallingly bright. 'Announce yourselves! Witnesses! Or suffer the fate of the Impure!'

'We witness!' Imid squealed. The babe wisely added a bubbling burble.

Triumphant, the Paladin of Purity marched on, driving his flock ever onwards.

Something near the Grand Temple was burning, smoke twisting and billowing in dark, almost black clouds.

A figure approached in the wake of Invett Loath, and Imid was startled to see Elas Sil, moving furtively towards him.

'Elas Sil!'

'Quiet, you fool! Did you see him? He's gone mad!' She paused. 'That baby's not yours!'

'I never said it was.'

'Then why are you holding it? Don't you know how dangerous that is? It might void, it might wail, or worst of all, thrash about!'

'Someone dropped it.'

'On its head?' She came closer and peered at it. 'That smudge – is that a bruise?'

'It might be—'

'By the Lady, is this a Saint? Imid, you have discovered the youngest Saint of Glorious Labour!'

'What? It's just a baby—'

'A Saint!'

'What labour? Babies don't work! Elas Sil, you've lost your senses!'

'Look at its face, you fool – it's working right now!'

Something warm squelched against Imid's lap, and then the stench struck him.

IN THE MEANTIME, THE MOB OF THE ADJUDICATED HAD GROWN. four hundred and twenty-six and counting, charging in a stampede up Greentongue Avenue. Whilst, on each side, down alleys and side streets, the riot spread like runny sewage.

A drover who had been leading thirty oxen to a seller's compound lost control of his terrified beasts. Moments later, they were thundering madly, straight into a number of heavily burdened wagons that had been backed up and were sitting directly beneath the Monument of Singe – an ancient solid brick edifice, twenty storeys tall, of dubious origin and unknown significance.

Loaded on to the beds of the wagons were caskets of jellied oil, which had been sweating out the entire day, forming a glistening patina on the sodden wood. Arto the Famous Fire Eater, whose fame had dwindled to pathetic ashes of late, was passing by at that moment. He had time to turn and see the wall-eyed oxen stampeding towards him, then was struck by a massive horned head, the impact throwing him back, the stoke-pot slung from his right shoulder wheeling outward, spraying its coals in all directions.

The subsequent explosion was heard and felt by every citizen in Quaint, and those crews out in the bay, throwing four-finned fish from their nets, looked up in time to see the skyward pitching fireball and at least three oxen cart-wheeling above the city, before the Monument of Singe dropped from sight and flames lit the dust clouds a gaudy orange.

BAUCHELAIN SLOWLY WIPED THE BLOOD FROM HIS KNIFE BLADE with a bleached cloth. He glanced down at Ineb Cough for a moment, then away, westward to where the sun was crawling down into its cave of night. Poised, like a figure in some heroic tapestry.

The demon was lying prone, trapped into immobility by the straits of the puppet's clothes.

'All right,' Ineb growled, 'cut me loose. But carefully!'

'You need have no concern there, demon,' Bauchelain said, crouching down and extending the dagger. 'However, if you continue to squirm . . .'

'I won't move, I promise!'

The brief flapping of wings announced the crow's return. A pungent, musty smell wafted over Ineb, then a second figure appeared at Bauchelain's side. A huge man, bald, his skin the tone and pallor of a hard-boiled and peeled egg, likely as clammy to the touch, as well. Small, flat eyes regarded the demon with cold curiosity.

Ineb tried a toothy smile. 'I know what you're thinking,' he said. 'But no. Not me. Not a homunculus. Not even a golem. I am a real demon.'

The man licked his flabby lips.

Ineb fell silent, mouth suddenly dry.

The tip of the dagger slipped beneath the demon's jacket just above Ineb's straining belly. Began slicing upwards.

Bauchelain lifted his other hand, offering his companion the bloodied cloth. 'The sun has set, Korbal Broach,' he said. A snip, and the jacket parted. The sorceror began working on the sleeves.

Korbal Broach took the cloth and held it to his face. He breathed deep, then, smiling, he turned away and walked off a short distance. He tossed the cloth down at his feet, made a few gestures in the air with his right hand, then faced Bauchelain and nodded.

'And the unclean ones, Korbal Broach?'

The man's round face pinched in disappointment, almost petulant.

'Ah, of course,' Bauchelain murmured. 'Forgive me, friend.'

Three more cuts and the clothes fell from Ineb. The demon clambered upright and drew in a savage, satisfied lungful of air. 'Excellent! Much better. I'm a new demon.'

Storkul Purge staggered over. 'I'm bleeding,' she said in a high, wavering voice.

Ineb sneered at her. 'He pricked your finger, woman!'

'I think I'm going to faint.'

Bauchelain sheathed his knife. 'Please, sit, Miss Purge. Ineb, pour the unwell Knight some wine.'

TUNIC SODDEN AND FOUL, IMID FACTALLO RAN DOWN THE street, Elas Sil at his side. The baby squirmed in his arms, but its expression was content.

Behind them, a long distance runner, returning from a six league sojourn out of the city and his mind understandably befuddled, ran into a burning building. And did not re-emerge. Panicked animals and frenzied citizens scampered in all directions through the smoke, sparks and ashes. The lamp-lighters had not appeared, leaving only the conflagrations in various districts of the city to fight against the encroaching darkness.

Elas clutched at Imid's arm and tugged. 'This way!' Down a narrow, winding alley.

'Don't hurt us!' A piping, squealing cry from somewhere up ahead.

They halted, looked round in the gloom.

'Leave us be!'

Imid Factallo edged forward, eyeing the two small figures lying in the rubbish two paces in front of him. Absurdly tiny, the both of them. On the left, a man, his skin a mass of wrinkles, like a golden fig. Beside him, a woman, tiny but nonetheless a woman in the adult sense, as if some perverted inventor had fashioned a breastly, slim-legged doll upon which to lavish sick fantasies.

'Bridges of the Abyss,' Elas Sil whispered. 'What are these?'

The wrinkled one said, 'I am Corpulence, known to my many friends as Nauseo Sloven. And my companion here is Sloth,

Senker Later by name. And do I smell something? Something . . . imminent? Enlivening? Oh yes I do. Can you smell it, Senker?'

'I can't be bothered to sniff.'

'Ah yes! Ennui returns . . . belatedly!'

Imid Factallo said, 'That smell would be baby turd.'

'Not that. Something else. Something . . . wonderful.'

Behind them, sudden shrieks sounded from the street.

'What was that?' Nauseo asked.

Elas Sil pulled Imid's arm again. 'Let's get out of here.'

They edged round the two demons.

'Where to?' Imid asked.

'Grand Temple. To hand the baby over to the nuns.'

'Good idea. They'll know what to do with it.'

In their wake, Nauseo Sloven crawled closer to the Demoness of Sloth. 'I'm feeling better, did you know that? Better. It's strange. Changes are coming to Quaint, oh yes.'

The screams came closer.

'We should run,' Senker said.

'Run? Why?'

'Oh, you're right. Why bother?'

EMANCIPOR REESE WALKED OUT OF THE THRONE ROOM. although, truth be told, it could hardly be called a throne room, unless an iron-framed, geared and pulley-strapped mechanism as large as a room could be called a throne.

Then again, why not? Was not the apparatus of state a repetition of balances, weight and counter-weights? Of course it was. Metaphorically. With the king in the middle, burdened by birthright and suspended within a structure founded upon the delusional notion of hierarchical superiority. As if inequality could be justified in the name of tradition and the underlying assumptions were self-evident and therefore unassailable. And was not this zeal for fanatical health an identical delusion of superiority, this time bound to moral tenets? As if vigour was innately virtuous?

Sadly, it was part of the sordid nature of humanity, Emancipor reflected as he walked down the wide, long colonnade, to concoct elaborate belief systems all designed to feed one's own ego. And to keep those with less obnoxious egos in check. An unending multitude of daggers to hold against someone else's throat—

Shattering glass scattered his thoughts. Glinting shards falling inward on either side of the grand corridor. Strange and ghastly shapes clambering free – the healthy dead – climbing out from their upright coffins, hands grasping, clutching at the air. Horrible moaning sounds issued from desiccated, ravaged throats, mouths gaping wide. Staggering free, their cries growing louder, more desperate.

Emancipor Reese stared, then he groaned, and muttered, 'Korbal Broach . . .'

A corpse reeled in front of him, its shrivelled eyes seeming to fix on Emancipor. It wasn't as far gone as many of the others, and strange fluids were weeping down its flaccid cheeks. The jaw worked for a moment, creaking, then it said, *'It's all a lie!'*

'What is?'

'We go. All of us. To the same place. The healthy, the sickly, the murderers, the saints! All the same, terrible place! Crowded, so crowded!'

The dead, Emancipor had long since discovered, rarely had anything good to say. But even then, no two ever said the same thing. He admitted to a growing fascination for the details of the innumerable private nightmares death delivered. 'What does it look like?' he now asked. 'This crowded place?'

'A giant market,' the corpse replied, fingers grasping at nothing. *'So much food. Treasures. So many . . . things!'*

'Well, that doesn't sound so bad.'

'But I have no money!' This, a rasping shriek, and the corpse clawed at its own face, then wheeled away, moaning. *'No money. No money. No money. Everybody else has money – even the murderers! Why not me? Oh, why not meeee?'*

Emancipor stared after it.

A dead woman staggered past, seeming to reach down and lift up invisible objects. *'This one's not mine!'* she wailed. *'This one isn't either! Oh, where is my baby? Whose babies are these? Oh! Oh!'* She moved on, picking up and discarding more invisible babies. *'They're all so ugly! Who's responsible for all these ugly babies?'*

The colonnade was filled with wandering corpses now, although there was a general, almost haphazard convergence towards the outer doors. Emancipor suspected they would soon begin seeking out their living loved ones, since that was what the undead usually did, given the chance. Driven to utter last regrets, spiteful accusations or maundering mewling. Mostly pathetic, and only occasionally murderous. Nonetheless, this was to be a night, Emancipor surmised, that few in Quaint would ever forget.

'ABYSS BELOW,' IMID FACTALLO WHISPERED, 'THAT MAN LOOKS decidedly unhealthy.'

Crouched in the shadows beside him, Elas Sil softly grunted, then hissed, 'That's because he's dead, you idiot!'

The figure, stump-like feet dragging, was making its irregular way across the plaza that sprawled before the formal entrance to the Grand Temple. The concourse was littered with rubbish and ominous puddles, but, apart from the lone undead, deserted. Somewhere behind the temple's rearing bulk, some buildings were on fire, and glowing smoke billowed in the night sky. Screams and shrieks of terror reached them from all sides, every street and alley, from tenements and residences.

'What has happened?' Imid asked in a tremulous voice.

'Try using that healthy brain of yours, fool,' Elas snapped. 'This is *our* fault. You and me, Imid Factallo.'

He blinked, then, eyes darting, he faced her. 'But it was all the saints, all of us! We were just the ones to deliver the coins!' He stared out again at the stumping corpse. 'They never said anything about, about, uh, raising the dead!'

'They're necromancers!'

'But how is this going to get rid of King Macrotus?'

'Hush! Are you mad? Not another word of that!'

Imid Factallo looked down at the baby, slumbering in his arms. 'By the Lady,' he whispered, 'what have we done? What life will this child find here?'

260

'Oh relax,' Elas Sil said, 'those corpses will fall apart eventually. Then we'll just pick up the pieces . . . and bury them somewhere.'

'Do you think,' Imid asked, oddly breathless, 'that *everyone* who was dead . . . ?'

Elas Sil eyed him sidelong. 'Got some secrets, have you?'

'No! Nothing like that. Only, well, there was Mother . . . I mean, I loved her dearly, of course. But, still . . .'

'Not charmed with the idea of seeing her again?' Elas gave him a particularly nasty smile, then snorted. 'Well, you think you've got problems. I pushed my husband down the stairs.'

Imid stared at her.

She laughed. 'Aren't we the perfect saints!'

He looked out into the plaza. 'Do you think – do you think he's out there?'

'Why wouldn't he be?'

'Why did you kill him?'

'He peed standing up.'

'What?'

She glared. 'It's messy, isn't it? I kept telling him to wipe the chute rim after. But did he? Never! Not once! Finally, well, I'd just had enough! Why are you looking at me like that? It was justifiable, a mercy killing, in fact. Imagine, being a man who can't aim! It must have been humiliating!'

'What, not peeing straight or never wiping up?'

'I had multiple arguments prepared, all sufficiently valid. Just in case the Guard got suspicious. But they weren't interested, not after I bribed them. This was in Necrotus's time, of course.'

'Of course.'

'Look, the way is clear. Let's go.'

They rose from their hiding place and scurried out on to the concourse.

INEB COUGH HOPPED FROM ONE LEG TO THE OTHER, EYES ON THE fires bathing the underside of smoke over the city. He shot Bauchelain a glance. 'I'm sensing hunger in there. The desire to . . . indulge!'

The sorceror nodded, his arms folded, and said, 'That would be the *un*healthy dead.'

Storkul Purge looked up with drunken suddenness. 'But there is no alcohol in Quaint! Not a drop! And no rustleaf or durhang! No whores, no gambling establishments!'

Bauchelain smiled his half-smile. 'My dear Knight, your naiveté is charming. How many floorboards are being pried up right now, I wonder? How many long-locked cellar doors are squealing open? And when the living see what their dead visitors have uncovered, all those well-hidden hoards, well, even a saint such as you will make the correct conclusions.'

Ineb Cough capered over to squat beside Storkul Purge. 'More wine?' he asked.

She held out her cup and Vice poured, careful not to spill a drop despite his burgeoning eagerness to return to Quaint's now or soon-to-be-delirious streets. When he was done he scampered away again, and noticed that Korbal Broach was nowhere to be seen, and indeed, Bauchelain was adjusting his cloak and examining the polish of his boots. 'Blessed sorceror,' Ineb said, 'are you going somewhere?'

The man regarded him a moment, then nodded. 'Oh yes. The time has come to enter your beloved city.'

Ineb jumped up and down. 'Excellent! Oh, it shall be such a fete! The living, the dead, everyone will be there!'

'Korbal Broach's work is done,' Bauchelain murmured. 'Now, mine begins . . .'

Ineb Cough leapt to the man's side. He did not want to miss this.

Storkul Purge tottered to her feet and stood, wobbling. 'Hurla's Brothel. It'll be re-opening for business. Hurla's dead, but that shouldn't matter. Much. Her clients won't know the difference. My room's still there – they'll be waiting for me. Oh, let's hurry!'

CLEARLY, EMANCIPOR OBSERVED, THE VEIL OF CIVILIZATION was thin indeed, so easily torn away to reveal depravity waiting beneath, waiting, as such things always did, for the first hint of turbulence. Even so, the burgeoning of anarchy was something to behold. The vast concourse fronting the palace was filled with figures, most of them dreadfully dead and in terrible states of decay. Which seemed little more than a minor inconvenience as they staggered about, waving dusty bottles in their bony hands, fluids leaking down their legs. One woman was sprawled on the palace steps, drawing rustleaf smoke in from a hookah, the smoke then swirling out through various rotted holes in her chest. A long-deceased prostitute chased an all-too-alive man through the crowds, demanding long overdue monies from some past transaction. His shrieks of remorse filled the air.

Citizens fought with dead relatives over possession of various indulgences, and in these cases the corpses usually fared worse, since the living were able to tear arms off and break brittle shins, which seemed an egregious thing to do to relatives, whether they deserved it or not. But now that the locks had been let loose on all manner of desires, the ensuing war was entirely understandable.

Still, Emancipor wondered as he stood at the top of the palace steps, it was all rather . . . sudden. The raising of the dead, healthy and unhealthy, should not have so easily triggered such a hedonistic conflagration. Had Bauchelain done something to add spice to the mix? Probably.

More buildings had caught fire, and the air was bitter with smoke and drifting ashes. He considered what to do next, then sat down on the rough stone. To stare out, bemused, on the macabre frenzy in the square.

INEB COUGH, BAUCHELAIN AND STORKUL PURGE STOOD ON THE road before the city gates, staring up at the row of impaled figures on the wall. Animated yet spiked in place, their legs jerked and kicked about, heels cracking against the battered stone.

'I have seen,' Bauchelain said, 'a dance, in a far land, much like this.'

'And are those dancers spiked to a wall, too?' Ineb asked.

'No, but they might as well have been. And indeed, as my man-servant might concur, they *should* have been.'

Ineb stared up at the row of kicking figures. Some had their hands on their hips. 'I see his point,' the demon said.

'Well,' Bauchelain sighed, 'there are no guards visible at the gate, suggesting that our entrance will not be challenged.' The necromancer set off towards the rubbish-strewn passage. Then halted. 'But first, I must fulfill a promise.' He looked up at the wall again. 'Ah, there he is.' A gesture, and Ineb Cough watched as one of the dancing corpses lifted clear of its impaling spike, then slowly drifted down, still kicking and with its hands on its hips.

The corpse's mouth opened wide. 'I can't stop!' it shrieked. 'Oh, help me stop this infernal dancing!'

The demon stared as what had once been King Necrotus finally settled on the road, and promptly pranced sideways into the ditch.

There was a thump and a flailing of limbs, then the deathly head rose into view, wobbling on its scrawny neck.

'Dear King,' Bauchelain said, 'you are free, and so I invite you to join us. We march into Quaint.'

The corpse scrambled upright and stood wavering. 'Good! Yes. I want that bastard's head! I want to rip it free and fling it into the air, then kick it down the street. Oh, let's visit my dear brother, yes, let's hurry!'

'It would seem,' Bauchelain said as he led the others through the gateway, 'that much of the present fabric of comportment has frayed in your city, King Necrotus, nay, torn asunder, and none of it through my doing. I am pleased to discover said evidence of my own cherished beliefs.'

'What?' Storkul Purge demanded drunkenly, 'are you talking 'bout?'

'Why, to transform the metaphor, that piety is but the thinnest patina, fashioned sufficiently opaque to disguise the true nature of our kind, yet brittle thin nonetheless.'

'Who cares about all that?' Necrotus demanded. 'I just want my throne back!'

'Ah, but will the citizens of your city accept the rule of an un-dead king?'

'They accept inbred brain-dead ones easily enough, sorceror,' Necrotus said in a rasping growl, 'so why not?'

'Well,' Bauchelain said, 'it is true enough that the common people delight in scandal when it comes to royalty. I suppose this could well qualify.'

They paused in the street just inside the gate. The citizens were out tonight, both breathing and breathless, trim and vigorous and decrepit and disintegrating. Hoarse shouts and ragged, pealing screams, wild laughter and the shattering of empty bottles. Fires raging against the night sky, smoke tumbling and billowing. And, Ineb Cough saw, all manner of dramas being played out before their eyes.

A dead artist pursued a gallery owner, demanding money in a

voice so whining and piteous that the demon felt compelled to kill the man a second time, not that it would do any good, but might well prove satisfying anyway. Even as Ineb considered setting off in pursuit, the two passed out of sight down a side street. Whilst from another a mob of mossy children – who'd clearly climbed out from some secret cemetery in someone's backyard – had found their murderer some time earlier and now marched into view, singing badly and waving about like trophies dismembered limbs. An odd detail that Ineb noted – the now torn apart murderer appeared to have been singular in having three arms, unless the children had grown careless, as children are wont to do, or perhaps did not know how to count very well. In any case, the urchins were happy and happy was good, wasn't it?

'This is sick,' Storkul Purge said after a time. 'I'm off to find my broth'l, where the sane people are.'

Bauchelain bowed slightly in her direction. 'Dear Well Knight, I thank you for your contribution to this night. I trust the wine has restored you?'

She blinked at him. 'Restored? Oh yes. Restored, enlivened, invigoratedly enstored, lively, even.' She then looked wildly about, meeting each set of eyes regarding her, fixing at last on the dead set. 'Oh, you're not well, are you?'

The desiccated face twisted. 'You just noticed?' Then Necrotus smiled. 'Actually, I like that. You're my kind of woman . . . I think . . . now.'

Storkul drew herself up. 'Just so you don't make any wrong assumptions,' she said haughtily, 'I don't come cheap.'

'Disgusting,' Ineb Cough murmured, 'but lovely.'

'Shall we proceed?' Bauchelain asked Necrotus, who twitched in answer, then nodded.

Storkul Purge staggered off, presumably towards her old brothel.

King Necrotus made a brief, spasmodic effort to comb down his overlong, snarled and bird-dropping-gummed hair, then set out in a lilting half-step, feet kicking out. 'Oh, I'm going to dance! All the way to the palace! Oh! How mortifying!'

The necromancer glanced over at Ineb Cough, brows lifting.

The demon nodded. 'Absolutely. I'm with you two. Wouldn't miss it, no sir, not a chance.'

'Actually,' Bauchelain said, 'I would you do something else for me.'

'Is it sordid?'

'Why, yes, I suppose it is.'

'All right, I'll do it.'

I MID FACTALLO, THE BABY AND ELAS SIL CAME TO WITHIN SIGHT of the Grand Temple of the Lady's sprawling front entrance, and all three stared owlishly at the scores of bodies lying on the broad steps leading up to the dais and its altar.

'There's been a slaughter,' Imid said in a quavering voice.

Elas grunted, then shook her head. 'Not necessarily. See any blood? I don't see any blood.'

'Well, it is rather dark—'

'No, even beneath those torch-stands.'

'No one's moving.'

'I'll grant you that – it's damned odd, is what it is. Come on, Imid, let's get closer.'

The two set out across the concourse. A tenement building two streets behind the temple was burning, showering sparks into the sky, making the Temple of the Lady a backlit silhouette that seemed sealed tight as a tomb, since no light was visible.

Snorting, Elas Sil said, 'Typical. Drawn up as if under siege, which, I suppose, they are. Guess we won't be hearing any eerie proclamations from the altar any time in the near future, eh? The goddess is likely cowering in some hole.'

'Shhh! By the Abyss, Elas, are you mad?'

'Mad? Yes, I am. Exceedingly mad.'

They approached the steps and the scatter of bodies, bodies that then began to stir at the sound of their voices. Heads lifting, bleary eyes fixing upon them. Imid and Elas halted, fell silent.

'She won't save us!' one woman gasped. 'Unhealthy people . . .
everywhere! Drink . . . and smoke – everywhere! Ah, I feel sick.
Just seeing them! Sick, nauseated, ill, unwell!'

'Sick, nauseated, ill, unwell!' a few others chanted.

Then they were all moaning the refrain. *'Sick, nauseated, ill,
unwell!'*

'Lady below,' Imid whispered, 'Do-gooders! And look, they're
withering before our eyes!'

'Remember our schooling as saints,' Elas said. 'Licentiousness,
when all about, is a plague. A deathly, devouring host of demons,
corrupting minds, bodies, souls. Licentiousness is the lurid escape
from natural misery, when natural misery is the proper path to
walk. Why? Because it is the only *honest* path.'

Imid stared at her. 'You didn't believe all that rubbish, did
you?'

'Of course not, but these people do.'

'And their convictions are killing them?'

'Precisely.'

'But that's insane!' Baby mewling in his arms, Imid Factallo
stepped forward. 'Hear me! I am a Saint! Listen to me, all of
you!'

The moaners fell silent, hopeful eyes gleaming in the firelight.

'Can't you see?' Imid demanded. 'Sobriety means clear-eyed,
and clear-eyed means you see the truth! You see just how unjust,
cruel, indifferent and ugly your life really is! You see how other
people are controlling you, every aspect of your miserable
existence, and not just controlling you – they're screwing you
over!'

Gasps and a single muted shriek answered Imid's careless
curse.

'You can't say that!' 'Foul, foul!' 'No no no, I don't want to
listen, no!'

The baby wailed.

'It's all lip-service!' Imid shouted. 'Nobody in charge really
gives a flying—'

'Silence!'

This last command was stentorian, ringing clear and loud from the temple's entrance. The do-gooders on the steps twisted round with cries of relief. Imid and Elas stared, as a grey-swathed nun marched up to stand to the right of the altar.

'It's the Stentorian Nun!' someone shouted.

The baby wailed again.

Imid's knees quivered as the grey woman stabbed an accusing finger at him. 'You!' she hissed.

'Me!' Imid answered instinctively.

'Decrier of false truths!'

Elas Sil said, 'What?'

'Blasphemer! Proclaimer of all that is Not to Be Known!'

'Well!' Imid shouted, suddenly, inexplicably emboldened, 'too late for *that*, isn't it?'

More gasps. Worse, a crowd was gathering in the concourse behind them. Dead and living both.

'Oh,' Elas said behind Imid, 'you're in for it, now.'

The nun lifted her arms out to the sides. 'Adjudication is demanded!' she cried out. 'The Lady of Beneficence shall speak! From her most Holy Altar, she shall speak!'

A strange, grinding noise came from the blockish stone beside the woman, then, a quavering voice, 'Do I smell baby?'

ONE SLAP AGAINST THE MASSIVE, FLABBY CHEEK, THEN another, and another and another and—

'Stop! Please! Don't hurt me!'

'Nauseo? You awake?'

Bleary, sated eyes blinked up, the woeful expression dwindling away, to be replaced by a scowl. 'Ineb Cough. What are you trying to do, kill me?'

'I was trying to wake you!'

'Was I asleep? Not surprising, you know. I'm filled to bursting – what a night! So unexpected!'

Ineb Cough was standing on the Demon of Corpulence's chest, or he thought he was – might have been just the left breast, since Nauseo Sloven had burgeoned to fill the entire alley, flesh piled up against either wall, more flesh sprawling and tumbled down to just short of the alley-mouth. 'Even so,' Ineb said, loosing a beery belch, 'I need you up and around. We've a journey to make.'

'A journey? Where?'

'Not far, I promise.'

'I can't. It'll be too hard. I'm ready to explode – gods, where did all that greed come from?'

Ineb squatted down and scratched his pocked jaw. 'All pent up, I suppose. Hiding, lurking. As for the food, well, seen any dogs in the streets? Cats? Horses? Me neither. The night's been a blood-bath, and it's not even half done. Who could have imagined all this?'

'What's happened, then?' Nauseo asked.

'Someone in the city's gone and hired two necromancers, Nauseo, to bring down this reign of terror.' He pulled at his nose, which was itchy and runny with all the powder stuffed into it. 'Seems they've made quite a start.'

'Necromancers?'

'Yes. One of them's a conjurer and binder of demons, too, which makes me very nervous. Nervous, Nauseo, oh yes. Even so, he's yet to try for me, which I take as a good sign, weak as I was back then.'

'No worries now, though, is there?' Nauseo shifted slightly and mounds of flesh rumbled and rolled beneath Ineb. 'We're too strong, now. There's not a binder alive who could take us, emboldened as we now are.'

'I expect you're right. So, it does seem as if these necromancers are staying true to their word. Pluck Macrotus from his throne, prop someone less horrible in his place, and Quaint returns to its normal, sane, decrepit state. Might even be Necrotus himself – the other one raised him, you know.'

'Oh, joy!'

'Anyway, we've got to go. Have you seen Sloth lately?'

'Why, she was here earlier—'

From somewhere below, came a faint moan.

THOSE AMONG THE DENIZENS STILL CAPABLE OF MOTION HAD moved on by the time Emancipor Reese spied Bauchelain, his master slowly walking with hands clasped behind his back, pausing every now and then for a word or two with various crippled dead and undead citizens, as he made his casual way towards the palace steps where sat the manservant.

Bauchelain peered up at Emancipor. 'Is King Macrotus within?'

Emancipor nodded. 'Oh yes, he's not going anywhere.'

'I was in the company of King Necrotus,' the necromancer said, looking round, 'but it would seem we have become separated – there was a mob . . . well, the details aren't relevant. I take it, Mister Reese, that you have not been accosted by a corpse intent on entering the palace?'

'Afraid not, Master.'

'Ah, I see. I am curious, has it struck you, Mister Reese, that events have quickened with a decidedly rapacious pace?'

'From the time that Invett Loath charged out of this building behind me, the whole city seems to have lost its mind.'

'Invett Loath?'

'The Paladin of Purity, Master. Lord of the Well Knights. I am afraid . . .' Emancipor hesitated, 'well, uh, I loaned him a kerchief. He'd bloodied his nose, you see. It was just common courtesy, how can I be blamed for that? I mean—'

'Mister Reese, please stop. I so dislike babbling. If I understand

275

you, one of your many kerchiefs is now in the hands of this Paladin. And this is, in your mind, in some way significant.'

'Master, do you recall that D'bayang field we passed through, oh, five, six days past?'

Bauchelain's eyes narrowed. 'Go on, Mister Reese.'

'Well, the buds were open, yes? They call 'em poppies but they aren't really poppies at all, as I am sure you know. Anyway, the air filled with spores—'

'Mister Reese, the air was not filled with spores, provided one remained on the road. As I recollect, however, there was some tumult, in your mind, at least, that resulted in you running madly through that field – with a kerchief covering your nose and mouth.'

Emancipor's face reddened. 'Korbal Broach asked me to carry that woman's lungs, the ones he took that morning – Master, they were still breathing!'

'A small favour, then—'

'Forgive me, Master, but it wasn't small in my eyes! Granted, it was unseemly, my horror and the ensuing panic. I admit it. But anyway. As you know, I so dislike enlivening alchemies – stupor and oblivion, yes, of course, at every opportunity. But enlivening, such as comes from D'bayang poppies? No. I despise that. Hence, the kerchief.'

'Mister Reese, the kerchief you loaned the Paladin was not the one filled with D'bayang spores?'

'Alas, Master, it was. I'd meant to wash it, but—'

'The Paladin was afflicted?'

'I believe so. Of a sudden, zealousness overcame him.'

'Possibly leading to . . . indiscriminate adjudication?'

'That's one way of putting it, aye.'

Bauchelain stroked his beard. 'Extraordinary. The guise of reasonableness, Mister Reese, permits all manner of intolerance and indeed, pernicious attack. Once that illusion is torn away, however, the terror of oppression becomes a random act, perhaps indeed an all-encompassing one.' He paused, tapped one side of his nose with a long finger, then remorselessly continued, 'That chest of coins rightly belongs to you, Mister Reese. Raising the dead? Entirely unnecessary, as it turns out. All that was required was a single, subtle push, at the hands of an innocent, somewhat naïve manservant.'

Emancipor stared at the necromancer, desperate to refute the charge, to deny all culpability, yet unable to speak. In his mind, a risible refrain: *no, not me, no, no, it wasn't me. It was him. Who him? Anyone him! Just not me! No, not me, no, no . . .*

'Mister Reese? You have lost all colour. Did I mention that I have not before seen your eyes so clear, the whites veritably startling? It is a force of nature that draws all things down to the earth. I therefore imagine the flow of a multitude of toxins now swelling your poor feet. They must, I fear, be bled. Thoroughly. Of course, now is not the time – no, make no entreaties otherwise, Mister Reese. Now, if you please, lead me to King Macrotus.'

Emancipor frowned, then blinked. Feet? Bleeding? Macrotus? 'I am happy to lead you to Macrotus, Master, and you may speak to him all you like, I am sure, although I suspect it won't do much good.'

'I rarely speak in order to do good, Mister Reese. Now, shall we be on our way?'

INVETT LOATH HAD NEVER FELT MORE ALIVE, SO ALIVE IT WAS killing him, but that was fine since it seemed he was doing a fair share of killing himself, if the blood smeared on his sword was any indication, and he was reasonably certain that it was indeed fairly indicative that he had been practicing holy adjudication upon the unwholesome unwashed cretins who dared consider themselves worthy citizens of Quaint, adjudication that was only proper, as was his right, nay his obligation as the Paladin of Purity, the Paladin of Perfection, leading the vanguard of vigour to their healthy, thankful deaths, and if he and his blessed vanguard trod on a few babies, toddlers and weak-boned old folk along the way, well, there was nothing to be done for that, was there, not when the cause was just, so just it blinded like the sun's own fire, all-consuming, scouraging the meat from the bones and yes, he was sure scouraging was a proper word and why shouldn't it be, was he not the Paladin of Proper, he most certainly was and look! the night's still young, exceedingly bright, in fact, given all those burning hovels and their burning denizens, none of whom deserved a less sordid, less scorching death because adjudication came in all forms, in all sizes including ratty blankets swaddling shrieking undeniably irritating whelps all laid out plump and yummy by the nuns who might well be pretty behind those veils who could tell not that such thoughts were acceptable, they being nuns and all, and he the Paladin of Probity marching down this street of flame was there not some cavern in the underworld that was nothing but fire and torment, maybe not but there should be, as far as Invett Loath was concerned, some preserved place of eternal pain just for all those unhealthy turds badly clothed in human skin, the fires could crinkle it back, rupturing the meat beneath, and how they would writhe and spit and heave up vile fluids in an endless torrent of foul toxins and all the flesh would tumble out, fold upon fold, gelatinous and pocked with big, suppurating pores, the flesh filling the street and how was he to get past this? By the Lady, it lived!

'Oomph!' the massive body gusted at the sudden impact.

Invett Loath's wild charge was brought short. He plunged into flabby folds, then popped back out to land on his backside, blinking water from his eyes, fresh blood streaming down from his swollen nose.

'That hurt!' a piping squeal.

The Paladin leapt to his feet, cloth at his face. He could get around this! He had a sword. Cut, cut and dice and chop and cleave and hack in twain! With a roar, Invett Loath raised his blade high.

Twenty-odd paces away, the barrel-sized, misshapen blob that was Nauseo Sloven's sweaty face, spread out to the sides and above and below in a expression of terror, the tiny eyes widening and bulging sufficient to push away the puffy flesh, and the demon screamed.

And flinched back, narrowly avoiding the descending sword.

Iron rang on cobbles.

Panicked, Nauseo Sloven lunged forward, heaving his mass to grapple with the Paladin before he could swing again. Stretched, oily skin slimed over Invett Loath in a desperate embrace. Pores sprouting curly hairs, the flesh around them enflamed and raised up like tiny volcanoes, pressed indiscriminately against the struggling Paladin, squirting volcanically foul juices.

Nauseo's arm drew inward once again, dragging the squirming figure into his right armpit.

Where all manner of horrors resided.

Invett Loath could not breathe. But he didn't need to breathe!

He was the Paladin of – of – he was asphyxiating! Swallowed in fleshy darkness, matted hairs like worms sliding across his face, pimples bursting, a crevasse of skin spreading to smear years-old greasy dirt across his lips – oh, the taste, what was it? What did it remind him of? Yoghurt?

Yoghurt. Invett Loath's last conscious word, sobbing dreadful in his mind.

'GIVE ME THAT BABY!'

Imid Factallo flinched back at that reptilian hiss. In his arms, the babe fell silent, eyes suddenly wide as it stared up at the saint.

'Give it to me!'

Imid looked across at the Stentorian Nun. Their public debate had collapsed into a ruin of vicious insults which, while entertaining to the crowd, were otherwise worthless. One rather strange consequence of the exchange was that the nun's clothing had become dishevelled. Even her veil had begun to sag at one corner, revealing half of the hate-twisted mouth.

In which Imid now saw pointy teeth. He stabbed out an accusatory finger. 'She's got filed teeth! She wants my baby! *She's a cannibal!*'

Mobs were unpredictable beasts, particularly after a night of unspeakable trauma. Among this one could be found mothers who had lost their young ones to the Temple, to nuns just like this one. With her hungry snarl and shark-like teeth. The shouted proclamation from Imid Factallo required a moment of stunned silence in which to do its work, time sufficient for various terrible details to fall in line.

Then – screams, a surge of vengeful humanity, grasping hands, ugly animal sounds.

The nun bleated and made to flee.

She did not get far.

A horrifying scene ensued, Imid Factallo's witnessing thereof cut short when Elas Sil used both hands to pull him away, round to the other side of the altar, then stumbling onwards towards the temple doors. Seeing their destination, Imid pulled back. 'No! Not in there!'

'You idiot!' Elas Sil hissed. 'Those teeth weren't filed! They were rotten! Just stumps! That woman *slurps* her meals, Imid! Understand me?'

He looked back, and saw very little left of the Stentorian Nun. 'I could have sworn they were pointed—'

'They weren't!'

'Then . . . baby soup!'

'Oh now, really!' They approached the doors, and Elas Sil added, 'Mind you, what a great way to close a debate. I'll have to remember that one.'

'They looked pretty pointy to me,' Imid persisted in a grumble.

Elas Sil grasped the iron ring and tugged.

To their surprise the door swung open. They peered into the gloom. An empty chamber, longer than it was wide, the ceiling arched and sheathed in gold leaf, and no one about.

'Where is everyone?' Imid wondered in a whisper.

'Let's find out,' Elas Sil said.

They crept into the Grand Temple.

KING NECROTUS THE NIHILE WAS FEELING DECIDEDLY UNWELL. For one, his left arm had fallen off. And he'd found bats nesting in his crotch. They'd fled, thankfully, some time during his frenetic dancing on the wall. Even so, the little claws from which they had hung were sharp, and now that brittle sensation raced through his withered flesh, sensation so painfully reawakened, he found certain parts aching abominably.

Stumbling over his own arm was an unexpected development. One moment swinging amiably at his side, the next fouling his feet, resulting in a face-flat fall that broke something in his jaw, where things now rattled loose whenever he turned his head. All of this in consequence to his panicked flight from that mob, a mob that had been perniciously hunting down the dead and tearing them apart. Base prejudices hid beneath even the most placid of surfaces, which came as little surprise to the king known as the Nihile, but had proved inconvenient nonetheless.

And now he was lost. In his own city. Hopelessly lost.

There were no burning buildings nearby, and so he stumbled along in darkness, right arm tucked under his left (the Royal Seamstress could do wonders, assuming she still lived), in search of a familiar landmark.

Unexpected, therefore, the strange transformation of the street he walked down, the sudden swirling of mists, the leaden smear of sky, and the massive arched gate appearing at the far end, a gate composed entirely of bones, from which a hunched, scrawny figure hobbled into view.

Necrotus halted twenty paces from the figure, who also stopped, leaning heavily on a gnarled cane. The figure then lifted a skeletal hand, and beckoned.

Overwhelming compulsion tugged at Necrotus and he found himself slowly drawn forward. 'Who are you?' he hissed.

Hooded head cocked to one side. 'The Lord of Death? Harvester of Souls? The Bony Fisherman who casts his all-encompassing net?' A sigh. 'No, just one of his minions. Have I not great potential? I keep saying so, but does he ever listen? No, never. I keep the path swept clean, don't I? Polish the skulls of the Gate, yes? Look at them – blinding, even the teeth are entirely devoid of tartar! I am no slouch, no sir, not in the least!'

Necrotus struggled to escape, yet watched, in horror, as his feet were dragged forward, one then the other, again and again, closer to that dread gate. 'No! I've been raised! You can't have me!'

The minion grunted. 'Korbal Broach. One abominable act after another, oh we despise him, yes we do. Despise and more, for I am tasked to pursue him. To capture him. That must mean something! Great potential, and so I must prove my worth. I have gathered a legion – all of Korbal Broach's victims – and we will find him, oh yes, find him!'

'Go away!' Necrotus cried.

The minion started. 'What?'

'Go away! I hate you! I'm not going through that infernal gate!'

In a small voice, 'You . . . *hate* me?'

'Yes!'

'But what have I ever done to you?'

'You're compelling me to walk through that gate!'

'Don't blame me about that! I am only doing my job. It's nothing personal—'

'Of course it's personal, you scrawny idiot!'

'Oh, you're all the same! I drag you out of your miserable existence, and are you ever grateful? No, not once! You and your precious beliefs, your host of conceits and pointless faiths! Your elaborate self-delusions seeking to cheat the inevitable. And you hate me? No, I hate you! All of you!' With that the minion spun round and hobbled stiffly back through the gate.

There was a loud slam and the scene in front of Necrotus dissolved, revealing the slightly more familiar street of Quaint he had been stumbling down earlier. He stared about, bewildered. 'He . . . he didn't want me!' Well, that was good, wasn't it? Then why did he feel so . . . offended?

King Necrotus the Nihile resumed walking. He still needed to find out precisely where he was.

A double thump at his feet. He halted and stared down. Two arms were lying on the cobbles. 'Shit.'

Then his head rolled off, left temple crunching hard on the stones, his vision tumbling wildly.

Oh, this was not going well at all.

BAUCHELAIN HAD CLIMBED INTO THE APPARATUS, DEFTLY ducking rocking levers and edging round ratcheting gears until he was next to King Macrotus.

Standing near the spilled supper left on the floor by the servant, Emancipor Reese watched with reluctant admiration. The necromancer was not one for exercise, yet remained lean and lithe, ever in fighting form on those rare occasions when sorcery, guile, deceit and back-stabbing failed. Physically, he looked to be about sixty, albeit a fit sixty, yet he moved with a dancer's grace. The result of good living? Possibly. More likely alchemy.

'Well, Master?' the manservant called. 'How many days, do you think?'

Bauchelain leaned forward for a closer examination. 'At least two weeks,' he said. 'I believe his heart burst. Sudden and indeed catastrophic.' The necromancer glanced back. 'How did you know?'

Emancipor shrugged. 'He wasn't eating.'

Bauchelain made his way back. 'Proponents of vigorous exercise are mostly unaware,' the sorceror said, 'that exercise as a notion, discrete from labour, is a gift of civilization, derived from tiered social status and the leisure time thus afforded. True labourers care nothing for exercise, naturally.' He stepped cleared of the clanking, wheezing apparatus, paused to brush dust from his cloak. 'Accordingly, one salient fact that labourers well know, but appears to be lost on those who fanatically exercise, is that the body, its organs, its muscles and its bones, will inevitably wear out. I believe, Mister Reese, that, for example, there are a set number of beats of which a heart is capable. In similar manner all muscles and bones and other organs are allotted a specific limit to their functioning.' He gestured grandly back at the labouring corpse of King Macrotus the Overwhelmingly Considerate. 'To hasten one's own body to those limits is, to my mind, the highest folly.'

Emancipor grunted. 'Master, I really need to get out of this city.'

'Ah, that would be withdrawal.'

They stared at each for a moment.

Then Bauchelain cleared his throat. 'One last task awaits me. Given the unexpected turn of events this night, Mister Reese, I believe your tasks within Quaint are done. Thus, I grant you leave to, uh, leave.'

'I can't thank you enough, Master.'

'No matter. One final thing. Can you give me directions to the Grand Temple of the Lady of Beneficence?'

'Of course, Master.'

ARM IN ARM WITH REVELLERS AND IN THE MIDST OF A BAWDY, drunken crowd, the Demon of Vice staggered into the vast, seething mob filling the concourse fronting the Grand Temple. He was singing, at the top of his voice, a song he had never heard before. Life was wonderful, again, and this was a night Ineb Cough would not forget in a long while. Or not remember at all. It didn't matter which.

They stumbled over pieces of corpses, many of them still eager to party, if the twitching and writhing of dismembered limbs was any indication. A number of tenement fires had leapt closer to the temple, bathing it in lurid light. Near the steps was the mass of putrescent but doggedly throbbing flesh that was the Demon of Corpulence. He was surrounded by impromptu feasting, huge slabs of undercooked, dripping meat making the rounds, greasy smeared faces splashed with the light of rapture, and people were being sick everywhere, unaccustomed as they – well, no, Ineb corrected himself – they were sick with excess, glorious excess.

He saw Sloth being carried in atop a score of hands. Seeing Ineb Cough, she managed a faint white-gloved wave.

So, all were gathered, and need only await their brilliant saviour, Bauchelain, on his way to pronounce upon the city its fate. Ineb was delirious with anticipation.

'SWEETIES, I'M HERE!' STORKUL PURGE SPREAD HER ARMS OUT to her sides and held the gesture. Before her, in the Orgy Room on the top floor of Hurla's Brothel, shapes moved about in the gloom. Lots of shapes, she realized, all seemingly on their hands and knees. A good sign. In fact, judging from the grunting and squeaking, lots of good signs.

Except, of course, for the smell.

One figure rose up hesitantly before her.

Tragically, her eyes had begun to adjust to the darkness. 'What is all that smeared on you?' she demanded.

A wavering voice, 'Keeps them happy, you see.'

'Who?'

'Why,' the little man gestured behind him, 'my pigs, of course.'

Pigs? By the Abyss, they *were* pigs! 'But this is a brothel! Worst, this is the third floor! What are all these disgusting animals doing here when I wanted the *normal* disgusting animals!'

'I'm hiding them, of course! Everyone has gone mad! They want to slaughter all my beauties, but I won't let them! Who'd look on the top floor of a brothel? Why, no one! No one but you, and you're not here to lead my pigs to slaughter . . . are you?'

She considered for a long moment, then slowly lowered her arms, and sighed. 'Fine, I'll just hold my breath. Get undressed, old man, this one's on the house.'

'I—I can't do that! They'll get jealous!'

Too much pent-up frustration by far. Storkul Purge screamed.

289

WANDERING BEMUSED IN THE SUBTERRANEAN CHAMBERS and corridors beneath the temple, Imid Factallo, his baby and Elas Sil could all hear the roaring from somewhere overhead. Ominous, as if a terrible slaughter was taking place in the city's streets. Or so they believed, since their last sight of the above world had been the horrid death of the Stentorian Nun.

Yet here, below, there was naught but silence. Where were the nuns? The confiscated children? They had found no one, no one at all.

'Shh!' Elas Sil's hand clutched his arm.

'I didn't say anything!'

'Shhh!'

Now, close by, a gentle murmuring of voices. They were standing in a corridor. Before them was a T-intersection, with a door directly opposite them. Faint lantern light leaked from its seams, musty with scented oils.

Elas pulled him along, up to the door.

'This is it,' Imid whispered.

She looked across at him.

'Where they prepare the babies,' Imid explained, his heart thudding hard in his chest. He licked his lips, his mouth suddenly terribly dry. 'They lead them in by the hand, the smiling nuns. Then *whack*! Down comes the cleaver! Chop chop, bones into the cauldron, some old hag stirring with a huge iron ladle, spittle hanging from her toothless mouth. All those tiny voices, silenced forever!' He stared down at the slumbering child in his arms. 'We've come to the wrong place, Elas!'

'You've gone mad! You sound like . . . like a *parent*!'

And she flung open the door.

Light spilled over them.

A sea of faces. Cherubic faces, countless children of all ages.

All of whom cried out, 'Inside, quick! Oh, shut the door!' More of a cacophony of voices, truth be told, but both Imid and Elas comprehended those two commands at the very least.

They stumbled into the domed chamber.

And the door was slammed shut behind them.

Children rushed forward upon seeing the swaddled baby. 'Ooh! Another one! He? She? Is it well? Not sick yet, oh blessed Lady, not yet sick!'

Imid recoiled slightly at the upwards grasping hands. 'Get away, you horrid creatures! Sick? No one's sick! No one, I tell you!'

'What,' Elas Sil demanded, 'are you all doing here?'

'We are being well!'

'Well what?'

A slightly older girl stepped forward. 'We're being protected. From the outer world, that horrible, dirty, sickly place!'

'Sickly?' Elas repeated bemusedly. 'What do you mean?'

'There are foul things out there – things that will make us sick. Animals, to make us sick! Flies, birds, bats, mice, rats, all diseased and waiting to make us sick! And people! Coughing, snivelling, wiping themselves everywhere! There are wayward fumes, emanating from anuses and worse. And wagons that might run us over, stairs we might fall down, walls we might walk into. You must join us, here, where it's safe!'

'And healthy,' another piped up.

'What's it like?' a third child asked.

Elas Sil blinked. 'What is what like?'

'The world?'

'Stop that, Chimly!' the first girl scolded. 'You know that curiosity is deadly!'

Someone in the crowd coughed.

Everyone swung round, and the first girl hissed, '*Who did that?*'

'Now!' Imid shouted. And, thankfully, Elas Sil understood. In unison they turned and scrabbled at the door latch.

Behind them: 'Look! They're getting away!'

Then the door was open, and the two saints with their charge fled out into the corridor.

'Get them!'

They ran.

King Necrotus the Nihile was seeing things from a new angle. Sideways, slightly upside-down. He had tried locomotion by wiggling his ears, but the effect had been meagre. Clearly, his facial and scalp muscles weren't designed to aid in the physical transportation of his head. That's what the body normally attached to it did. It had been a pathetic conceit.

A large polished boot stepped into his view.

'Hello?' Necrotus called up.

The boot shifted, then the heel drew upwards and a hand settled on the king's head, tilting it to one side. Necrotus found himself looking up at a crouching Bauchelain.

'Abyss averted!' the king sighed in relief. 'I am so glad you found me. Can you see my body? It's the one without any arms – and no head, naturally. It can't have gone far . . . can it?'

Bauchelain collected Necrotus in both hands and straightened. There was something oddly disturbing about the necromancer's expression as he studied the king.

'Am I speaking only in my head?' Necrotus asked. 'Uh, as it were. I mean, can you hear me?'

'I can hear you fine, King Necrotus,' Bauchelain replied after a moment, angling the head this way and that.

'Just a little off the top?' the king asked in a half-snarl.

'I have,' Bauchelain said, 'a glass case that would fit you nicely.'

'You wouldn't!'

'Yes, a nice fit indeed. Well, this is a bonus, isn't it?'

'That's diabolical!'

'Why yes, thank you.'

Necrotus was tucked under Bauchelain's left arm, affording him a jostling view of the street they now walked down. The king was furious, but there was little he could do about it. Oh, his kingdom for a body! 'You'll keep it wiped clean, won't you?'

'Of course, King Necrotus,' Bauchelain replied. 'Ah, I see the edges of a crowd. I believe we approach the Grand Temple.'

'And what are we going to do there?'

'Why, a grand unveiling to close this fell night.'

'IT'S A TUNNEL OF SORTS,' IMID FACTALLO SAID.

'I can see that,' Elas Sil snapped.

'We've no choice. I can hear those terrifying little whelps.'

'I know I know! All right, I'll lead, and close that panel behind us.'

They had stumbled on the secret passage only because someone had left the small door wide open. From somewhere up the corridor behind them came the dread, blood-curdling sounds of excited children.

Imid followed Elas into the tunnel's narrow confines, then twisted about to tug the panel back in place. Sudden darkness.

'By the Lady's never-sucked teats!'

'Elas Sil!'

'Oh shut up! I'm a woman, I can curse about things like that. Wait, it's not as dark up ahead. Come on, and hasn't that baby of yours been asleep a long time? You sure it's not dead?'

'Well, it peed on me halfway down that last corridor, and last I looked it was smiling.'

'Huh. It ever amazes me women get talked into motherhood.'

'Talked into it? Don't be ridiculous, Elas. They're desperate for it!'

'Only once and that once is the first time.'

'I don't believe you.'

'I don't care what you believe. You're a man, after all. All I know is, I happen to value a full night's sleep a lot more than flinging another urchin into this all-too-crowded city, then sagging everywhere as my only reward. No thanks. I intend to stay pert forever.'

'I'm pretty sure it doesn't work that way,' Imid said.

'You've only your mother for comparison and she had you, didn't she?'

'So how come you don't get pregnant – I mean, what we did this afternoon—'

'Willpower. Look, it's getting lighter – there's some kind of room up ahead.'

'Hear all that noise above us? Something awful's happening in the concourse, Elas Sil – and it seems we're getting closer to it, or maybe it's getting closer to us.'

'Abyss below, Imid, do you ever stop moaning?'

They clambered out into a strange circular room, the floor set with pavestones except in the middle, where rested a single slab of polished wood that shifted beneath them, as if unanchored. The domed ceiling was barely high enough for them to kneel any-where but in the middle, and it turned out the extra room in the centre came from a square shaft leading straight up, as far as they could see. Off to one side sat a lantern, burning out the last of its oil. The room smelled of sweat.

'Now what?' Imid asked.

'Put that damned baby down,' Elas Sil said, oddly breathless.

Imid adjusted the blanket's folds, then gently laid the baby to one side, on to the pavestones. It cooed, then rolled on to its side and spat up. Briefly. Once done, it settled on to its back once more, closed its eyes and was asleep. Imid backed away.

The lantern dimmed, then winked out.

Hot skin – arms, thighs – 'Elas!' Imid gasped as he was pulled round. 'Not in front of the baby!'

But she wasn't listening.

THE NECROMANCER HAD THAT CERTAIN QUALITY, INEB COUGH reflected, to clear a path before him, seemingly effortless and without a word spoken. Sounds died away, as if Bauchelain was a pebble of silence flung into a loud pond. A pond filled with loud fish, that is. Perhaps. In any case, Ineb marvelled at the way things got quiet as Bauchelain, an extra head tucked under one arm, made his way to the temple steps and ascended to the platform, positioning himself to the left of the altar as he faced the now rapt crowd.

The necromancer cocked his head (his own, the one atop his shoulders) for a moment, and Ineb Cough felt a subtle outflow of sorcerous power – power of such terrible magnitude that the Demon felt his knees weaken beneath him. For all his confidence, and Nauseo Sloven's, it was now clear that Ineb, Corpulence and Sloth were as babes before this man. 'He could take us,' the Demon of Vice whimpered, a bottle of wine falling from his hand to crash on the cobbles. 'He could bind us and not raise a single bead of sweat in the effort. Oh. Oh no.'

Bauchelain raised his right hand and a sudden hush descended upon the massed citizens in the concourse. Under his left arm, King Necrotus's head faced outward as well, bizarre grimacing expressions writhing on its withered features. The necromancer spoke, 'People of Quaint, hear me! You have, until this night, been the victims of a terrible deceit. Said deceit will be revealed to you here, and now.' That upraised hand then slowly closed into a fist.

A muted scream from . . . somewhere, and nowhere.

A figure blurred into being directly beneath Bauchelain's hand.

Ineb Cough started. 'That!' he shouted. 'That's Lust! The Demoness of Lust! That's Agin Again!'

The voluptuous, naked woman, bound in place by Bauchelain's conjuring, shrieked in terror.

'An imposter!' the necromancer bellowed. 'Hiding in the guise of the Lady of Beneficence! Do you think Lust thrives only in matters of sex and sordid indulgences? If so, my friends, you are wrong! Lust is born of obsession! Obsession begets zealotry! Zealotry breeds deadly intolerance! Intolerance leads to oppression, and oppression to tyranny. And tyranny, citizens of Quaint, leads to—'

'The end of civilization!' a thousand voices roared.

Lust cried, 'I'm sorry! I'm sorry! I didn't mean it!'

'Indeed,' Bauchelain said in response to the crowd's proclamation, ignoring Agin Again, who now wept unconvincingly. 'And so,' the necromancer continued, 'wisdom returns to Quaint. Your faith had been subverted, twisted into hateful fanaticism. But of that, no more need be said. It does grieve me, alas, to inform you now of the death of King Macrotus.' He shook his head. 'No, not by my hand. He is dead of exercise. And has been for some time. Alas, he could not be here to tell you himself, for the chamber where his body resides is warded, and so he cannot be raised. But it would do you all well to pay a visit to his Royal chamber. Consider it a worthy shrine to ever remind you of the deadly lure of lustful activity left unrestrained.'

He paused then, looking about, studying the upturned faces, then nodded as if to himself. 'Citizens, I shall now proclaim your new rulers. Worthy individuals indeed, iconic representations of all that is proper, individuals you will be delighted to emulate in all matters of behaviour and comportment.' Another gesture, and

Agin Again was suddenly released. Wailing, she leapt upright, then fled.

From the altar came a heavy grinding sound.

Bauchelain half-turned, twitched a finger and the altar rose into the air.

In time to reveal, rising from a subterranean platform, Quaint's new king and queen.

Locked into a most amorous embrace and momentarily oblivious to their own arrival, so intent was their missionary zeal.

A draft such as is common during the night alerted them to the change of venue. And two heads lifted clear, looked out dumbly upon the vast crowd.

Who stared back in shocked silence.

Then went wild.

T HE SUN WAS CLEAR OF THE HORIZON BY THE TIME BAUCHELAIN returned to the wagon and the camp on the hill outside the smoke-wreathed city.

Emancipor watched him from a low to the ground, sideways perspective, lying as he was on his back with his bared feet propped high against the side of a wagon wheel.

The necromancer was carrying a head under one arm, and he strode up to the manservant. 'Dear Mister Reese, may I ask, what are you doing?'

'It's the toxins, Master. I'm draining my feet. No need for bleeding, no, no need at all.'

'I can see by the murky cast of your eyes,' Bauchelain said, 'that such medical intervention would be pointless in any case.'

'True enough,' Emancipor replied.

Bauchelain strode to the back of the wagon, and Emancipor heard him rummaging about for a time. After a moment, he reappeared with a glass case that Emancipor had never seen before. 'Now, Mister Reese, assuming your feet are now cleansed, as best as they can be, might I suggest you prepare to break our fast?'

Emancipor lowered his legs and struggled upright. 'Gods below,' he swore, 'my legs have gone numb.' Even so, he managed to hobble over towards the hearth, which was still smouldering. 'I have mulled wine, Master. Shall I pour you a cup?'

'Hmm? Yes, excellent idea. And for yourself as well.'

'Thank you, Master.' Emancipor paused to light his pipe. 'Ah, much better,' he said, blowing smoke. Cut short by a hacking cough, forcing him to launch a slimy ball of stuff into the fire, where it flared into strangely hued flames for a moment before sizzling in the more expected manner. Emancipor stuck the pipe back between his teeth and puffed merrily as he poured the wine.

A flutter of wings nearby announced the arrival of Korbal Broach. The crow hopped over to watch as Bauchelain set King Necrotus's head inside the glass case, then placed the container on the buckboard. The king looked to be talking, but no sound issued forth, for which Emancipor was thankful.

The manservant rose and handed Bauchelain a cup. 'A toast, Master?'

'A toast? Well, why not? Please, proceed, Mister Reese.'

Emancipor raised his cup. 'The Healthy Dead!'

Bauchelain almost smiled. Almost, but not quite, which was about as much as Emancipor had expected. 'Indeed,' the necromancer said, raising his own cup, 'The Healthy Dead.'

In the glass case, King Necrotus smiled broadly, as the dead are wont to do.

INTRODUCTIONS

Stephen R. Donaldson, James Barclay and Paul Kearney
on Steven Erikson's Bauchelain and Korbal Broach stories.

These three stories were first published in collectors' limited
editions by Peter Crowther's award-winning small press,
PS Publishing. Each volume opened with an introduction by
a fellow fantasy novelist, and these are reproduced
in the following pages.

An introduction to
BLOOD FOLLOWS
by
STEPHEN R. DONALDSON

Brace yourself. You're about to enter the strangely compulsive world of Malazan, Steven Erikson's magic-raddled creation. If you continue beyond this point, your life as a reader will never be quite the same again.

After only two instalments, *Gardens of the Moon* and *Deadhouse Gates*, Erikson's 'Tales of the Malazan Book of the Fallen' has already become the kind of epic narrative that will leave you scrambling for more. It certainly has that effect on me. And I know I'm not alone: every reader I've talked to who has made Malazan's acquaintance has the same reaction. After *Gardens of the Moon*, I was hungry for more. After *Deadhouse Gates*, I find myself wondering whether Steven Erikson has any creative limits.

Of course, the novella here, *Blood Follows*, doesn't precisely happen in Malazan (here Mell'zan), and it isn't exactly a tale of the fallen. The story takes place on the same planet that the Malazan Empire occupies: it has the same rules, and the same rich power, as Erikson's larger narrative. But the insecure and imprecisely-legitimate Empress of Malazan doesn't rule here. Instead, darker forces hold sway amid the barrows and alleys of the Lamentable City of Moll. Creatures long dead – very long dead – have taken a particular interest in Moll's doings. And there have been the kind of murders that make bluff soldiers and jaded mages question their sanity.

Meanwhile, Emancipor Reese manoeuvres in his peculiar way to avoid the strident affection of his redoubtable wife, Subly. Princess Sharn indulges a new-found taste for the pleasures of torment. And Master Bauchelain's friend, Korbal Broach, seeks to devise a son.

I say 'compulsive', but that's not the perfect word, I admit. I'm trying to suggest a range of characteristics that all have one quality in common: they take hold of the reader and don't let go.

In part, of course, this compulsiveness arises from the sheer complexity and intensity of the action: there's a lot going on, and it obviously matters. But that's an over-simple view of Erikson's work. We've all read books which offer us a murder-a-minute, and which still put us to sleep.

On a more substantive level, Erikson's characters tend to be rather likable – and extremely obsessive. These are people who do not give up or let go, who do not acknowledge limits or quail at dangers. And because they are likeable – and because Erikson makes them vivid – their clenched commitment to their own agendas clenches us as well.

This is not as easy to do as it might sound. Prose that lacks fire, richness, imagery, cannot hope to convey the urgency of the men and women – and beings – who people Malazan. But prose that is too full of its own poetry tends to obscure the storytelling: obliquely it shifts attention from the characters' needs and emotions to the author's rhetorical gifts. The compulsiveness at which Erikson excels requires a fine balance. In part, his narratives grip us because he so seldom wavers.

And on a still more substantive level: ah, how to explain this? Some of Erikson's compulsive hold arises from the sensation, so acutely conveyed to the reader, that his invention is spinning out of control; that his imagination is so rife, so fecund, that it can't be contained within the normal structures of storytelling. Reading him is like watching two massive locomotives powering towards each other on a single track: you find that you simply cannot look away from what will inevitably be a spectacular and hideous catastrophe. And yet, somehow, astonishingly, the inevitable does not occur: at the last instant, a hand rises to the instrument panel, a lever is pushed, a switch closes; and the locomotives howl past each other with frightening velocity, full of force and intention, and – you can see at last – perfectly under control.

After you've watched Erikson's ideas proliferate for a while, you'll find it almost scary to realize that he knows what he's doing. That all this vast profusion actually fits together.

I say 'strangely compulsive' because I can't think of a better description. But be warned. Once you enter this world, you'll have a hard time winning free again.

If you're like me, you won't want to.

Stephen R. Donaldson, 2002

An introduction to
THE LEES OF LAUGHTER'S END
by
JAMES BARCLAY

Someone once told me that they didn't think fantasy could be 'done' in short form. Look around the fantasy bookshelves and you are bound to have a certain sympathy with that view. Let's face it: a good percentage of fantasy writers have trouble getting through a story in three great doorsteps.

But enough of that. The fact that you're reading this means you hope that this someone is wrong. Or *know*, as I do, that this someone is wrong. Oh yes, my friends, very wrong indeed. Fantasy in novella form is alive and well. And if you've already picked up an Erikson novella, you'll know that he is a fine exponent of said form.

That reminds me. Chronology. This novella is the centrepiece of a trilogy, not that it matters to you right now because as a stand-alone it works beautifully. And in case you want to know, the novella that prefaces this one is *Blood Follows* (and readers of this first part will find some familiar characters returned), and that which comes after is *The Healthy Dead*. Can't have too much of a good thing, can you?

So that's all the administration up to date. What about this, *The Lees of Laughter's End*, then? It is a piece that unleashes a terrifying force in a confined space from which there is no escape; and it stresses, to breaking point, the indomitable nature of the human being in peril. It is set in the Malazan world but in a far-flung corner inhabited almost exclusively by the wretched and the ill-fated.

But is it up to the standard of a full-size Erikson tome? Can the man really cram all the characterization, action, excitement and atmosphere into something so relatively diminutive? Here's another question with the same answer; is the Pope a German? (Now clearly this hilarious response question will only work for the lifespan of Benedict XVI, but it's better than bears and woods, etc.)

You see, there's this thing about Erikson that allows him to distil the essence that makes him a first-class novelist into his shorter works. Not every author can achieve this and retain a cohesive narrative structure. What you get with Erikson, though, is a complete episode that hints of greater things around it. You get characters that can tell you half their life-story in a single line of speech. You get unrelenting action, finely judged dialogue and that wonderful sense of humour that fans of the Bridgeburners will know and love. And you know, you just *know*, that the author had enormous fun writing it.

Make no mistake; the characters absolutely make the story here. And not just the humans, the creatures too. Before I'd reached the end of page three I was already feeling sorry for the hapless crew. And *that* was before I knew what was coming. But whatever was eventually to be revealed, there was the powerful feeling that those in the way were, through no particular fault of their own, wholly unprepared and entirely inadequate to face it.

There are great creations to enjoy. The lich is particularly satisfying. The inhabitants of the crows' nest, the bunch of irritable souls, the mysterious and enigmatic passengers, the poor individual losing his extremities one by one in increasingly bizarre circumstances. And as for what swims in the sea or resides in the chest, well... Appetite whetted? I hope so.

What impressed me most about *The Lees of Laughter's End* was that there was so much happening in such a small space; so much was imparted while the action raged. Any followers of *Fawlty*

Towers will be familiar with this. Each half-hour programme had enough material for three standard sitcom slots. Remember the episode called 'The Germans'? Well, they don't even appear for the first twenty minutes. I think you get the point.

Sudden shocks rebound around eye-watering trench humour. Magnificent mayhem covers every timber while we learn intimate details about the poor unfortunates we so want to survive. Even the names speak loud about the individual. Nickname or real name, it doesn't matter. They are imbued with life history in a way I haven't quite managed to fathom just yet. And they exist in an atmosphere so sinister that you fear for what will happen to them next even while you are laughing at their fecklessness.

These are people for whom the phrase 'poor unfortunates' was coined. They are on a journey from which there is no turning, no escape. And here is something else well handled. That part of the human spirit which, when it is presented with no choice but the one it fears most, reacts in remarkable and courageous ways. When there is nothing else to do but fight the seemingly invincible; when every door is closed but the one to lying quivering and waiting for the end, even the feckless can rear up. But do so with great reluctance and with little thought other than self-preservation.

The Lees of Laughter's End is a splendidly outrageous offering. It is utterly fearless and compelling. Most of all, it is hugely entertaining. Erikson in this mood is a joy to read. So please, sit back, get your favoured liquid near you in sufficient quantity together with your favourite snacks, and enjoy this fantastic voyage.

James Barclay, 2007

An introduction to
THE HEALTHY DEAD
by
PAUL KEARNEY

Fantasy – now, how would one define it? There's a lot of it out there, it must be said, hecatombs of high-falutin' tales sprung from the fevered imaginations of a fervent band of devotees. Some might think it's an easy genre to master. Up springs a callow youth of uncertain heritage, his childhood leavened with the usual omens and uncanny coincidences, and then lo and behold, he discovers a yen to wander, to take a look at the wide world the author has made up around him. Throw in a sidekick, a magic sword, and preferably a dragon or two, et voila – simplicity itself.

There's a lot of it out there, as I said, and there are those who think that the rules of the genre are inescapable. This chap you're about to read though, this Erikson fellow, he drives a freight train through the rules. He leaves you wiping dust out of your eyes and wondering what the hell just went by.

Wizards, sure. Warriors by the thousand. Assassins, nobles, beggars, eccentrics, gods, demons. We've seen them all before – but not done like this. The world of the Malazan Empire is jaw-droppingly complex, and the folk who inhabit it no less so. It may seem a deceptively obvious thing to say, but they are *real* people whose motives are mixed, whose souls are contorted by the travails of their everyday lives. I like that – I always have. To take fantasy and make it as *real* as possible – in this genre, that is the sign of real artistry.

A handful of examples, out of the teeming multitudes: firstly, Erikson's magic. It is the most complex, believable (if that's the right term) and *visceral* system of magic I've ever encountered, in any book, anywhere. It *feels* right. It also feels incredibly dangerous.

His fighting men – they are soldiers. They speak as soldiers should. They are not heroes, but men of work, professionals. Their calling makes them tired and old and sets a canker at their heart.

His primitive peoples – and here I will confess to sheer, unadulterated envy at his knowledge and the use of it – are authentic down to the dirt beneath their nails. Erikson knows how these civilizations operate at a basic level, how it feels to kindle fire in a wilderness and listen to the night-noises whilst the stars blaze overhead. It is a knowledge that cannot be assumed, but must be integral to the writer's psyche.

This story – *The Healthy Dead* – is lighter in tone than most of the material which concerns the Malazan Empire, its rise and fall, but the invention and sheer panache on display are no less impressive. It is a tale which begs to be read out loud amid a crowd of like-minded folk in a fire-lit pub, preferably with clouds of pipe-smoke winding through the air (and no doubt some would-be Well Knights looking on in disapproval). The wealth of the ideas within are staggering, but they troop on stage in so modest and winsome a fashion that it is easy to pass them by, to take for granted the ingenuity and sheer originality of their crafting. Reading Erikson, one begins by thinking that he has started a hare for the hell of it, just because he's been distracted by an idea, a concept, a character. After a while there are a litter of these things up and running, all bright-eyed and full of beans, but by the end of the story he has them all in the bag again – he's brought them to the end he had in mind at the beginning. He makes it look easy, and it's anything but.

To put it another, more personal way – and speaking as a

writer – again and again upon reading Erikson I find myself grinding my teeth, slapping my forehead and groaning, 'Damn! I wish I'd thought of that!' In such an egocentric profession as this, there can be no higher praise.

Paul Kearney, 2004

Stephen Erikson is an archaeologist and anthropologist and a graduate of the Iowa Writer's Workshop. His debut novel, *Gardens of the Moon*, marked the opening chapter of his epic 'The Malazan Book of the Fallen' sequence which has been hailed as one of this millennium's most ambitious and significant works of fantasy. He lives in Cornwall. To find out more, visit **www.malazanempire.com** and **www.stevenerikson.com**